PRAISE FOR W. L. RIPLEY

"Cole Springer is a comer...and so is W.L. Ripley."

— *NEW YORK TIMES* BESTSELLING AUTHOR
ROBERT B. PARKER

"Ripley is the blue-collar Elmore Leonard."

— *BOOKLIST*

"I've been a fan of W.L. Ripley for a good long while. One of my go-to, must-read authors."

— *NEW YORK TIMES* BESTSELLING AUTHOR
ACE ATKINS

"Ripley ably juggles humor and violence."

— *PUBLISHERS WEEKLY*

"Ripley succeeds at creating characters whom we care about."

— *WASHINGTON TIMES*

NOBODY'S FAVORITE

ALSO BY W. L. RIPLEY

Double Down

Cole Springer Thrillers

Cole Springer Trilogy

Springer's Max Bet

Jake Morgan Thrillers

Home Fires

No Badge Required

NOBODY'S FAVORITE

A JAKE MORGAN THRILLER
BOOK THREE

W. L. RIPLEY

WOLFPACK
PUBLISHING
— EST 2013 —

"I may stand alone but would not change my free thoughts for a throne."

— LORD BYRON

* * *

"No man in the wrong can stand up against a fellow that's in the right and keeps on a-comin'."

— CAPTAIN BILL MCDONALD, TEXAS
RANGER

NOBODY'S FAVORITE

CHAPTER ONE

Everything was perfect so far. He could not believe his luck. Caught the moment perfectly. His job would be easier now. Cleaner.

Then, in the distance, the main doors echoed, followed by the sound of footsteps in the hall and now the panic starts. Who was that? *Why now?* He didn't wait to see who it was, couldn't wait or the plan was ruined and he would pay a heavy price. He did what he came to do, and hurried out of the office, down the rear hall. He burst out the back door and ran through the dark night to the place he had parked the vehicle he had taken for this one job.

He was sure he wasn't seen. He *could not* be seen. Just get away and make the shit storm in his head stop. The piece of shit deserved it and wouldn't fuck anyone over again. The best part? He was getting away with this and they would surely blame someone else. And now it was done, and he deserved a medal for ending the man and his reign of bullying. Nobody liked the son of a bitch.

Nobody.

* * *

Jake Morgan stopped his County Unit, sighed, and stepped out of the Ford Explorer with the Paradise County Sheriff's badge emblazoned on the door. The rotating red-and-blue lights whirred and painted the scene and pierced the night air. He had stopped the 2002 Chevy pick-up, reddish-brown from age and lack of washing, numerous times and knew it was going to be the same thing as always, almost like it was scripted.

"Well," Jake said to himself, approaching the driver's window. "Here we go again."

The pick-up belonged to Cecil Holtzmeyer, a retired factory worker whose wife died of cancer five years ago. Cecil never remarried and Cecil only had two hobbies— watching major league baseball on TV and drinking beer.

Paradise County Undersheriff, Jake Morgan, had stopped Cecil heading south on highway 27. Jake had picked up on him just outside the city limits two blocks from the Blue Ribbon liquor store. They were in a bad spot on the down side of an incline in the road.

"How many times do we have to go through this, Cecil?" Jake said. "It's become so routine I should put it on my day planner; you think you can drink and drive, then I stop you and you tell me it'll never happen again."

"What?" Cecil said, while making an attempt to push a Jim Beam pint down between the seats of his Dodge Ram pick-up. "I don't know what you mean, Jake." Cecil was a large man in a short man's body, axe handle wide and jowls like a bulldog.

"You're too sharp for me, Cecil," Jake said, shaking his head and trying to be serious. "Pretty slick the way you're hiding the bottle. Look, I just don't want to scrape you off the highway some day and neither do I want you to kill someone else. Are you getting this?"

"Jake, I've only had one beer," Cecil said as if the Whiskey pint between the seats had ceased to exist. "Honest."

"C'mon Cecil, I thought we were friends. Why lie to me? Do you really want me to have you get out, see if you can walk a straight line."

"Hard for me to walk a straight line because of my bunions. Besides, I'm on my way home."

Jake drummed fingers on top of the truck cab, amused. Police work is so glamorous. "Taking the scenic route, right? Your house is dead East in the other direction."

Cecil looked out his window and said, "Oh yeah, guess I got confused. Let me go, Jake. I promise to give up drinking you let me off this time. This time I mean it. Honest."

"This is a preventive stop," Jake said. "I know you haven't had time to suck too much out of that bottle. If you'll just turn your vehicle around and head home, I'll let it go this time. When you get home, call my cell from your landline and…"

Jake heard the roar of a vehicle bearing down, moving fast and cresting over the hill, then its headlights blinding. Jake's County unit was parked at an angle, as per policy, and his lights danced against the dark night. Cecil had pulled over in a bad place on the downside of an incline of highway 27.

The vehicle boomed over the rise and was on Jake before he could avoid being hit. Too late to do anything but jump into the pick-up bed of Cecil's pick-up.

The speeding car clipped the fender of Jake's angled Ford Explorer and slammed the SUV into the pick-up which sent Jake rolling across a pick-up bed filled with beer cans, bottles, various tools and garbage. The sick sound of crunching metal, whine of taxed vehicle motor. The out-of-control car careened off the road, jumped a ditch, and ripped through a barbed wire fence and into Aaron Yoder's cow pasture.

Jake, helpless against the impact, was tossed across the floor of the pick-up bed. His head cracked against the metal bed and his shoulder banged against the walls. In the distance, he heard the thud of the car hitting turf, the shriek of twisted metal and then it was quiet.

Jake heard the sound of a second vehicle running hard and whipping air as it passed by the parked vehicles. Jake sat up, winced when he did and saw the second vehicle's tail lights disappearing in the distance. They were pick-up tail lights. F-150 maybe a Chevy Silverado. He didn't get the license number. What was their hurry? Most people stopped or slowed when they came upon these things.

Not this guy.

Jake called out, saying, "You okay, Cecil."

"I'm okay," Cecil said. "Not drunk neither."

"Dammit, Cecil I don't care about that right now. Just want to know if you're all right."

"What was that, Jake?"

"I don't know but I'm going to find out."

Jake took stock of the bruises and scrapes he'd sustained while rolling around on the floorboard. Head and shoulder hurt, pants ripped and shirt torn. Various cuts and bruises. He reached up to touch behind his left ear and felt wetness. Blood? He removed his hand and confirmed the find.

With all the beer cans, bottles and rusty junk, he knew he had been lucky but would need medical attention and a tetanus shot. Jake clambered over the side of the truck bed, took a look at the damage to his vehicle, and saw the sheared silver of exposed metal on the front fender of his unit.

His police radio boomed to life. "Jake, this is dispatch, respond immediately." His cell phone rang that same moment and it was a call from Sheriff Buddy Johnson.

Jake answered, "This is Morgan."

Sheriff Johnson was Jake's best friend and had been an all-state offensive lineman who had saved Jake's bacon a dozen times back in high school, said, "We got one for you, Jake. Homicide. This is in the city limits so it's Chief Bannister's jurisdiction with my assistance."

Jake was the dual investigator for both Paradise PD and the Paradise Sheriff and both benefitted from his Texas Ranger training as a major crimes specialist. Jake had returned to his hometown and decided to stay on. The dual authority afforded him a decent salary though not as large as he had earned as a Ranger.

"I was sideswiped by a speeder while I was making a stop. The driver lost control and crashed his vehicle into Aaron Yoder's cow pasture. A second vehicle also at a high rate of speed passed by seconds later. Somebody needs to let Aaron know in case he has cattle in this pasture. I'll check on the driver, then I'll come in."

"You're not going to believe who the victim is," Buddy said.

"Who is it?"

"Martin Saunders."

"The teacher?" Jake remembered Saunders, from his days at Paradise High School. "Never liked the guy."

"Somebody else didn't like him, either. He's dead."

"My Explorer's damaged so I'll need a ride. I had stopped Cecil Holtzmeyer when the vehicle popped over the hill and struck my unit. Then a second vehicle, a pick-up came but he missed us."

"You okay?"

"I'm fine, few scrapes, so's Cecil. It's dark but it doesn't look good from here, so get me some techs out here. Also a wrecker, two of them. The wrecked vehicle looks pretty bad. Going to check on it. I'm out."

Jake retrieved the first aid kit out of his Explorer and told Cecil to wait in his truck. "You're a witness and we'll need a statement from you."

"Can I drink while I wait?" Cecil said.

Unbelievable. "No, you can't."

"My vehicle's too damaged to drive."

"It was already too damaged to drive. How does this bucket of rust pass inspection?" Jake ran a hand through the hair on the back of his head, winced when he touched the damaged ear. "Okay, Cecil, I'll arrange for a wrecker and someone will take you home and not to Hank's bar, understood?"

"If I'm going home and I can't drive what difference it makes if I drink?" Cecil asked, his face hopeful.

Jake shook his head. "Cecil just...Just sit there, until I get back."

Jake left Cecil, crossed the ditch and stepped over the ripped barbed-wire fence into the pasture. The damaged fence sagged in both directions from the impact. He shined his flashlight on the ground, saw the gouge marks made by the flying car. One fence post was sheared in half and another flattened by the impact on the wires. The fence line was sagging for fifty yards either direction from the point of entry.

A bright harvest moon hung in the sky so the visibility was good. Jake was able to reach the vehicle without stepping in cow piles.

He reached the late model Nissan Maxima, amazed it was upright and looked in on the driver.

It was Pete Stanger. Stanger was the head maintenance man at the high school. A soft moan from the injured man. Jake shined his flashlight on Pete and the interior of the car.

"You all right, Pete?"

More moaning, no response. Pete had not secured his seat belt and leaned at a bad angle from the door, his arm caught in the wheel. Due to the position of Pete's arm and body, Jake decided not to touch him.

"Ambulance on the way, Pete. Just take it easy until then."

Pete stopped moaning and Jake checked his pulse which was strong. Pete's arm was bent just above his left wrist and a goose egg mushroomed on his forehead. While he waited for the ambulance, Jake stepped off the distance from the point where the vehicle went through the fence. He heard the sound of ambulance sirens and saw the lights against the evening sky.

Who was driving the second vehicle? Was he chasing Pete? And what was Pete's big hurry? 27 highway was a state highway which ran fifteen miles before you hit another town. It was not usually a busy avenue this time of night.

The ambulance techs arrived and extricated Pete Stanger from the wreckage of his Maxima. Pete was unconscious so Jake was unable to get information. The Techs treated Stanger's injuries.

Two tow trucks arrived to hitch up Jake's unit and Stanger's Camry back to the county lot. One of the two trucks was Angus Wilson, an old friend of the family.

"Hook up Cecil's truck and take him back with you," Jake said to Angus.

Angus eyed the old truck and said, "I don't have to Jake. Looks like Cecil's truck is drivable."

"Not by Cecil," Jake said. "Take him home and drop off the truck at his place. I'll pay the tow if he doesn't."

Angus laughed, and said, "That's a white man who loves his booze. He smells like a brewery."

"That's quite a shock since he told me he only had one. Hard to believe Cecil would lie about such a thing."

Angus laughed. "That's Cecil for sure and for certain. He asked if he could drink on the way back to town."

"I give up." Jake shrugged. "Let him drink if he wants."

"Boy, Jake," Angus said. "You are a different kind of cop."

"Serve and protect."

As Angus pulled away, Cecil gave Jake a big smile and waved the Whiskey bottle in triumph.

Oh well.

* * *

Jake bent over the body of Martin Saunders sprawled across an upended executive chair in the Paradise Superintendent's outer office. It looked posed. The killer wanted it to look like he had been knocked out of the chair and there was ample indications Saunders' had been badly used. There was bruising along the side of the man's face and neck. The late Martin Saunders was a speech and drama teacher who had been teaching at PHS for over ten years, Jake could not remember when the man started.

Police Chief Cal Bannister was on the scene. Cal stood back to give Jake room. Paradise PD officer, Buster Mangold, sat in a visitor's chair off to one side. Mangold, a big man, was not a favorite of Jake's. Mangold should have been stationed outside the office to prevent outsiders from entering the office and worse, Mangold was drinking a coke and holding a golden apple in his hand, the type given to teachers when they retired.

Jake looked at the apple, looked at Mangold then

raised his eyebrows in Cal's direction. Cal didn't miss the meaning behind the look.

"Dammit, Buster," Cal said. "Where'd you get the apple?"

"It was on the floor. I figure it was knocked off the desk during the struggle."

"Put it back where you found it and tape off this office."

"Okay, boss."

"Don't call me boss. Get out of here."

Mangold made a face, placed the apple on the floor, and stepped out of the office.

"We'll need Buster's fingerprints to eliminate them," Jake said. "I wonder what else he touched."

"Problem here," Cal said. "Is that the fingerprints of every teacher, every staff member and many people in the community will be present."

Jake nodded and returned to his examination of the body and the crime scene. Chair overturned and the bruises suggested a nasty end to the man's life. Beaten to death? In any homicide or accidental death, Jake would need an autopsy to determine death by blunt force trauma and that meant county Medical Examiner, Dr. Montooth.

"Cal, where's Zeke the Sheik? Somebody called him, didn't they?"

"I'm right here, buckethead," Zeke said. Dr. Ezekiel Montooth, a long, lanky high school buddy of Jake's, walked into the room, his tie askew, wearing a wrinkled short-sleeved shirt and a cigarette dangling from the corner of his mouth. "Buster acted like it was the first time he'd seen me. Who pissed him off?"

Jake looked up from the floor and said, "I hope you don't think you can smoke up my crime scene, Zeke. Also, this is a school and they have rules about that."

Zeke leaned down, looked at the body and said, "Yeah, but apparently there are no rules about killing teachers."

"All the guys with medical degrees in the world and I get Smelly McSmokesalot. Take a look at this guy, Zeke, and tell me what you think?"

"I am looking." Zeke took his time, at first eye-balling the corpse, without touching him and said, "My professional medical opinion is he's dead."

"I knew you were the right guy for the job," Jake said.

Zeke said, "Did you get a look before I got here, Jake."

Jake said, "Yeah, I've been looking. Just started. Some bruising, no cuts I can see."

"Can I move the body?"

"Sure, go ahead."

Zeke probed the neck and examined the eyes. Zeke was a fine M.E. and Jake knew they were lucky to have him. Despite his disheveled appearance, Zeke had been organized and meticulous as a student, valedictorian of his class at P.H.S. who graduated magna cum laude before pursuing his medical degree at M.U. where he graduated third in his class.

Zeke rolled the body over to reveal a tiny pool of blood from a cut under his lip. A shard of gold leaf appeared to have caused the cut. There was also a small wooden trophy base with something torn from it. There was a brass plate with writing on it. Jake looked at the golden apple on the floor.

Buddy closed his eyes, as if in pain, leaned his head back and said, "Son of a bitch."

"What is this underneath the body?" Zeke asked.

"The gold apple thing on the floor?" Jake said, nodding at the apple. "The leaf broke off of that apple. Mangold had it in his hand when I arrived."

"Shit," Zeke said. "The victim has a cut lip. Perhaps

from the broken leaf. Mangold, huh? Buster's the kind of guy who pisses in sinks."

"Exactly."

"It looks like blunt force trauma. For now, let's assume the leaf shard caused the cut on his lip. The only blood I found is from his lip. From the shape of the bruises, the killer used the apple and was trying to make sure there were no broken bones. I'm surprised there isn't more blood which indicates the victim expired soon after hitting the floor. When the heart stops arterial pulsation stops with it. The lack of blood issue is unusual. I'll know more during the autopsy."

"Appreciate it."

Zeke had been intent on examining the corpse and now let out a cry of recognition. "Hey, that's Mr. Saunders, isn't it?"

"Give the man a cigar," Jake said. "You've been looking at him for five minutes and you just now recognize him?"

"I just examine them," Zeke said, standing up. "It's your job to make sure they don't end up like this. Too busy eating donuts and busting high school kids for speeding?"

"See? You know nothing about police work. Eating donuts is required and harassing high school kids is one of the perks. I have it written into my contract. You realize county coroner is an elective position and I could use my influence to remove you."

"I ran unopposed, dumber-than-me. Since you come to town, nobody else wants the job."

Cal Bannister saying now, "I believe there's an inscription on the trophy plate."

Dr. Zeke looked closer and read the inscription, "Kudos to Mr. Saunders for the theatre department production, 'Failure can be Deadly'. Class of 2015." Zeke sat back and said, "Damn, worked him over with his own award. I saw that play. Looks like a clue."

"You examine the body, I'll decide what a clue is," Jake said as he examined the apple. "And…a…it is my opinion that's a clue. Cal, I'll need to know who was in that play. Can you put somebody on that who is not Buster Mangold?"

"I'll take care of it," Cal said. "This is bad business, Jake."

Zeke stood and said, "When can I get the body?"

"I won't take too long," Jake said. "Something's wrong here, though. I can feel it more than know it. Thing is, I have to read this scene and not work anything else into it except what I can see and what I can prove. How soon can I get a cause of death?"

"Looks like a beating death but I'm like you in that something seems out of place here. I'll get on it right away and try to have it for you by morning," Zeke said. He shook a cigarette out of a package and placed it between his lips. That done he produced a Zippo lighter.

"I appreciate that," Jake said. "I need to get Wiley in here for some photos. Zeke, you can't smoke in a school."

Zeke fired up the zippo and said, "I dunno, did it all through high school."

CHAPTER TWO

On the way in from working the wreck on 27, Jake had contacted another best friend, Leo Lyons, the football coach at PHS. Jake figured Leo could provide some background on Saunders. He met Buddy and Leo outside the entrance to Paradise High School, a place of many memories for all three men.

While Chief Bannister and Buster Mangold secured the crime scene with yellow police tape, Jake took the opportunity to get some background.

Buddy was clean shaven, his shirt perfectly pressed; he was an imposing figure at his six-foot-six height. Leo was wearing coaching shorts and a Paradise Pirates Sweatshirt with the sleeves cut off. Leo looked like he had been put together using different body parts—lumber-jack arms, short legs, piercing eyes and a D'Artagnan mustache. On his head was a black baseball cap emblazoned with the crossed cutlasses he designed for the football team's helmets.

Jake said. "Anything you guys can tell me about the victim?"

"He's an asshole," Buddy said.

"And a bad teacher," Leo Lyons said. "Also, he failed at having me like him."

"So which one of you killed him?" Jake said. "I'll need alibis and your whereabouts at the time of the crime."

"Screw you, Morgan," Leo said.

"Well, someone disliked him enough to kill him. You guys have any suspects that come to mind?"

"Anyone who ever met him," Buddy said.

"And the only people who didn't dislike him, never met him," Leo said.

"How did he keep his job?" Jake asked.

"Tenure. Two uncles on the school board," Leo said. "One uncle, Foster Taylor, is the board president and the other uncle is also an asshole. Assholery runs in their family like a flushed toilet, but don't quote me, I need a new sprinkler system for the football field and I'm in brown nose mode."

Leo told Jake that Saunders was not popular with the students, but put on good, even excellent quality, school plays. Saunders was known to torment students he didn't like and had his favorites. There had been rumors over the years about Saunders' lifestyle. Saunders had briefly been married but now his private life was extremely private. He did not keep a landline and did not socialize in Paradise.

"Saw that your father-in-law is here," Leo said. "Cal's daughter is the best girl in the county. Also the prettiest."

Buddy said. "Jake'll figure out some way to screw it up."

"It's his nature," Leo said.

Cal Bannister's daughter was Harper Mitchell, divorced, who Jake had been seeing off-and-on for several months. For Jake, Harper was sunshine and apple blossoms. Never met anyone like her and didn't think he would again. They were engaged but Harper's previous marriage had been a disaster so they were slow-walking the wedding date.

Jake saying now, "When you guys are finished being not funny I think I'd like to have Buddy take a look at the scene. Leo, hang back okay? I want to get more background on Saunders and the faculty."

Jake and Buddy re-entered the superintendent's office to get Buddy's take. Buddy had a good eye for these things and it was Buddy who had talked him into working for both law enforcement authorities. Being a law officer in Jake's hometown was not always an easy thing; though it was more easily acceptable for Jake than for some of the people he had grown up with. Old friends wanted favors and tickets fixed which Jake would not do. Telling old friends 'no' didn't always sit well.

There is a saying in law enforcement that after five years you make no new friends just new enemies. Today was no different when the School Superintendent showed up while Jake was still working the scene.

Dr. Winston Vestal was a peacock of a man, dressed in a grey suit, crisp white shirt and a maroon silk tie. He had a wispy dark mustache. This was Vestal's second year as head of the school district and he thought well of himself and walked right by Buddy's outstretched arm.

Vestal started to enter the inner office, *his* office when Jake put up a hand and said, "Whoa, don't go in there. In fact you shouldn't be in here. Somebody get this dirty old man out of here. Dammit, Cal, what is Mangold doing out there?"

Cal left the room and there were footsteps in the hall, then angry voices in the hall.

Vestal stopped, looked perturbed and said, "I'm the superintendent and I just need to get some things out of my office."

"Well, this scene has been compromised enough without you adding to it."

Vestal took another step into the room and again Jake said, "Dr. Vestal, this is a homicide investigation. I'm sorry but you're going to have to step outside and stay outside."

"I need to get some things out of my office."

Jake wondered why a man with a doctorate degree could not understand English.

"Nothing leaves this office until Jake says so," Buddy said. "Any activity by you compromises the investigation."

"It'll only take a second and I simply must get some papers from my desk."

"No," Buddy said.

"It's my office."

Jake said, "But, it's my crime scene and…" Vestal, undeterred, continued to move towards the inner office whereupon Jake rose and confronted him. "What do you think you're doing? Get your ass back out of the crime scene or I'm going to arrest you for obstruction."

"You can't tell me what to do in my office."

"Telling you what to do is most of my job right now. If being perp-walked from school is on your bucket list, take another step and you can cross it off."

Cal Bannister returned, red-faced and asked, "What's going on here?"

Vestal pivoted towards Cal and said, "Chief Bannister, this man will not allow me to enter my office. He is threatening to arrest me."

"Well," Cal said, and thumbed back his cap. "That's what's going to happen if you don't do everything he tells you just as soon as he tells you."

"I don't like this, Cal," Vestal said.

"Winston," Cal said. "I can't begin to tell you how

little I care what you don't like. Jake is in charge and he has full autonomy."

"I'm not going to touch anything germane to your investigation," Vestal said.

"That's right, because you're not going to be here. I'm going to cordon off this office, Saunders classroom and the theatre until Monday at the earliest. Mr. Vestal you may wish to cancel school tomorrow."

"Cancel school?"

"Maybe you won't have to. That is, if you don't mind me, three or four county deputies and maybe a state trooper and a forensic guy I know walking in and out of classrooms and in the halls carrying equipment, interviewing students and faculty, with the students asking questions about, you know, 'why are they—'"

Vestal threw up his hands and said, "Okay, all right. I'll make an announcement."

"I will need faculty and staff to show up Monday or I can interview them at their homes."

"The only thing I ask in return is that you allow me to get some items out of my office, okay?"

Jake looked at Buddy in disbelief. Jake slowly shook his head and said, "No."

Vestal put a hand to his chest and asked, "I'm a suspect? Is that it?"

Jake smiled and raised his eyebrows.

* * *

People change and Jake had changed during his ten years in Texas. He had left Paradise an angry young man, with a reputation as a rounder and now returned to become city and county investigator. His father, Alfred Morgan, had been known around the community as a drunk who during Jake's high school years had been emotionally abusive to Jake's mother who was dying of cancer. Jake and his father had been estranged during that time and Jake did not forgive his father until Alfred was dead and buried.

Deep inside the rift between father and son was scar tissue where a young man stored his memories. It had healed some, calloused over for the most part, but still a part of who he was. He was and always would be Alfred Morgan's son. Alfred had been a good role model for Jake as a kid but when Jake entered high school Alfred fell victim to a smoldering anger inside his soul that was exacerbated by Kentucky Bourbon. It bubbled up from deep inside Alfred Morgan and Alfred would lash out at those he loved. His wife, dying of cancer, withered under his dark moments, but young Jake had bulled his neck and fought back and these fights wore Jake's mother down as quickly as the cancer that ate away inside her.

After graduation Jake left Paradise County and headed to Texas and eventually to the Texas Department of Safety to become part of an organization widely known as the Texas Rangers. Jake demonstrated an aptitude for law enforcement and rose quickly in the Ranger ranks, but as Herman Melville once wrote, 'Life is a voyage that's homeward bound'. And so it was true with Jake.

Jake released the Saunders' body to Dr. Zeke who zipped up the corpse in a body bag. It was a ceremony Jake had witnessed too often as a Texas Ranger and its finality was chilling.

"I'll give you a call in the morning," Zeke said, standing outside the ambulance which was waiting to take Martin Saunders to Zeke's office.

Jake nodded and the two men shook hands. That done, Jake pulled Leo Lyon aside and said, "I've got some more work to do here yet but school is canceled for tomorrow. Come by Hank's tomorrow afternoon. I'll buy you a beer and you can tell me all there is to know about Martin Saunders."

"So, I'm your C.I.?" Leo said.

"No, C.I. means 'criminal informant'," Jake said. "But the way you coach football could be considered criminal."

"It's that attitude right there," Leo said. "It's the reason you have no friends."

"I have you."

"I have very low standards," Leo said. "I have an affinity for the weak and the useless."

* * *

Hank's was an old school bar in Paradise, with worn hardwood floors and a jukebox that played hits from a previous century. Paradise had tripled in population and growth since Jake left for Texas and all the new lions, wannabes and commuters frequented the franchise bars out on the new highway bypass whereas locals, like Jake and Leo, were hardcore Hank's patrons.

Hank as usual was happy, in his own way, to see the pair.

"What are you two losers up to?" Hank asked, as he approached the friends. As was their tradition, Hank already had a beer in hand to give to Leo the Lion. Also as was traditional, Leo insulted the offering. "Is this one going to be less flat than the one you brought me on Tuesday? You should avoid freezing your beer."

"You can't imagine how it pains me that you were served unacceptable beer," Hank said. "And that pain is only exceeded by the hemorrhoids I contracted starting with the first day you came into my place, Leo. What'll you have, Jake?"

Jake ordered a beer and Hank had one sent over by a server.

"You worked with Saunders," Jake said. "Tell me about the guy. Enemies, friends, anyone have a grudge against him?"

"Like I said before, almost everybody," Leo said. "He tried to run over everyone on our faculty."

"What about you?"

"I said 'tried'. I ignored him. Football team had a better year than the Drama club. He got into it with parents, administration…"

"How about the central office?"

"You mean Vestal?"

Jake nodded.

"Yeah, they hated each other. Vestal couldn't fire him because of Saunders uncles, so there was friction and a large amount of resentment. Saunders would go over Vestal's head when he didn't like decisions from central office. Vestal would respond by cutting items from Saunders' budget. Typical school politics."

"Anyone else have problems with Saunders? I know you said everyone, but I need some that are more likely than others."

"Bill Tompkins, the baseball coach. They had some run-ins. Tompkins is a good man but like all good school people he believes he's hired to teach his class instead of just coach baseball. He teaches Biology and he's good at it. Saunders took some Bio students out of Tompkins' class to work on a play last year before the state achievement tests. Tompkins told Saunders not to do that again…ever. Said he 'didn't take students out of Saunders' classes to practice baseball'. Tompkins was right, of course, but Saunders whined to Vestal, Vestal skipped over our Principal and allowed Saunders to continue the practice."

"I thought Saunders and Vestal hated each other."

"It doesn't make sense, does it? There's a rumor that Saunders has something on Vestal and, here's the best part, Vestal also has something on Saunders, sort of a mutual destruction pact."

"You're hearing this in the faculty lounge?"

"Never go in there," Leo said. "Unless of course there are brownies. As a Championship Football coach and the Big Kahuna of classroom pedagogues I am above the rarified air of the faculty lounge."

"I'm staggered by your humility."

"It's awesome, isn't it? Some others might include Brenda Sutherland. Brenda has been here longer than Saunders but they, meaning Vestal and Saunders' Uncle, Forrest Taylor, passed over Brenda and named Saunders department head."

"Does that job include a boost in salary?"

"It does," Leo said. "There are many more. Are you really going to shut down access to the school?"

"Most of it," Jake said. "Also the central office. I'll have to. There are too many people in and out of the place."

"Even my office and locker room?"

"Especially your office. It's not like anything productive is happening in there." Jake took a last swallow of his beer, leaned forward, and said, "No, I don't think I'll find anything in the football locker room so you may continue to befoul the air in that place. Leo, is there anyone else you can think of that might have wanted to kill Saunders?"

"Saunders treats support staff like serfs, no like indentured servants. There are a few more on the faculty that don't like him and some in town but there's one staff worker in particular he treated badly."

"Okay," Jake said. "Who?"

"Pete Stanger."

"You're kidding," Jake said. "I just pulled Pete out of wreck out on 27."

"Is he okay?"

"He's badly hurt, maybe comatose so I didn't get to talk to him. But, Pete Stanger, huh? That's a...that's interesting. Tell me more."

"You want interesting you're in the right place. As always the old professor has his finger on the pulse of the community."

"Just tell me without grandstanding."

"Pete Stanger is Martin Saunders' brother-in-law."

Jake started to pursue that tidbit when his cell rang and he was called away.

Jake raised a finger and said, "More on that later. Got a domestic call."

"Leave your tab open, okay?" Leo said, raising his beer glass.

CHAPTER THREE

The domestic squabble was handled without much work on Jake's part. It was an older couple that had gotten into a row about a spaghetti recipe. Jake threatened them with arrest and they settled right down. Never a dull moment.

Jake called Leo who said he was in his football office. Jake wanted further information about Pete Stanger and his sister's marriage to Martin Saunders.

"How's that for interesting?" Leo asked, as he leaned back in his office chair. Leo the Lion's desk was cluttered with travel mugs, a stack of playbooks, and various papers with football diagrams strewn about. His walls were lined with clipboards hanging from nails, seven years of framed Paradise Pirates Football team photos and another photo of Leo with the State Second Place Class 3 trophy. There was a worn wooden table with an unwashed Mr. Coffee Machine and a large red container of Folgers coffee beside it.

Jake nodded and then said, "Not bad. I forget how intertwined lives are in small towns."

"You moved away and missed out on some entertaining small town jealousy and doomed dramas. This place makes General Hospital look like the Andy Griffith show. Saunders married and divorced Pete's sister, Melanie Stanger. Melanie was a bright student in my classes and became a successful insurance agent. It seems, or Melanie claims, that Saunders was emotionally abusive and there is evidence to support her. The divorce proceedings were nasty and Melanie wound up clinically depressed and hospitalized and now receives outpatient care in Columbia which required her to move closer to the clinic and Saunders maneuvered to take the house in court and tried to get her institutionalized. He failed at that but drained their bank accounts without her knowledge."

Jake ran a thumb along his jaw and felt the stubble on his unshaved face. He had been on the clock for most of the past 36 hours and his eyes felt grainy and raw.

"So, Pete didn't like that and had reason to go after Saunders."

Leo nodded and said, "He did go after him once but his friends broke it up before it went too far and Saunders filed assault charges because Martin Saunders is a chickenshit. Pete is nobody to mess with. He played for me a few years back. All conference outside linebacker. He was a tough kid."

Was Pete running from something or somebody when he hit Jake's Explorer? It made him wonder. Was he running from the second vehicle, the unidentified pick-up? He made a note to touch base with Cecil Holtzmeyer and see if Cecil could i.d. the make of the second vehicle.

"If Pete went after Saunders, how did Pete keep his job at school?"

"Pete's Uncle, Forrest Taylor, is the school board

president," Leo said. "He's also Martin Saunders' uncle. How do you like that?"

"They're both related to Taylor?"

"And Dr. Knox Taylor is also Saunders' uncle but I don't know the blood connection. You know this place, half of the population is related to the other half. Town's bigger but the entrenched local gentry still occupy all the big fish positions."

Jake thought about that and said, "Do the uncles get along?"

Leo placed his hands behind his head, leaned back in his chair. He smiled and said, "They have mutual financial interests so there is a tenuous cease-fire pact. Sutherland needs Taylor more than the reverse. I told you, doomed dramas."

"Anything else?"

"It's almost endless but check with Dr. Sutherland's ex-wife, Brenda Sutherland. She was passed over in favor of Saunders for the department head job. That despite the fact she has been here longer, was well-thought of and more deserving. She can give you more insight about Saunders as well as Knox and she will be considered a suspect in your cop head. Also, get some rest," Leo said. "You look like shit. Not that you don't ordinarily look like shit, it's just that sleep deprivation exacerbates your shit-like appearance."

"Sleep would be good," Jake said, he stood, pointed at his friend. "To be continued."

* * *

Felicia Jankowski caught the news of Martin Saunders murder and though it surprised her, it didn't make her sad. She bit into the rubbery rice cake. She was watching her weight, not that she was overweight, but she was considering divorcing Frank, in prison now, on conspiracy and obstruction, and a girl needed to keep her options open.

She had been involved with Martin Saunders recently, a brief affair that wasn't satisfying for her. Mostly it had been a bad choice and she had other options.

With men who were more financially set.

Besides, the indiscriminate shithead had been cheating on her. Well, as much as someone could be cheating on a woman cheating on her husband while she was seeing others. She giggled at the thought. She was being a bad girl and enjoying every minute.

She sipped her decaf, another bad choice, and noted that, Jake Morgan, the asshole that had thrown her husband in prison was investigating the murder. She did not want him coming around and asking about an affair with Saunders, but would need to be prepared if he did. She got up, opened a cabinet door, removed a bottle of Amaretto, poured some into the tasteless coffee and took a sip. That was better. She'd brush her teeth and wash out the lingering aroma of Amaretto before her city council meeting later that day. She had recently been appointed to take Frank's place on the council which was the second best thing about Frank in prison.

The best thing about Frank in prison was that she was now in control of Frank's Real Estate/Development Company which gave her some juice around the community.

So Martin was dead, which meant sooner or later, someone, hopefully not Morgan, would be around to ask her about it. She'd had a little flirtatious thing with Saunders which was sort of creepy. Life sure got complicated when she was just trying to cut through the curtain of boredom of small-town Paradise. She did have a contact within the police force and would check with Buster Mangold as things progressed.

She poured more Amaretto, this time into a glass rather than her coffee cup, and took a good swallow. She let it slide back against her throat. Nice start to the day before she called her former undercover buddy, Winston Vestal, and see what he knew about this.

Also, why he hadn't called her recently.

* * *

Jake was up early. He called Dr. Zeke who had an autopsy report in record time. Zeke was a talented M.E. and Jake knew the county was lucky to have him. Jake grabbed a travel cup of coffee and a donut in town and drove to Zeke's office.

Jake decided to take the scenic route through the older residential areas of Paradise on his way to Zeke's office. As his County Explorer was in the shop, he was driving the vintage Lincoln Mark IV Alfred Morgan had restored for him. A token from a dead father, reaching out to his estranged son. He sailed the majestic vehicle past second generation homes with mature Maple trees turning red and gold. He passed by old men walking small dogs, men and women leaving houses for work, coffee cups in hand and the morning dew glistened as the sun warmed and cheered on the day. The morning sang with promise.

Zeke was drinking a cup of hot tea and chewing on a frozen sausage biscuit he'd heated up in a microwave. Zeke alternated bites from the sandwich with sips of Chai tea. Cheese drizzled along the side of the sandwich.

Zeke held out the mangled breakfast sandwich and said, "Want a bite."

"What do you think?" Jake said, making a face as he

leaned away. He looked down at the lifeless form on the examination table. "Was it blunt force trauma?"

The County Coroner covered the body of the expired teacher, Martin Saunders, who appeared to not only have zero friends, but likewise seemed to be a pariah among the faculty and staff of Paradise High School.

Zeke removed his gloves, stepped on a garbage can lever, and tossed the used gloves into the can. "Yeah that could've killed him," Zeke said.

Jake looked up from the examination table and said, "Could have? What are you telling me?"

Zeke shook another cigarette from a rumpled pack of Marlboros, placed one between his lips, lit the cigarette, took a languid draw and exhaled a blue-grey cloud at the ceiling. He offered the pack to Jake who shook his head. Jake had the habit but was making an attempt at quitting the sticks. Again.

"Congratulations on your ability to resist," Zeke said.

Jake knew Zeke liked drawing things out.

"Some time before the earth cools, Zeke. I want your take on cause of death?"

"The injuries sustained in the assault were extensive yet insufficient to cause his death." He paused to take another drag on the cigarette. The cigarette remained on his lips as he spoke. "Many were superficial and a hair-line fracture of his jaw was the only broken bone. Much bruising to the chest, arms and neck, but no internal bleeding, no brain hemorrhaging. There is nothing that would indicate a killing blow."

Jake looked at the lifeless body of Martin Saunders, partially covered with a white sheet, then back at Zeke. "How about it with the suspense, Montooth?"

The tall M.E. stabbed out his cigarette in an Aricept promo mug and said, "Unless I missed something while I was probing, your guess is as good as mine."

Jake put his hand on his gun belt, shook his head and said, "Well, that's just great. I'm giving some thought to a second homicide. C'mon, Zeke, I know you have some ideas on this."

"I do but I can only enter facts on a death certificate. There are contusions and bruises, on the chest, shoulders, jaw, cauliflower ear on the left side and a contusion on the back of the head. As I said before none of them were killing blows. I'm not even sure I can officially call it a homicide."

"You're kidding?"

The lanky M.E. shook his head. "I can't. It's the job, Jake. I have to be clinically and factually correct to call it a homicide. The assault didn't kill him but something did."

"Heart attack?"

"No. Well, sort of. His heart stopped, but there was no previous damage."

It was quiet between the old friends for a long moment. Jake chewed on his lower lip and Zeke scratched the back of his head.

"However," Zeke said. "I was thinking perhaps some type of paralytic like Succinylcholine or a synthetic cathinone, which you would call bath salts, but I didn't find any trace of it. Succinylcholine is dosed at 1-1.5 milligrams and even the smallest amount more is a killer."

"Had a case like that in Texas. Fortunately, they found the hypo nearby with trace elements. Did you find any succinylcholine in your autopsy?"

"There were other complications I encountered when I examined the body. There were—" The office phone rang. "Hang on," Zeke said. "I have to take this."

While Zeke was on the phone, Jake donned a pair of latex gloves and pulled back the sheet covering the remains of Martin Saunders. Dead bodies look exactly like dead bodies. Jake thought that if it was a paralytic it would have to be injected so he was looking for needle marks, though sure Dr. Zeke probably had already done so. Zeke didn't miss much. It would have had to have been administered quickly, while Saunders was dazed from the assault. But if you're beating a victim why the need to kill him some other way. Jake needed a blood sample examined and waited for Zeke to get off the phone.

Zeke hung up and before Jake could pose the question, the M.E. said, "I have a blood sample I'm going to send off to the Highway Patrol."

"You read my mind, Sheik."

"It's such a tiny thing, but a shame to let it go to waste. Oh, one more thing that's interesting," Zeke said, pausing for effect, a wide grin on his slender face.

Zeke the Sheik liked his little games. Jake waited half-a-beat before he said, "Okay, what is the other thing?"

"Saunders had a venereal disease in its early stages."

CHAPTER FOUR

Friday morning, Jake sat in the central office of the Paradise School district, secured by police tape and compared crime photographer Wiley's many photos with the crime scene in front of him. He had set up interviews with faculty and staff workers, dividing them up between Buddy, Cal, Deputy Bailey and himself. He would start the interviews today and continue over the weekend. They had fingerprinted, a futile exercise, as every employee and hundreds of people in the community had been in the office; not to mention Buster Mangold playing with the gold-plated apple, Jake wondering how anyone could be that stupid.

School was cancelled but the faculty and staff were asked to come in and make themselves available to law enforcement.

Earlier he had asked Cal to authorize Leo the Lion to assist Jake when he examined the school building and in particular, Saunders' room, office and the multi-purpose room when Saunders' directed his plays.

"Why Leo?" Cal had asked.

"Because nobody knows this school and this town

like Leo. The guy is like a travelogue for Paradise and he will know the school and who has keys. He'll be able to point me in the right direction."

Jake posted Deputy Bailey overnight to ensure the integrity of the crime scene. Bailey wasn't imposing but she knew her job. Jake had Leo relieve her in the morning when Jake visited Dr. Zeke. After that, Jake returned to the central office building to take another look at the scene.

Leo sat quietly while Jake worked the crime scene. Jake had taken measurements the night before and written down notes. It was his hope the light of day would reveal something he had missed.

Jake looked at Wiley's photos and then at the room, holding the pictures up and looking back at the office floor and the body outline and the card that noted the blood speck on the floor. Something was bugging him.

It was the blood, rather the lack thereof, which was on his mind.

There was no blood except for the droplets which had occurred after Saunders had fallen out of the chair and then on top of the trophy base, the apple, and broken apple leaf. Jake wasn't buying the toppled chair as it looked staged. Nothing else in the room was disturbed.

If Saunders fell on the Apple commemorative plaque that made the cut then he wasn't dead yet when he fell out of the chair. A corpse stops bleeding when the heart stops pumping. But he could've fallen out of the chair and expired when he hit the floor, but that would be an amazing thing. Still, in his time with the Texas Rangers, Jake had seen some unusual things in homicide investigations.

"You've stared a hole in those photos," Leo said. "What're you thinking?"

"Something's wrong. Something about this scenario.

Somebody tuned him up pretty good and yet there's no blood. Also, the room isn't in disarray like you might see. Somebody knocking him around would've made a mess."

"There's some papers on the floor."

"They were scattered purposely, be my guess," Jake said. "Like they were interrupted and had to get out of here."

"You think somebody else came into the building?"

Jake stacked the photos neatly and placed them back in the envelope. "Yeah I do and I'm thinking it may have been Pete Stanger."

"Okay," Leo said. "I'll be your Dr. Watson. Why do you think that?"

"Because right now I don't have anyone else."

* * *

Harper Bannister's best friend, Sherry Hammersmith, was excited about her plans for opening a coffee shop so she invited Harper to her house to tell her about it.

"I think it's a good idea," Sherry said. Sherry was a copper-blond with a smile for every occasion and had grown up in Paradise as had Harper. They had been close friends since their middle school days. "We can make some money and God knows you can't get a decent cup of coffee downtown."

Harper spooned a tiny measure of sugar, not sweetener, she hated fake stuff, and watched it dissolve in her coffee cup. Harper and Sherry had been talking about going into business together for years. Harper wanted to revitalize downtown Paradise, which many now referred to as "old town". The Paradise community, once a small farm town in Western Missouri, had blossomed into a neo-boom town with newer businesses including national chain fast food stores, restaurants, and hotels.

"What do we do about Starbucks?" Harper said. "They can undercut us with name recognition, inventory and speed of service."

"They're out on the highway. I think we can syphon off some of the old-timers who sit at McDonald's. We can brew gourmet coffee for the young professionals and serve Folgers coffee for the old-timers."

"Some of the old-timers still hang-out at the Dinner Bell just a block off the square."

"But the DB doesn't make finger foods. We'll come up with some pastries that are tasty and easy to handle, not like the mass produced junk they carry. We'll get the wives who just sent the kids off to school. Heck, I've already found an old cracker barrel we can put inside, give it nostalgic appeal. We'll get the downtown business crowd and the Paradise lifers. Plus we're close to the mill, the grain elevator and the bank. I think we'll get carry-out business. C'mon it'll be fun. We'll get some investors."

Harper smiled at her friend. Sherry had always been a dreamer and a hard worker. Sherry had thought this through. It could work but there were other problems.

Harper saying now, "I'm still working on my law degree and I don't have much free time to devote to a start-up and besides that, coming up with the capital for equipment and inventory well..."

"I have some money from my divorce, the only good thing that came of that. I can train some young people to work it and I'll manage it until you're freed up. We can put together a syndicate, some investors and then buy them out when it gets going."

There was no stopping Sherry. She continued, saying, "What about your boyfriend, I heard he inherited some money and making money off renting out his farm."

She meant Jake Morgan. Jake's late father had

invested wisely and while Jake was no millionaire he did have a chunk of change left to him. Now that he was a full-time investigator for the town and the county he didn't have much time for such things. Worse, he had little time for their relationship which was wearing on her. She loved Jake but his work and sometimes his disposition was keeping her at arm's length. She had already been through a nasty divorce and did not want to make a mistake again.

She loved Jake and she knew he felt the same way. Harper also knew she was a big reason Jake had left the Rangers and settled back in Paradise County again. While that was nice it also made her wary and even cast a shade of guilt on her if things didn't work out between them. Jake had been a star investigator in Texas with a rosy future and pension ahead of him and the weight on her thoughts was always there which led Harper to say this to Sherry.

"I would be uncomfortable asking Jake to invest in this."

Sherry turned her head to one side and said, "Why? Everybody in town knows you two are going to close the deal and live happily ever after."

Harper thought about that often and hoped Sherry was right but for now...

CHAPTER FIVE

Dr. Zeke Montooth, AKA "Zeke the Sheik", a nickname from his basketball days as a Paradise High Schooler, heard his cell phone buzz, looked at the read-out and saw the name, 'Jake Morgan'. That meant the investigator wanted more information or had a question. Once Jake was on the case it went like this.

Without a greeting, Jake said, "The blood from the cut on Saunders? Was it from an outside cut or from the inside of his mouth?"

"That's interesting," Zeke said. "Hang on a second." There was a sound of pages turning and then Zeke said, "The puncture wound was from his gums and inside his cheek."

"What if he wasn't beaten at the school but died after he was moved there?"

Silent on the other end for two beats. "Hmmm. That's a wild theory, Jake. Why would someone beat him up and then drag him into the office and then kill him."

"Send a message," Jake said. "I'm thinking maybe the killer wanted us to see the apple thing. I'd know more if Buster Mangold wasn't a moron. Or, just I don't know why. Hell, I'm guessing but making that guess on what I've seen so far."

"There is a possibility I may not be able to determine the cause of death. I can't pinpoint anything other than his heart stopped and he expired. What you're not going to like is I cannot do much with the death certificate. He didn't commit suicide unless he decided to beat himself up and drink poison and poison I would've found. Yes, there was an assault but I cannot conclusively tie that to his death. Further, Martin Saunders has no medical record of heart disease or stroke. Accidental death by unknown means or heart failure may be my final determination. You can still indict someone for 'assault with intent'."

"He was murdered, Zeke."

"You know that and I know that but we don't know how."

"Can't be the assault?"

"It's possible, just not likely. Somebody knew what they were doing. You may be looking at someone with the intelligence of human anatomy and maybe medical background. Regardless, it is somebody educated and that isn't much help to you as every faculty member is educated. Jake, unless I can find a cause of death we are stuck with heart failure."

"Why not heart failure exacerbated by assault?"

Zeke nodded absently, rubbed his forehead with his free hand. Jake Morgan was not going to let go of this, no way. Jake had always been this way; stubborn even as a kid. When they were freshmen, it was a tradition for the upperclassmen to haze the freshmen. One tradition was that ninth grade football players had to carry the seniors' helmets out to the practice field. Failure to do so meant twenty-five push-ups over a sweaty senior's jock-strap or a pretty good whipping from an older player.

Most Frosh were resigned to their fate, not Jake. He wouldn't go along with it and was more than willing to break tradition no matter the cost.

"I'm not your servant and I'm not doing push-ups for you or anyone else. You put your hands on me, I'll get a baseball bat and break it over your head."

They believed him. All except one guy, Marty Young, a running back who decided he wasn't going to put up with an uppity ninth grader. Young took off his sweaty jock strap, walked up behind Jake and wrapped it around Jake's head.

Then it was on. The other players broke up the fight. Jake had a cut lip and a swollen jaw but had taken a toll on the older boy. When they were separated, Young pointed at Jake and said, "This ain't over, little boy."

Jake, glared through bloody teeth said, "You are right about that."

Sometimes it was hard to watch Jake's rebellions.

The next day, Young told Jake to carry his helmet, Jake again declined and refused to do the push-ups. Another fight ensued, this time Jake did a little better but still ended up the loser, still defiant.

"I'll do this every day," Young said, when the fight was, once again, broken up.

"You'll have to," Jake said, wiping blood from his face. "Not kidding. And the day's coming where I'll be bigger than you and I'll kill your ass."

The third day Young again commanded Jake to carry his helmet. Jake shook his head, put up his fists, and said, "Come on, let's do it."

Young looked at him, shook his head, waved a hand at Jake and said, "Forget it, kid. It ain't worth it."

That was the end of that tradition.

Zeke saying now, "Jake, the beating could've exacerbated and generated a heart event but Saunders was forty years old and in excellent shape. Unless you can come up with something I can't rule it a homicide."

"You have anything on Pete Stanger's condition?"

"Last I heard, he is semi-comatose, that is he swims in and out, but is not aware of what is around him. Pretty good bump on the head. I'll check with the hospital and keep you updated."

"Another thing. Could you check and see if there is any bruising or cuts on his hands?"

"There's going to be cuts and—wait, you are looking for damage from hitting someone."

"Just covering the possibilities. He was running from something and...I don't know. Can't help thinking or at least wondering if it had something to do with Saunders homicide?"

"Well, we know Pete didn't like Saunders and let's not call it a homicide just yet."

"So, I'm supposed to believe that Saunders was soundly beaten, maybe by a memento taken from Saunders room, dumped in the Superintendent's office and it's...Dammit, it's a homicide, Zeke. List it that way."

"Excuse me, I completely forgot that you had a medical degree. Tell you what, it's still early, I'll hold off on a determination for twenty-four hours."

"Forty-eight hours," Jake said.

Zeke held the phone out away from his ear, chuckled to himself and then said, "You never change. You are still an impossible asshole. What the hell is wrong with you?"

"I'll let you know when I figure it out," Jake said. "Until then, forty-eight hours."

"You're like a Chinese water torture, Morgan. What the hell, it's only my career as a trusted medical professional which I scrimped and saved to attain."

"Your dad taught at the University. You went free."

"What a fucking pest you are. Okay, you got forty-eight hours."

"How about seventy-two?"

* * *

Saturday morning, Deputy Sheriff S.G. Bailey, called 'Grets' or 'Bailey' by her fellow officers was relieved at 7 AM by a Paradise uniformed officer. Sharon Gretchen Bailey had been on overnight duty protecting the crime scene at the Superintendent's office where a teacher had been killed.

"Nobody," Jake Morgan, "And I mean nobody comes inside this building."

Bailey was chosen by Morgan over other deputies and police officers. Sheriff Buddy Johnson told her, "I'm lending you to the local police at Jake Morgan's request. He told Chief Bannister and me that he trusted you to do it right. He has a high opinion of you, Bailey."

She knew there were officers in both departments with more experience; men who were bigger and tougher than her, but she liked that Morgan chose her and had confidence in her.

Night duty protecting the integrity of a crime scene was generally a boring post but last night had been different. More than one person had come by and wanted to gain entrance and asked questions. Questions Bailey was not at liberty to entertain.

There were even a couple of interesting visitors and Bailey knew Morgan would be interested in who they were.

Very interested, in fact.

CHAPTER SIX

Jake met Chief Cal Bannister and Sheriff Buddy Johnson at the old storefront which had been modernized and made into Paradise Police Chief Bannister's office. They were sitting in the break room that connected Cal's office with the main Police Department HQ. They met to compare notes and each man had a paper cup of coffee in front of them.

"What've you got?" Cal asked Jake.

Jake briefed both men on Zeke's findings and that the Sheik was holding off on a final determination of Saunders' death.

"That's going to bring some heat from city council to come up with more than that," Cal said.

"Yeah," Buddy said. "Forty-eight hours of questions from the press. Fortunately, it's a weekend so it does give us some time. You have any thoughts on what caused the death if it wasn't due to having the shit kicked out of him?"

"No," Jake said. "I don't. Well some." He took a sip of coffee before continuing. "What I'm thinking isn't solid and not for publication. There may be some foreign agent administered that stopped his heart, but even that is conjecture. I want to say he was assaulted and then brought to central office."

"That sounds crazy," Buddy said.

"It does, doesn't it?" Jake said. "I wish I had more but maybe after we interview some people and compare notes we can pare down the possible avenues and hopefully limit the number of suspects."

"Which is quite a list," Cal said.

Buddy said, "I don't want the community to be panicked but this is a small town and you know how people are around here. They'll start talking and we'll be deluged with tips and rabbit trails to run down."

"'Deluged' huh?" Jake said, brightening at his friend's choice of words.

"Plus they will start thinking we're incompetent," Cal said, and reflexively reached for a pack of cigarettes that wasn't there. Cal had quit a month ago. Jake was also trying to quit and wanted one now. Something about a cup of coffee and a cigarette appealed to him but he wasn't going to light up in front of Cal, a man he respected and could possibly be his father-in-law if things worked out.

Buddy asked, "What about drugs?"

"Zeke mentioned that," Jake said. "But so far nothing. He sent off lab samples to the Highway Patrol and County Medical but that'll take time. As for suspects, Leo the Lion is right. Nobody liked the guy." He looked around the room. "Why are the donuts always gone when I show up?" He smiled at Buddy before saying, "Dammit, Buddy, did you Bogart the donuts again? You believe this, Cal? I tremble when someone brings a box in. You gotta stay clear or get trampled if you get between Buddy and—"

"Give it a rest, Morgan," Buddy said. "I'm a high

energy machine and require fuel. You said something about Pete Stanger. Where are you with that?"

"I hate to use the word, 'hunch', its clichéd, but Pete was high-balling like he was running from something and then another vehicle, a pick-up, flew by soon after. You know, people usually slow down or even stop when they see something like a wreck, especially with Pete running through a fence and into a field, but this truck never slowed."

"You think the person was chasing Pete?" Buddy said.

"Or Pete was chasing someone," Cal said.

Jake stared off and nodded his head thinking about it. "I hadn't considered that but…"

The door to the break room opened and the Dispatch operator, Gail Thurman, entered and right behind her was Felicia Jankowski. Thurman put her hands out and shrugged as if saying, 'couldn't stop her'.

"Well, this is nice," Felicia said. She was wearing skinny jeans and a pair of suede half-boots topped with a long-sleeved cotton shirt with the cuffs rolled back. Felicia was in her early forties but stayed in shape and could still wear jeans like a college coed. "We have a murder and you three are sitting here drinking coffee. You should be out arresting the killer."

"We would've had donuts with the coffee, but we're out," Jake said. Buddy shot him a look.

"What is it you want, Felicia?" Cal said.

"I want to know where you are as far as the investigation into the killing of Martin Saunders. You are aware he was murdered, right?"

"I'm sorry," Jake said. "We were discussing a possible BOLO for a produce guy selling apples without a license. We have our priorities."

"I know you." Felicia's eyes narrowed. "The same smartass that put my husband in prison."

"If I remember correctly, I think he put himself there," Jake said. "But you seem to be doing okay for yourself."

She ignored Jake's remark and turned to Cal. "Cal, where are we in this investigation? People are not going to like it if there is no statement or information forthcoming. As a council member I have a right to know."

"You know I can't tell you that. It's an ongoing investigation and being on the city council does not change that. I'm not trying to be rude or difficult but that's the way it has to be. Now, if there's nothing else I can help you with..."

"We'll talk about it this afternoon with the rest of the council members."

"That's fine, you do that, Felicia," Cal said. Cal had kind eyes and the type of personality that allowed him to say things that sounded conversely soothing and combative at the same time. "Now, if you'll excuse us, we were discussing the case you are concerned about."

Felicity turned on her well-appointed heel and left the room.

"She's still a good-looking heifer but Jankowski is having the vacation of his life in prison," Buddy said. "Can you imagine being married to that?"

"She's right though," Cal said. "I'll have to make a statement and with what we have it isn't going to be much."

"That could work to our advantage," Jake said. "The killer will be waiting on that statement and the less said could make him...or her...edgy."

"Her?" Buddy said. "How could a woman beat Saunders and drag him into the superintendent's office."

"Well, I hadn't gotten to this part yet. There may be two individuals involved in this thing. One for the assault and a second person who administered the coup-de-grace. Saunders called in sick the two days before he was killed. I got some information from Bailey before I came in and Winston Vestal once again tried to get into the building."

Cal smiled and shook his head. "That man's persistent, isn't he? Bailey turned him away, right?"

"You bet she did," Buddy said. "She's the real deal. Does her job and does it right. She gets a CJ degree, we'll lose her to the highway patrol or Kansas City and that'll be a pity."

"Vestal wasn't the only one who wanted to know what was going on. Also Buster Mangold."

"What the hell was Buster doing there?"

"Said he dropped by to relieve Bailey."

"Why would he do that?"

"Good question. I'll ask him about it when I see him. Bill Tompkins showed up asking Bailey questions."

"Tompkins, the baseball coach?" Cal said.

"Yeah, and it gets better," Jake said. "I checked and Tompkins owns a Dodge Ram pick-up."

CHAPTER SEVEN

Jake considered the order of interviews. Bill Tompkins, the baseball coach; Brenda Sutherland, the English teacher passed over in favor of Saunders for Department head and Winston Vestal, the superintendent determined to gain access to his office despite police tape and threats of arrest.

Those three were the ones Jake took. Other teachers were assigned to Buddy, Cal and Deputy Bailey. The latter trio were to begin their interviews, dividing possible suspects along with possible leads and witnesses. Bailey was canvassing neighbors close by Saunders' property to learn if they'd heard any disturbances the night of Saunders' death.

The first thing Jake did was make Saunders' house inaccessible to the public and setting up police tape and mounting a cop to guard it until he could get there.

Jake had checked Saunders' house. Jake had hoped Saunders being a Drama/Theatre teacher would have security cameras. There were cameras but they were disabled. However if they had bluetooth connections they could be uncovered in Saunders' computer which was password protected. Jake was no tech wizard so he would need to find someone who was or get a court order to have his server company reveal it.

Jake had reason to interview Winston Vestal last. He wanted Vestal to worry about what his employees might say. Vestal had twice tried to bypass police restrictions which raised Jake's antenna so he wanted employee information as ammunition against Vestal.

Jake had set up his interviews in the Paradise school board room. Sheriff Buddy Johnson would use the Principal's office while Chief Cal Bannister would receive his people in the faculty lounge.

First up was Bill Tompkins, the baseball coach who also served as the middle school football coach. Leo had told Jake that "Bill is a solid guy, hard worker. Good classroom teacher. Drinks a bit."

"How much is a bit?"

"A bit more than you and me."

"As a sum total? Don't equivocate, Leo,"

"All right. He drinks too much because he's going through a break-up with his wife. I'm not sure what that's about as he doesn't talk about it, but he has not been himself lately."

"When he is himself, what is that like?"

"Turned our baseball program around and is a good hand as an assistant football coach. Glad to have him on staff. Has a great sense of humor, likes the students and they like him. He's a young guy, who likes what he's doing and has a promising career ahead and he's going places. Lately though, he's been morose and doesn't seem involved with the school or really anything. Shows up late, leaves as soon as possible, drinks too much. Shows up with dark rings around his eyes. A divorce would do that to anyone."

Jake said, "Women, huh? God love 'em."

"Amen, brother. So how's it going with Harper? Has she wised up and dumped your useless ass yet?"

* * *

The interviews were set, and Jake ran into Buster Mangold who Chief Cal Bannister had posted in the parking lot to prevent intrusion from the media and gawkers. Mangold, was a big man, late thirties, twice divorced and an imposing figure. The PPD officer was dressed in his uniform and on duty. Jake walked up to him.

"How's it going here, Buster?" Jake said.

"So far, it's cool. Couple young guys tried to sneak through but I 'Bustered' them." Mangold liked to verbalize his name whenever he made a bust.

"Good," Jake said, and started to walk away, turned around and said, "Buster, why did you come up here last night? Bailey had secured the area."

"I didn't have anything on. Was bored sitting around and thought maybe she wanted to have a break."

Jake shrugged and said, "Oh, okay."

"You checking me out, Morgan?"

"Do I need to check you out?"

"Who the fuck you think you are, Mr. High horse? I don't work for you, I work for the Chief. I would never work for you."

Jake walked away, smiling to himself. Back over his shoulder he said, "You're right about that."

* * *

Bill Tompkins entered the interview room, introduced himself and shook Jake's hand, a good firm handshake. Tompkins was twenty-five, sandy-haired with the kind of physique young guys had when they worked the weight room. He was middle-class handsome, the kind that probably had the cheerleaders after him when he was in high school. In contrast to his obvious health, Tompkins eyes were bloodshot at nine in the morning.

And...his knuckles were swollen and marked by scabs.

"Have a seat, Coach Tompkins," Jake told the young man. "And relax, this is just background information to eliminate anyone who is not a person of interest. Are you a person of interest, Bill?"

"Could be. I hated that son-of-a-bitch Saunders and he's dead and that's good all the way around."

"Aw, c'mon, Bill, don't be so guarded." Jake was taken back by Tompkins' blatant honesty. "You just ruined most of my clever interrogation techniques designed to trick you into just such of confession. So now I've got to skip on down my list. Why did you hate that 'son-of-a-bitch'?"

"Everybody hates him. The kids, the other teachers, he's an asshole."

"An ex-asshole at this point. Any specific incident or confrontations between the two of you? Coach Lyons already told me about the thing with the achievement tests. Is there something else?"

Tompkins looked uncomfortable and began to rub his injured hands. "I'd rather not say."

"I'm afraid you're going to have to, that is, unless you want to do this downtown with your lawyer present."

"Aw, shit...this on top of...Every. Other. Fucking. thing."

Jake waited on Tompkins. "Would you like some coffee, a glass of water?"

"No. I'm good. Listen, the thing I don't want to talk

about has nothing to do with your investigation. Really doesn't."

"Sorry, I'm the one who makes that determination. If it's personal and turns out to have nothing to do with his death I'm the only one who will ever know about it. So, I'll wait while you gather the words and straight up, I'll tell you this, if you try to hide something I'll know or I'll find out and things will get decidedly worse for you."

"I've heard you're tough," Tompkins said, giving a hard look. "But, I really don't have anything that'll help you. Understand?"

Jake met the baseball coach's look and waited some more. Pregnant pauses always worked in the interrogator's favor and Jake was pretty sure that Bill Tompkins was not a liar and therefore not used to hiding things. Top notch coaches were confident people who did not mince words and would be uncomfortable doing so. Career coaches were used to making split second decisions and doing so with assurance. No regrets.

"Okay, but this doesn't leave the room, Okay?"

"Again, if it is not germane to the investigation your secrets will die with me. That's my promise to you."

Tompkins took a deep breath, looked away as if wishing to be outside with a fungo bat sending baseball into the blue sky. He put his forearms on the table.

"I'm having some problems at home. You know, with my wife."

Jake nodded to keep him talking. He could tell this was hard for the man, telling a stranger about his domestic troubles when he hadn't told his friends.

"We fight a lot and…well Saunders has something to do with it."

"He seeing her?"

"What? No. That's not it. He's a fucking pussy. I

thought he'd even looked her way I'd beat the living shit out of him."

Jake pointed at Tompkins' hands and said, "How'd you hurt your hands?"

Tompkins started to move his hands from the table and then thought better of it. "That? Well, like I said, I'm having trouble at home. I got drunk, got mad and our house is brick and I took out my frustrations on the wall."

"Maybe the house had it coming. I'll write it as self-defense."

Tompkins smiled a little. "Leo said you're funny. But, my hands are something you wanted to know about. Did somebody beat him to death?"

"I haven't revealed the cause. What have you heard?"

Tompkins shrugged, seemed more at ease now. "You know how it goes. Rumor mill is running full-tilt. Some are saying he was shot, some say he was stabbed but I don't know. How did it happen?"

"Where were you last Thursday night, say between nine and eleven O'clock?"

Tompkins colored noticeably and his eyes widened with recognition. "Wait, am I a suspect?" He looked at his hands and put them in his lap. "I didn't kill him. Honest, hand on the bible."

"Where were you?"

"I've seen all those detective shows. You're wanting to know if I can account for my whereabouts, if I have an alibi."

Jake nodded again.

"This is going to sound like shit and you're not going to like it. Karen and I had a fight and I took off and drove around for several hours."

"In your pick-up?"

Tompkins mouth fell open. It had knocked him back

which was Jake's intent. Slowly, he began nodding his head, his eyes blank. "Yeah, in my truck. But, you knew that."

Jake only knew Tompkins had a pick-up, remembering the pick-up that had sped by the scene of Pete Stanger's wreck.

Jake said, "That's right, Bill, I know you left your house and I know where you went so you need to shoot me straight here. You lie or try to hide anything from me and things will go south quickly."

"You're not going to tell anybody?"

Jake sat, saying nothing. He knew Tompkins was about to make a confession of some type. Something that would complicate a rising coach's life.

"If you know where I went why do I have to say anything?" Tompkins said.

"That's the way it works. I have to hear it said. Here or downtown and if we go downtown no guarantees about sharing it with anyone."

"Brenda Sutherland," Tompkins said. The words came out like his last breath. "I was with her."

Jake remembered when Brenda Sutherland was hired during Jake's sophomore year. She was a looker and all the boys had the usual teen fantasies about their teacher. But that was fifteen years ago and she was in her late thirties now. Much older than Tompkins.

Jake lifted his chin and then he said. "And Saunders found out about the affair."

Tompkins sat, deflated, and nodded his head. "Yeah, he did."

* * *

Police Chief Cal Bannister was dressed in his official Paradise Police dark blue shirt, grey tie tucked inside his shirt, his badge clipped to his pocket and his braided PPD cap on the table in front of him. Jake had supplied them with coffee and donuts, a nice touch. Cal's first interviewee was Darla Spears, a sturdy built mid-thirties woman with plain features but a ready smile. Darla was a nice person who had worked as a janitor at the school since she had graduated, eighteen years ago. People in town liked her and she loved her job. Cal offered her a soda and she sat in a metal folding chair, across the table from Cal, with a diet soda in her lap, unopened, telling Cal she'd 'drink it later'. She seemed to enjoy being interviewed. Cal asked her how she was doing and if she liked her job.

"I like being around the school. Always have. I'm a Paradise Pirate for life, ya know?" She reached in the air and made like pulling on a bell cord. "Go Pirates."

"Darla, you know why I'm here and what has happened?"

"How did Mr. Saunders die?"

"We're not giving that information out. I want to ask you about a friend of yours, a man you work with. Pete Stanger."

"Oh, Pete. It's just awful that wreck he had wasn't it?"

"Tell me about Pete, could you? You work with him some."

"He's the best guy, Cal. Always polite to us girls, never bossy. If we have something break or can't figure out what to do he comes around and takes care of it, He doesn't have to do that you know, as he is the maintenance supervisor. He fixes the busses, the heating system, things like that."

"I guess I didn't know that," Cal said. "So, he doesn't do janitorial work."

"Environmental services," Darla said, big smile on her

face. "We don't call it janitoring anymore. We're right up to date."

"What about Martin Saunders. You have any dealings with him?"

Cal watched the smile run away from her face. "You know, Cal, I was raised not to say anything bad about people, especially them what has died but that Saunders, well, he's...he's a different story."

"In what way, Darla?"

"I don't like to talk about people like him."

"It would really help me if you would. I have a job I like just like you do and I would appreciate your help. Also, I'm a lifetime Pirate myself."

Darla laughed at that. "I know. Go Pirates again. Okay, well, it's like this, the principal, Mr. Howard, he's my boss, and when the teachers need something like a kid hurled their lunch, ya know, well they tell him and he tells me. The teachers are nice here but not Saunders. He comes right up like he was president of America or something and demands I clean something up for him and he means 'right now'. Teachers are not supposed to do that because we have other chores and Mr. Howard doesn't like it because it confuses things about who is our boss. Line-staff something he calls it. Mr. Howard told Mr. Saunders that one day and meant it. I overheard it." She kind of leaned forward, conspiratorially, and said, "I hear a lot of things people don't think I know."

Cal knew what she was saying was true. The support staff people are everywhere around the building and become unnoticeable, almost like furniture, to students and faculty. Cal had accessed information from janitors, nurses and support staff in several government settings over the years during investigations.

"Yes, Darla," Cal said. "I'll bet you have heard and seen things nobody else has seen or heard. What are some of those things, such as, well…" Cal tossed a hand in the air. "How about the superintendent, Winston Vestal."

Darla pursed her mouth and seemed to shrink away at the mention of Vestal. She looked down at her hands and said, "I…I better not talk about Dr. Vestal."

"Are you afraid of Vestal?"

Darla chewed at her lower lip with a tooth. "He can fire me you know."

"He won't. Nothing you say here will ever get back to him. You're not a suspect, Darla, so anything you tell me will be private and kept secret from him or anyone else. It'll be like you never talked to me."

"What if he asks me?"

"You tell him that I said your interview was privileged information and I told you not to discuss it with anyone or I would arrest you."

"You'd arrest me?" Darla said, sitting up quickly.

"Of course not."

Darla laughed. "Oh, I see. Yeah, I'll be very glad to tell you about Vest the pest, that's what we call him. Also, you might want to talk to Ms. Sutherland, the English teacher."

"Why's that, Darla."

Darla tilted her head, coyly and said, "Ask her."

CHAPTER EIGHT

Harper Bannister was sitting in the Dinner Bell restaurant waiting for Jake to show for their breakfast date, and he was fifteen minutes late. Where was he now? I know he had those interviews but said he would carve out some time for her.

*　*　*

Sheriff Buddy Johnson was digging the irony of sitting in the principal's office where he was about to interview the high school principal, Dr. Jackson Howard. Howard's office was neat, everything in its proper place. Walnut desk with a laptop sitting on the left-side of the desk as Howard was left-handed. And in-and-out basket on the right side of the desk and a large file cabinet on the wall behind the desk. There were PHS Pirates Football, Basketball, Baseball and Volleyball photos from various championship years, three with Leo Lyons. Buddy read Howard's wall plaques for 'District Principal of the Year', 'Outstanding Educator', and one that read 'Golden Gloves, St. Louis, 3rd place, 2001'.

Buddy and Jake had visited this very office a few years back when he and Jake had been invited at Mr. Howard's request, he didn't have a doctorate back then, regarding an incident where several dozen books were stacked up in the hallway after a basketball game.

They had never confessed to that prank.

Jake provided donuts, coffee, bottled water and soda for Cal and Buddy as the day could go long and also to share with those they interviewed. The Sheriff noted he had three dozen donuts whereas Cal and Jake only had one dozen each.

"Is this one of your attempts at being humorous?" Buddy said. He knew it was.

"Saves you having to come steal mine after you eat all of yours," Jake said. "I'm an experienced investigator and you are a practitioner of pastry pilfering, pardon the alliteration."

"You're not as funny as you think," Buddy said, shaking his head.

"I couldn't possibly be."

Jackson Howard, like Buddy, was a black man in a position of authority in a predominantly white community. Buddy had lived in Paradise all his life while Jackson Howard had arrived at Paradise High School, during Buddy's junior year and had been there since.

School was closed due to Jake shuttering the school for the investigation, so Howard arrived in jeans and short-sleeved T-shirt. It occurred to Buddy he had never seen Howard without a tie and jacket. Jackson Howard was a tidy man, his mustache clipped to perfection and his hair, greying at the edges had been recently barbered. Howard smelled of after-shave and Baxter pomade.

"Well, young Mr. Johnson," Howard said. "Here we are again and this time we have a role reversal situation."

When they shook hands, Howard winced and pulled his hand back in pain.

"You all right?" Buddy asked.

"It's nothing."

"You used to box didn't you?"

"Those days are over. I still work out some at home and that's how I hurt my hand. I didn't put on my workout gloves and caught the heavy bag in a bad way. Never had much of a right hand anyway. Getting soft and old."

"You look like you could go ten rounds still."

"I keep in shape."

Buddy returned to the principal's executive chair and Howard sat in the seat where dozens of young men and women had made confession to cutting class, skipping school and where Howard would inquire who started the fight.

"This is a tough time for the school," Howard said. "Something like this makes our district look terrible and we have a great high school here, Buddy."

"I agree, Mr. Howard," Buddy said. "Would you like some coffee or maybe a donut?"

Howard laughed and said, "Looks like you have enough donuts to feed an army, Buddy."

"I work with someone who thinks he's funny."

"That would be Jake Morgan, would it not? You two and Leo Lyons, wow, what a change for you three men. Leo, who I hired as football coach, has been an amazing employee. Sorry about your friend, Gage Burnell. Tough for you when he was killed."

"It was," Buddy said. "Look, you know why I'm here and we have a mess on our hands. Do you have anything or know anyone who might wish to see Martin Saunders disappear from the earth?"

"I believe I would like a donut and some coffee, if you don't mind."

Buddy held out the donut box and the PHS Principal selected a bear claw and helped himself to coffee provided by the Dinner Bell.

"Martin Saunders," Howard said, admiring the bear claw. "It's unfortunate to have to talk about him. Martin is not well-liked and that's an understatement but he is, well was, an outstanding drama coach and teacher. His productions were amazing for a high school. The sets, the preparation and the performances he elicited from his students, well, were as well done as you'll see anywhere."

"We're hearing there was tension between Saunders and, this may sound indelicate, your Superintendent, Winston Vestal. What do you know about that?"

Howard paused to take a sip from his coffee, sat the cup down on the edge of the desk, *his* desk, and said, "Buddy, we are both black men in high positions in our community." He pointed at Buddy then back at himself. "I am more than aware of the paradox of you sitting in my chair and here I am on the hot seat as it were. Both of our jobs are subject to the shifting sands of local politics. You run every four years, myself every two years and my contract comes up again this year. You're putting me in a position of sharing information about the man who gives the recommendation for my renewal and that is uncomfortable for me. Surely you understand my position."

"I ran against the previous Sheriff," Buddy said. "I even helped investigate him. Put your mind at ease, Mr. Howard, nothing you say about Vestal will leave this room unless it becomes important in court. One more thing, sir, and I say this as a man who respects you, always have, either you freely answer my questions or I will subpoena you. Do we understand each other?"

Jackson Howard was quiet momentarily, then suddenly erupted in laughter. It was a genuine laugh, up from the bottom. Howard removed his glasses and through his laughter, he said, "Buddy Johnson, I apologize, but this is the very kind of thing I've said to hundreds of students over the years. The humorous irony is not lost on me." Howard shook his head smiling for a moment, placed his glasses back on his face and said, "I will tell you want to know, so fire away."

"Vestal and Saunders," Buddy said.

"Yes, well, it's no secret they don't like each other, and the truth be told, I don't care for either of them. Saunders is a tiresome prima donna that I have tried to fire only to be blocked by the school board."

"Saunders's uncles."

"Correct. Winston is, I'm looking for the words here is a..."

"Primping penguin with short guy issues?"

Howard laughed again and said, "That's a leading question and as a former debate coach, I would have to caution you but as an intelligent man I applaud your insight. Winston blew in here two years ago and immediately began to alienate my faculty while schmoozing the school board. Don't get me wrong, for the most part our board is professional and genuinely wants the best for our students. However, Martin's uncles are two of the members and carry too much clout. Some of them are afraid to buck Martin."

Buddy scribbled some words on a notepad, lifted his head and said, "What about Vestal? What is his issue with Saunders?"

"Same as mine, he wants him gone but is frustrated that he can't get it done."

"Are you and Vestal on the same page regarding Saunders' employment?"

"Not really. As long as Martin does his job, I don't have to like him. My issues over the years are for the most part resolved. Martin knows I expect him to behave professionally, do his job and not show favoritism to certain students. Winston just doesn't like Saunders and vice versa. You can feel it when they're in the same room."

"Did Martin Saunders have favorites?"

"Yes and it has been a problem for me."

Buddy then said, "Anyone, say, a student or teacher complain about that?"

"Yes. Some more than others."

"Anyone in particular."

Howard looked down at the desk, in thought. He looked up and said, "I'm uncomfortable talking about my faculty but yes, Mrs. Sutherland for one. Bill Tompkins is another. Sadly, Pete Stanger, the man who had the wreck, is my maintenance man. Any word on his condition?"

"He's comatose."

"What is Mrs. Sutherland's complaint?" Buddy asked.

"She was passed over for department head in favor of Saunders. She didn't take it well and I don't blame her. She had seniority in the English department and I recommended her for the job."

"What happened?"

"Dr. Vestal over-ruled my recommendation and Forest Taylor, that's Martin's uncle, backed him up on it. I was furious and Brenda filed a grievance and then took it a step further by filing suit against the school district."

"What is the current status of the lawsuit? When will it be adjudicated?"

"It won't. Brenda dropped the suit."

"Do you know why she dropped the litigation?"

"She never gave an indication. She just dropped it."

"When was that?"

"Last week. Last Monday I believe."

Buddy thinking about that now. He didn't know if that made things more clearly defined or less so.

Buddy moved in his seat and said, "One more thing, Mr. Howard, and it will be uncomfortable for me, knowing our relationship over the years. Where were you between the hours of nine and eleven pm, Thursday evening?"

"Home."

"Can your wife or anyone verify that?"

"No. Cyntel is visiting her mother who is recovering from surgery. I was home alone. I would imagine that makes me a suspect?"

"Let's hope not. Anything else you can tell me or any questions?"

Howard smiled broadly and said, "Just one. Did you and Jake Morgan stack all those library books in the hall? Your confession will be confidential."

CHAPTER NINE

Pete Stanger was in darkness. Was it morning? Was it night? Was he alive or dead? Was he late for work? He heard voices…

"His vitals are good. Pulse low but that's normal for his condition."

"What about the injury to his…"

Blackness again.

Female voice saying, "Well, Mr. Stanger. Time to change your I.V. bag."

Male voice saying, "Any sign of consciousness?"

"Not so far."

"The swelling on his lip is pronounced. They sutured the…"

Blackness and then the dreams. He was at work, but far behind. He could smell the lunchroom and Mr. Howard leaving the room and Dr. Winston staying and the door slamming.

Footsteps down the hall and then…he was outside and flying through the air.

Darkness and a sense of falling.

* * *

After Jake dismissed his second interview of the day Jake was looking to compare notes with Dal and Buddy when he noticed a young lady walking his way. He did not recognize the woman and she wasn't on his list.

It was a media person.

Then his cell buzzed. It was Harper. He had lost track of the time and knew why she was calling. He held up a hand to the media lady and answered the call from Harper.

"I know. I'm late. Things are involved here. Can I call you back?"

Harper saying back to him, "I'll think about it."

"I'm sorry."

"No problem," Harper said. "I'm a cop's daughter and know what's going on."

"I'll grill you a steak later at my place."

The media lady moved closer despite Jake's raised hand. "You're Jake Morgan, right?"

Harper said, "Is that a woman's voice?"

"Yes, but she shouldn't be here."

"That's very true, isn't it?" Harper said. Jake was sure she was enjoying his consternation. "Oh well, I guess I'll just have to go back to the pick-up truck cowboys and the young lions of the legal profession."

"I have to go."

"Of course you do, darling boy."

Jake smiled, clicked off his cell and addressed the young media woman.

"I'm going to have to ask you to leave, ma'am."

"Ma'am? Nobody calls anyone ma'am anymore."

She was slender and tall, five-seven, sienna colored hair, late twenties, blue jeans, cream colored blouse under a dark tan blazer, high heels.

"Regardless," Jake said. "You have to leave."

The woman held up her cell phone and began speaking to it, "This is Melissa Vanderbilt for KCKS…"

Jake reached out and snatched the phone from her hand. It surprised her.

"Hey, you can't do that," Vanderbilt said.

"I just did, now what?"

"I just wish to ask you a few questions. First, how was the victim, Mr. Saunders killed? Do you have any—"

"No interviews. Not now, not today, maybe never with me. You're leaving."

"I can't believe this. What are you going to do, physically remove me like some troglodyte?"

"It would be easy. What do you weigh, about one-forty-five?"

"One-twenty-two, smartass."

Jake smiled. He pretended to talk to her phone and said, "Note to self. Melissa lies about her weight."

"I do not. Give me my phone back."

"Just as soon as you're off school grounds."

Vanderbilt put a fist on her hip and said, "Make me go."

Jake shook his head, keyed his communicator and said, "This is Morgan. I need Deputy Bailey."

Bailey answered, saying, "This is Bailey."

"I need you to come escort a woman off the school property."

"I'm canvassing Saunders neighbors but I can be there in ten."

Jake broke the communication, looked at the reporter and said, "Deputy Bailey, a seasoned female officer, who has taken down men twice your size will be here to remove you from these premises. Due to the fact you have trespassed in a restricted area, your TV station will need to send a different person to gather information."

"Are you threatening me?"

"No, I'm telling you. How are you missing that? Bailey will make you leave. So we can do this the easy way and I escort you, making it look like your idea, or Bailey will cuff you and you can spend the day in a holding cell, calling your station's lawyers to come get you out. Maybe you do a live remote such as, 'This is Melissa Vanderbilt, live from inside a jail cell in Paradise County. It'll do wonders for your career. Of course, the food's not the best and we're pretty busy, so there may not be anyone around to grant your release...'"

"This is bad publicity for you."

"Thus ending my dream of becoming a media superstar."

"Do I get my phone back?"

"As soon as you leave the campus or promise to. By the way, how did you get this far?"

"I don't give up sources."

"That's okay I can guess who did it."

"Okay," she said. She put her hands out. "I apologize. I would like to interview you later. May I please have my phone? I promise I'll leave."

Jake turned her phone off and handed it to her. "Talk to Chief Bannister, first. He's about five-nine, friendly eyes, looks like everybody's favorite uncle."

She smiled and shook her head, turned on her color-coordinated heels and left him.

* * *

Brenda Sutherland could pass for much younger than her age which Jake guessed to be early forties. "I remember you, Mr. Morgan," Brenda Sutherland said. "You were quite an athlete in your day. Although you were not in my classes I recall a paper you did for a class on the era of Romanticism in British poetry. It was quite precocious. You liked poetry."

"Still do."

"It is a contrast," Sutherland said. "You look more an oil field roughneck or a farmer."

"The latter. Grew up on a farm."

"I apologize for my attire," Sutherland said. "I just came from the gym. Took advantage of the day off to stave off age and weight."

And succeeding, he thought. Brenda Sutherland was dressed in workout clothes—tennis shoes, lavender body suit, and Nike shorts. There was a sheen of perspiration on her nose that she wiped away with a well-manicured finger. She glistened with health.

"So, Mr. Morgan, where did the love of literature and poetry come from?"

"I read a lot."

She sat and crossed her legs. Her eyes were bright, her face tanned and the aroma of Chanel wafted Jake's direction. She had an easy way about her. She was a confident, accomplished woman. Jake offered her coffee and donuts and she declined.

Jake said, "This is a tough thing to talk about, Mrs. Sutherland—"

"I'm divorced. Please call me Brenda, Jake."

Jake nodded and continued. "I need to ask you questions about Martin Saunders though you may not have knowledge of anything that helps me. There may be things you won't wish to answer."

Jake held back his knowledge of her affair for the moment in order to spring it upon her though there was a strong possibility that her younger lover had filled her in despite being told not to discuss their talk with anyone. Interrogation is a hard exercise when you had to bear down on nice people but Jake had learned that anyone from any class, race, religion, or demographic, is capable of murder in the right situation. In Texas, Jake had worked a homicide case where a hundred-pound librarian, a nice lady, killed her husband's mistress with a load of #4 buckshot and then waited for her husband to come up and greeted him in the same manner.

Jake saying now, "Brenda, you were passed over for department head in favor of Saunders. Did that upset you?"

"Very much. I filed a suit against the district due to being passed over."

"Was the suit filed due to sexism...or ageism?"

Sutherland looked at Jake for a long moment, her green eyes flashed and she pursed her lips before she said, "I think I will have some coffee, please. One sugar if you don't mind."

Jake considered whether to say, 'help yourself', as this was a woman used to having her way and it might back her up a step but thought better of it, choosing to serve her and put her at ease.

"I'll be happy to," Jake said. He poured coffee into a Styrofoam cup, emptied a packet of sugar into the coffee, stirred it with a plastic spoon and handed it to Mrs. Sutherland. Jake sat down again.

"Tell me about Martin Saunders, Brenda?"

"He was a brilliant man, wonderful play director, everyone simply loved him...What?"

Jake smiled and said, "Sarcasm isn't helping me, Brenda. Or, perhaps you're the only person in town who liked him."

"He was vile and insufferable," she said. "But he was brilliant, probably a genius in his own way but, you're right, I didn't like him."

"Did you have any other reason to dislike Saunders? I

mean, I've heard why others didn't like him but want to hear your reason."

"You mean my affair?" she said and raised a perfect eyebrow.

"You're getting ahead of me here."

"I doubt anyone gets ahead of you very often, Officer Morgan."

"Jake."

"Okay."

"How long have you been divorced, Brenda?"

"Three years."

"Is your ex-husband still around?"

She smiled at Jake and said, "Yes, you don't know who he is?"

Jake shrugged.

"He's on the school board. He's Martin Saunders' uncle, Knox Sutherland, another insufferable person."

CHAPTER TEN

After his interview with Brenda Sutherland, Jake stepped outside, gave some thought to smoking a cigarette and remembered he had quit. A kid Jake had seen around town came up to him on his bicycle. His name was Eddie Oswald.

"Are you Mr. Morgan, the detective?"

"Investigator," Jake said, and shook Eddie's hand. "Do you go to school here?"

"Yeah. Thanks for the day off. Can you do that again?"

"Just one more day I think and then you're back on Wednesday. Sorry. That it, unless you want to take up a collection?"

"Yeah." The kid laughed. "Say, I may be able to help you out on your case."

"Yeah?" Jake said. "I could use the help. What have you got?"

"You know a guy named Ron Manners? They call him Rowdy Manners?"

Jake did. He had stopped him a few times for speeding, parking his motorcycle on the sidewalk, running his mouth and busted him once for trafficking, but it didn't stick. Beyond that, Manners imagined himself a tough guy and was a known drug dealer who kept some bad actors around to help him collect on overdue payments. "Yes, I know Mr. Manners."

"Well," the kids said, looking around. "You won't tell anybody I talked to you."

"Sure. Snitches get stitches. It'll be our secret."

"You should talk to that guy."

"Why?"

"He came up to school one day and argued with Mr. Saunders in the hall, but Mr. Howard, that's the principal, ran him off."

"I'll do that," Jake said. "Thanks for the tip."

* * *

Jake's next stop was the home of one Chaz Conway Carlester, also known as 'Triple C'. Carlester's house was a post WW2 board home, run down, contrasted by the new Lincoln Navigator parked on the gravel drive. Carlester, a white guy was a wannabe gangsta, and known for shoplifting, reselling collectibles on ebay, and buying beer for high school kids. Carlester knew where things were when nobody was watching, knew how to flourish on unemployment checks, food stamps and keeping his criminal activity outside Paradise County.

Jake figured Carlester would know something about what Rowdy Manners was up to these days. Jake pulled into the drive, knocked loudly on the front door and quickly walked around to the back of the property and waited.

Thirty seconds later, Jake heard footsteps, before Carlester burst out a back screen door, buttoning up his black Levi's jeans and carrying a pair of motorcycle boots. He hurried down the wooden steps where Jake clotheslined him under his chin with a forearm.

Carlester's feet shot out from under him, his boots flew out of his hand and he sat down hard on the balding grass lawn of his back yard.

"God-dammit." Carlester clenched his eyes and opened them to see Jake standing over him. "Aw hell."

"How're you doing, Chaz?" Jake said. "Where're you going on such a fine day?"

"Jake Morgan," Carlester said, looking up and smiling big. "Good to see you, man. I was just going to call you, bro, got things to tell you."

"I know you were, Chaz, but I was afraid you lost my number. So I thought I'd drop by and see how you're doing."

Jake helped him up and Carlester finished buttoning his 501's, and then stuffed his 'Tech Nine' T-shirt, into the jeans. He had a spotty mustache and a spare black beard to go with his 'just-woke-up' haircut.

"Why you gotta come at me like that, Jake? Why not just ring the doorbell like a human?"

"I knocked. Your doorbell doesn't work. I want you to tell me where to find Rowdy Manners."

"I don't know nothing about Rowdy...whatshisname?"

Jake scratched the back of his head and said, "It just makes me tired all over when you lie to me. What kind of C.I. are you anyway?"

"The kind that don't get paid, I guess."

"Also the kind I overlook their petty crimes like buying beer and marijuana for the underaged. Also, you selling powdered sugar and flour, telling kids it's cocaine."

"Marijuana is legal in Missouri, now."

"Not for fourteen-year-old girls, like LeAndra

Robinson and her boyfriend LeMayne but thanks for the update."

"You knew about…I mean, I don't know what you're talking about."

"Just tell me how I find Rowdy Manners and we'll overlook that little incident. I hear Rowdy and his band of merry men are running a meth lab north of town near the county line. You know anything about that?"

Carlester put a finger to his lips for quiet, looked around and put his hand out and shook them as if warding off spirits. "Man, Jake. Shit, what're you doing to me? If you heard about it why ask?"

"To see if you'll tell me the truth."

"And to hold it over my head. I know how you work. Where'd you get such a mean streak, dude? Man, what am I getting out of this relationship with you, anyway? You roust me, mess with my head, and put me in jeopardy with the powers-that-be."

"You have my undying gratitude. You can't put a price on that, Chaz."

"Well, I could but you wouldn't pay."

"You're learning. I heard Rowdy is moving into the big time. That he's got some new muscle-bound recruits."

Chaz nodded. "Yeah, okay so far that's right. You know them. You already know about Gower and Frankie Boy, but he's also picked up a couple big guys, one of them named Frye."

"Good. Now, where's the meth lab? Be specific."

CHAPTER ELEVEN

Jake seared the ribeye steaks for two minutes at 475 degrees before he turned them and shut the hood on his grill. He had built a deck addition on the back of his house, a house left him by Alfred Morgan, his father, along with two-hundred twenty-five acres of good farmland.

He reached down into a Yeti cooler and produced an ice-sweated can of Coors, cracked open the tab and took a good swallow before he pressed the can against his forehead. The morning had been cool but the temperature had risen into the 90s by mid-afternoon. There was a bag of unopened potato chips and an ice bucket with the neck of the Chardonnay bottle sticking out, on a wicker table with a glass top and matching chairs. Jake had green beans, seasoned with bacon bits and garlic simmering on the grill's side burner.

Miss Harper Bannister, the ex-Mrs. Tommy Mitchell and daughter of his boss, Police Chief Cal Bannister, sipped cold Chardonnay and said, "Tell me, were you Barney Fife today or Dirty Harry today?"

"Little of both," He said. He pressed the tongs against

one of the steaks, thinking a little longer on the ribeyes. "Learned some things and found out others I wasn't expecting. I can't tell you much as it is an on-going investigation."

"I'm the Chiefs' daughter so I get an exemption."

"And you're a possible suspect."

"Really?" Harper wore a crisp lemon-colored blouse, white shorts and Ked's sneakers, no socks. Harper looked like she was sitting in an air-conditioned room rather than the Indian Summer heat of October. She crossed tanned legs, the only legs in the world Jake was interested in, and smiled up at him. "Why do you suspect me, copper?"

"I suspect you of many things, like those shorts. I'm not sure they are regulation length for an unmarried woman. Are you trying to seduce me?"

"Need I?"

"Also, as a former student of Martin Saunders, you become an automatic suspect because as it turns out, everyone in the school, including students, faculty, and staff, disliked him. I've seldom encountered anyone so universally unpopular."

"He was nobody's favorite," Harper said. "But he was smart."

"I heard brilliant and that from someone with reason to despise him. Did you know Brenda Sutherland, the English teacher, was getting 'boinked' by the baseball coach?"

"'Boinked'?"

"I'm quoting the current teen vernacular. I'm an up-to-date guy."

"Save it for the teeny-boppers," Harper said. "In the future I would prefer the more traditional terms such as, 'banging' or 'doing it'."

"Hmm," he said, and tested the steaks. Done. "So how're things going with the law school thing?"

"Don't try to change the subject. Tell me more about the case. Better yet, who was the female voice I heard?"

"Media." He plated the steaks from the grill to let them rest. "Said her name was Melissa Vanderbilt."

"You're kidding?" Harper said. "Well, aren't we rising in the world? She's big stuff. So when are you on? Tonight?"

"Nope. I didn't answer questions and I took her phone."

"Why?"

"I didn't want to tell her anything."

"You're like that. Sometimes it's hard to get you to say anything."

"As for Saunders, I don't know how he died, yet."

"Thought he was beaten to death."

"That's what I thought but the assault was short of death. His death is the result of his heart stopping."

"Heart attack?"

"That's what it's made to look like." Jake placed the steaks on plates and set them on the round table. "Zeke won't sign off on homicide and I have limited time to demonstrate that it was the result of foul play as none of the injuries were life threatening. I'm waiting on lab results."

"That may come outside your time limit."

"You seem remarkably well versed."

"Chief's daughter."

They sat on the wicker patio chairs and ate their steaks and talked about their day. Jake asked how her studies were going towards her law degree.

"I still have another year to go and then there's the bar. Between that and working as a paralegal, as if I didn't have enough on my plate, now Sherry Hammersmith wants me to invest in a coffee shop downtown. I have money from the divorce settlement and that intrigues me but…well, it's a lot to ask."

Jake nodded. "It is. What do you want to do?"

"I could ask you the same question. What do you want to do?"

"Marry you."

She smiled. "I know, Jake. But we both have a lot going on. I have mother issues and you have father issues. My mother left when I was very young and you and father never got along."

"That was his fault."

"See? Right there, that's one of our problems. When people are in close proximity to each other for long periods there are always going to be problems between them. You can't let go of it."

"I don't know if I agree with you on that. Yes, we had our problems but he made it up by leaving me well-off and restored my Lincoln."

"In absentia." She paused to sip wine. "You weren't around and he didn't have a chance to reconcile with you and he obviously wanted to. It was you, Jake Morgan, who harbored the anger while your father, whom you still refer to as 'Alfred', was grieving your estrangement and desired the opportunity to make things right. It makes me sick to think about that poor man wanting to be loved by his son and you…" She flipped the back of a hand in the air. "You would not allow him the chance."

Jake took a good swallow of his beer, crushed the can and reached into the cooler for another. "It's not an easy thing, I admit, and I handled it wrong but you don't know what it's like to have Alfred for a father."

"And you don't know what it's like to grow up without a mother, Jake. At least you had the opportunity. I didn't even have that. Your father left you a legacy and despite your differences he made a good man out of you. I didn't have a mother to hold me, to dress me up and teach me to be a woman."

"You turned out all right."

"Just all right?"

"Give me a break, counselor."

"As your attorney I would advise you to drink your beer and listen attentively. You didn't have to watch as your father, in my case my father, a man I love, watch him grieve over the loss of the woman he loved, never understanding why she left, and spend all his time raising a daughter without help."

Jake nodded slowly. "You're right. That was tough. And, your dad is a great guy and more than a father to me than Alfred...I mean, my father was."

"Don't put that on my dad, Jake. He has enough on his mind without having to raise a turkey like you."

"How did we get off track? I was talking about getting married."

"So was I. How did you miss it?"

Jake looked at her for a long moment.

"Don't try to read my face, Jake."

"I'm not doing that."

"Yes, you are and you're good at it."

He looked over towards the wooded draw past his yard and thought about quail hunting in the fall and wishing right now he was doing that. He took a good pop on the beer and said, "I love you, and that's all I know."

"And, I love you too, dummy. I'm ready to marry you but you're not ready for marriage."

Jake raised a hand. "Point of order. You're already wearing the engagement ring."

"And I like it and this thing will happen. I'm just

waiting for you to become marriageable. For now, I'll just ride this wave of being engaged. I'm enjoying it."

Jake started to speak, thought better of it, and took another sip of beer. Harper looked at him, her head tilted to one side.

"What?" he said.

She smiled at him, and said, "You're not very good with women are you, Mr. Morgan?"

"Slow learner."

"You're doing better than you think," She said. "With me, anyway."

CHAPTER TWELVE

After supper, they cleaned up the table and Jake told Harper about his interviews with Coach Tompkins and Brenda Sutherland and also about Winston Vestal who skipped his interview time. Instead of showing up, Vestal's attorney came in his place with a request to 'secure some effects' from Vestal's office.

Jake vetoed the request and the lawyer, a Medfield pleader with a weight problem named Kelton Sawyer, said he could get a court order.

"When you produce the order I'll let him in the office," Jake said. "Although at times I am hard to find and now I'm becoming more interested in the contents of his office."

"Officer Morgan—"

"Investigator Morgan, please," Jake said. Jake didn't really care about the title but the tiny correction would establish that the lawyer was not in charge.

"The…a…the death occurred in the outer office, not Dr. Vestal's office."

"Which is contiguous to Vestal's office and one cannot enter Vestals' office without passing through his secretary's office. I will see your client in my office downtown tomorrow morning eight-thirty. If he is not there, I will subpoena him and charge him with obstruction if he fails to appear."

"That won't stick."

"Maybe not, but it'll look really bad in the paper."

Sawyer made a sour face and said, "He'll be there."

"That will be wonderful. I'll have coffee and donuts ready."

"I heard you were a smartass, investigator Morgan."

"Jake. Please call me Jake."

Sawyer the lawyer, blew air between his lips and pushed his glasses up further on his nose and left.

Harper listened intently and said, "Do you enjoy being a smartass?"

"Why wouldn't I enjoy it?"

"Vestal has something to hide, doesn't he."

"Yes he does," Jake said.

* * *

After Attorney-at-law Sawyer left, Jake drove up to the school, donned latex gloves and examined Vestal's desk drawers and files. He didn't find a blackjack, a handgun with a spent cartridge or a signed confession. Disappointing. The file cabinet was locked and Vestal's laptop was password protected both of which would require a court order to check.

Jake did have access to the security cameras, but someone had disabled them. It was someone who knew there were cameras and how to disable them. Just like at Saunders' house.

Jake did get something on the outside cameras. But only got a quick look at a man leaving the office via a rear door of the school and running away. The camera quality was too grainy to determine the person. The man knew about the cameras and had avoided them so Jake couldn't get a fix on how he had entered.

Stanger, Tompkins, Vestal and Brenda Sutherland had keys to the building but did they have keys to Central office? Doubtful. Wondering now if any board members had access to a key. Jake called Leo Lyons and asked about the number of master keys circulating throughout the faculty.

"I've got one and there are several around," Leo said. "I know Bill has one and Stanger. I don't know if Brenda has one but it wouldn't surprise me. I'd guess Central office has little idea how many are out there among the staff and faculty."

Jake clicked off and thought about the rest of Brenda Sutherland's interview and was considering both the things said and the things not said when his County Cell lit up. It was Buddy Johnson.

"Morgan here."

"Jake, we've got a rumble out on county road H, you know that roadhouse."

"The Road Hogg?"

"Yeah, that one. I'm tied up here with my dispatcher out sick and Bailey is in class at her college. Some of the other deputies are scattered around the county and too far away to get there quickly. It's a bunch of wannabe Bikers causing problems with some local rednecks. The owner is getting worried. I need you to saddle up and Jake, it's a tough place so wait for back-up."

Jake grabbed his service weapon, and said, "Back-up? It's only one biker gang, right?"

"You wait for back-up like I told you."

"Hello...hello. You're breaking up."

"Dammit, Jake."

CHAPTER THIRTEEN

The Road Hogg bar had a reputation for drug deals, fistfights and selling beer to minors. Jake rolled into the parking lot with his lights dancing but his siren off. There were five motorcycles and six pick-ups in the raw gravel lot.

The air smelled of stale cigarettes, beer, and marijuana smoke. Jukebox sounds from inside the roadhouse belched neo-country sounds.

Jake, heavy flashlight in hand, stepped out of his county unit into the raw chat. They were waiting for him, probably after the owner called the Sheriff's office. He saw Rowdy Manners along with a couple other men he recognized—Deke Gower and Frankie Boy Degante. The other two were big belly guys with ZZ Top beards. Blonde beard was somebody new. Rowdy was recruiting.

He recognized the other big man. S.S. Frye, nickname, 'Super-Size Frye', if you can believe that. Frye was a known thumper who did a two-year jolt for assaulting two Medfield police officers. This was the new guy Carlester had mentioned. He was the guy to watch.

Rowdy was about Harper's age; a good-looking

young man, probably wowed all the gum-popping school girls who hated their parents. Rowdy had a can of beer in one hand, the other hand jammed down in his pocket, gave Jake his best 'give-a-shit' slouch. The others in his band of merry men were milling around, imitating thugs they'd seen in the movies.

A group of farmers, rednecks and wannabe cowboys stood on the deck of the Road Hogg yelling at the bikers. Rowdy and company shouted back and flipped the bird at the locals. Jake recognized a local farmer, Zeth Stokes, a man who hired out as a hand while running his own small farm. Jake had arrested Stokes a month ago for speeding and didn't write him. Stokes was slender, sunburnt and weathered from working outdoors.

Jáke called Stokes over and said, "What's up here, Zeth."

"Hey, Jake. These kids got mouth problems, 'specially Manners there. He and that sape he brought with them started bitching about the jukebox, you know, calling it shit-kicker stuff and one of our bunch asked if they 'wanted to see why it was called that'. Anyway things started with the name calling and cussing back-and-forth. Old Hogan, the owner, told everybody to chill and Manners got lippy so Hogan called it in. We been waiting to see who showed. Good to see you. You got anyone else coming?"

"Just me," Jake said.

"Good luck," Zeth said. "Holler if you need help."

Jake nodded and said, "Appreciate it but I won't need it for this bunch."

Jake walked over to his truck, his personal vehicle and retrieved some items from inside. That done he turned and confronted the group of bikers.

"Look here, boys," Rowdy said. "It's Jake the Snake Morgan, local yokel."

"County Mountie, tonight, Rowdy," Jake said, walking straight at the group. "Learn the appropriate appellations or you'll lose standing in the lock-up which is where you're going unless you and your playmates fire up your bikes, point them home and call it a night. Also, I've been meaning to talk to you."

"I don't see no fucking badge, Morgan," Rowdy said. "Any you guys see a badge? Deke you see a badge?"

"No, Rowdy, I don't see no badge," Deke said.

Jake aimed a flashlight beam at each man, eyeing the two ZZ Top guys, making mental notes so he would remember them later. Jake laughed happily and said, "Why would I need a badge to scare off a bunch of pups?"

"Get the light out of my face, pig," Super-Size Frye said, moving towards Jake. The men assembled on the wood porch leaned in to watch the action. Now he knew how Custer felt. Jake put the flashlight back in his truck, picked up a retractable baton and slipped it into his pocket.

Frye, bulled-up now, said, "I ain't afraid of you, badge or not."

"That's because you have no common sense," Jake said.

Frye moved closer now.

Jake said, "Don't close the distance on me."

"I'll do what I want." He moved even closer, but wary now.

Jake held out a hand. "Not another step."

The big man moved closer and said, "Whatcha gonna—"

Jake interrupted the man when he telescoped the baton and slashed it across the man's kneecap and then cracked the man's ear with the button end. The man howled in pain and slipped down to one knee, both hands now on his ear.

"I'm this way sometimes," Jake said. He moved quickly to cuff Frye. "When I tell you something, I'm not kidding. Stay down or I'll cripple you."

"Fuck," Frye said. "Cuff's are too tight."

"Tough."

Jake zeroed in on Rowdy, "Say good-night, Rowdy," Jake said.

"There's five of us," Deke Gower said.

"I can wait if you want to call some guys to even the odds up."

"What do you think you're gonna do?" Rowdy said, his head lolling to one side.

Jake said, "I could shoot three of you."

"Your gun is still on your hip."

"But I'm Wyatt Earp fast and I don't make threats. Think on that."

"Fuck you," said the other ZZ Top beard.

There was an explosion of lights from the road and the sound of a police siren. The Highway Patrol unit skidded into the parking lot with a spray of gravel and a muscular trooper stepped out of the vehicle and adjusted his Smokey the Bear cover. In his hand was a seventeen-inch Maglite that looked like a club in his knuckled hand.

Trooper Fred Ridley saw Jake and said, "What's going on, Morgan?"

"These children lost their way and are going home."

"They look pretty stupid, so we may have to spell it out," Ridley said. "What do you want to do, Morgan? You want to rope them and lock them up?"

"Aw, you know, they drink a little beer and forget they're guppies. Let's throw 'em back and see if they grow."

"Okay with me." Ridley looked at Rowdy and said, "You're getting a break here, Manners." Ridley moved closer to Rowdy and the latter shrunk away. Ridley had quite a reputation as a no-nonsense trooper. Nobody to try out. "Take it because I'm tired of corralling you."

Rowdy stepped back, looked around, searching for courage or a way to exit with what dignity he had left. "Yeah, we're just funning around. We'll go. We're not going to fuck with you state guys."

"And you, Super-Size," Jake said, pointing at Frye. "What a dumb name. You're going to spend a night at County. I apologize in advance for the beds but at least the food is terrible. As for you Rowdy, don't tear out of here because your feelings are hurt. Depart in an orderly fashion or I'll follow and you'll spend the night with double ugly here," Jake said. "And you will be in my office tomorrow morning at ten. I don't mean ten-fifteen, I mean ten sharp. This is only a request at the moment so don't make it a demand. Now get out of here and you ladies have a nice evening."

The people on the deck applauded and whistled at Rowdy and his gang. They fired up their motorcycles, revving them as loud as possible. Jake gave Rowdy and his bunch a look and slowly shook his head. They got his message and left without making a ruckus.

Jake watched them fade into the night and said, "Boy, am I glad to see you, Fred. I was just about to go full John Wick."

"I got a call from Sheriff Johnson, you remember Buddy, the guy you work for, your boss, right?"

"Black guy, six-six, two sixty, disarming personality?"

"He said you were supposed to wait for back-up but he knows how you think you're bulletproof. If he hadn't told me it was you I would've known anyway. Five guys? What were you going to do, shoot them?"

"Only three of them. I hate excessive violence."

"And then cite them if they didn't leave in an orderly fashion? God, I'll bet you give Buddy ulcers."

"I knew you'd arrive in the nick of time. How about a beer?" He nodded at the Road Hogg. "They're open."

"What was that thing about Rowdy at your office?"

"Got a tip from a reliable source that Rowdy has information about a case I'm working on."

"The Saunders' homicide?"

"Not a homicide yet, but yeah."

"Who's your 'reliable source'?"

"Fourteen-year-old kid."

Ridley shook his head and smiled to himself. "Morgan, at least you keep things lively. The way you go about your work though, how'd you ever qualify for the Texas Rangers?"

CHAPTER FOURTEEN

The next morning, Jake was in his office at 6:45. He leaned back in his swivel chair, boots on his desk, thinking about interview questions for Dr. Winston Vestal, Rowdy Manners and also to be briefed about a new suspect, Barnard Eberhard, known around town as Eb. Eberhard was turned up by Deputy S.G. Bailey, also known around the office as 'Grets'. Before she entered his office, Jake had coffee ready for her, two sugars with hazelnut creamer.

"How does Eb fit?" Jake asked Bailey. Bailey was a sturdy woman, plain features, brown-eyes, and a solid Deputy Sheriff. She was no beauty queen but Jake's pick when it came to research, canvassing, and technology. Bailey had a non-threatening demeanor that was disarming. She also had near total recall of events when she was at a crime scene.

Bailey telling Jake, "Word is that Eb accused Saunders of making fun of his kid, Ransom Eberhard, in an English class. Kept picking at Ransom until the kid exploded, and this boy is big enough to do some damage, but finally settled down. After class Ransom tried to talk to Saunders and Ransom slapped the kid and Saunders said he did it because the kid threatened him. Ransom and Eb deny it but Ransom was suspended and it knocked him out of an appointment to the Air Force Academy. Eb is still ticked off about that and isn't shy telling people about it."

Jake settled back in his chair and stroked the side of his unshaved face. "How about the school theatre and Saunders' office? You find anything noteworthy there?"

"Nothing on the stage or backstage looked like a clue. We're looking for clues, right?"

"That is correct," Jake said.

"I pulled all of Saunders' files and had a tech dust the room and especially his file cabinet and the inside of his desk drawers. There were, of course, too many fingerprints from students, etcetera, in the room but fewer in the file folders, his computer, and desk drawers."

Jake reached up and thumbed a scuff mark off his Lucchese boots. The expensive boots were a bit much, but Harper bought them and though he tried to talk her out of it she insisted and Jake knew he wasn't going to win that argument.

Jake saying now, "I've got Winston Vestal coming in this morning, which should be fun as he skipped out on me yesterday. He's going to like it less when I tell him I'm going to shut down his office for another day. I also have Rowdy Manners coming in for visit."

"What'd Rowdy do this time?"

"He and his buddies were liquored up, acting snotty out at the Road Hogg, then they got brave and I had to subdue one of them." He pointed in the direction of the holding cells. "That big guy you saw on the way in."

"You 'subdued' that guy in the holding cell?" Bailey said, incredulous. "What did you use, a whip and a chair?"

"I got a tip that Rowdy may know something could help us with the Saunders' thing. As for your guy, I've heard the name but don't know Eberhard that well. Tell me about him."

Bailey sipped her hazelnut laced coffee and then said, "He's a rancher. Big-time horse breeder and stud service. He's turned out some champion studs and has a national title with a Fox-trotter ridden by his wife. He also has had a boundary dispute over a home he bought for his daughter that abuts Saunders place. It's gone into court but that will be moot now that Saunders has assumed room temperature."

"Deputy Bailey," Jake said, in mock surprise. "'Room temperature'? That's cold. Anything else?"

"If the boundary thing wasn't enough, the school would not further investigate the incident at school. Eberhard has made no secret about quote 'catching Saunders out alone and whipping his ass' unquote. Eberhard is a big man and could do it."

"Okay."

"Can I offer up another…well, hunch? It concerns the manner of Saunders' death."

"We don't do hunches here," Jake said. "Well, I do, but the official word will always be we only deal with facts." He sipped his coffee and continued. "However, I do want to hear your 'informed conjecture'. I think you've earned the right."

"Well," she said. "We don't know what killed Saunders, right? It wasn't the assault so it has to be some foreign agent, perhaps a drug?"

Jake nodded, liking the way she was thinking as he had not posed that possibility to anyone except Buddy and Cal. Dr. Zeke was already looking into that possibility. "That's not bad. What're your thoughts?"

"Eberhard deals in high volume stock, horses and

cattle. He keeps medications on hand such as horse tranqs."

Jake said, "Get ol' Eb in here, you interview him and if you don't mind I'll sit in on it. Better yet, we'll go out there and maybe catch him and Ransom at the same time. "Better to talk to him out at his home so we can recon the place."

"For clues, right?" She was smiling.

"Always for clues," Jake said. "They are the puzzle pieces that we put together, move them around and then go with our hunches and hope the perps do something stupid. They often do."

"Another thing, I did background on one of the people you interviewed. The teacher, Brenda Sutherland, was a nurse before she went into education."

Jake nodded again, pleased with her work. "Horse Tranquilizers, PCP and other pharmaceuticals like it, would have shown in the autopsy. Zeke doesn't miss much. Interesting that Brenda Sutherland worked with prescription drugs."

"I also did some research into paralytics. One of these is Succinylcholine which is used as a short-term para-lytic. It's used to help with tracheal intubation but is used as a general anesthetic. Hospital people call it 'Sux' and tiny doses only are used. Bigger doses have been used in some obscure murder cases. Learned that in Crime-stopper school. Sux breaks down within minutes in the human body and is hard to detect, almost impos-sible without a quick toxicology screen."

"Zeke did a screen and he also sent off blood and tissue samples."

"Zeke would have to actively be looking for Sux to screen for it. It breaks down so quickly that the time may have passed."

Jake settled back in his office chair and put a boot up

on a desk drawer handle. "There's also antifreeze poisoning which is difficult to detect because it is quickly absorbed and breaks down…"

"And," Bailey said, interrupting. "It is chemically converted once ingested. There have been cases where killers have added ethylene glycol, the base chemical in anti-freeze, to sweetened tea and other drinks."

Jake had already considered antifreeze as a possibility and dismissed it as Zeke had not mentioned renal failure which is how it killed and Zeke would know that. "Hard to disguise antifreeze these days. In recent years manufacturers add a bitter additive that makes it unpalatable to pets and children."

"Correct," Bailey said. "What if someone had an older container? You know how people keep old paint cans and other chemicals around their garage and sheds. Farmers keep things around for years."

"Arsenic poisoning is easily available and often mistaken for heart attack. Large amounts are usually detected but smaller amounts over a period of time are difficult so the killer would have to have access to Saunders over a period of time."

"Like a lover?"

Jake said, "That's good work, Bailey. I better watch myself or you'll have my job."

Bailey made a face, snorted and then said, "I don't pack the crazy, Jake. Nobody wants your job. No one else is so colorful."

"I don't know whether that's a compliment or an insult."

Bailey stood, smiled and said, "A little of both."

* * *

Winston Vestal arrived at Paradise PD five minutes early in full battle array—Charcoal grey suit with a thin chalk pinstripe, power tie, fresh shave and grey leather dress shoes that probably set him back over two hundred dollars. Dressed for success and intimidation. Superintendents must make big bucks was Jake's thought. He wondered if Vestals' belt matched the expensive shoes. Jake offered a seat, no handshake, and Vestal sat, crossed knife-creased pant legs, adjusted his jacket and said:

"I hope we can conclude this quickly. I have work to do in my office."

Jake almost laughed at the man's overconfidence, knowing this was a person used to having his way with elementary teachers and staff. Then he thought about the attempts to gain entrance to the crime scene as though it was his right to do so. Jake had his doubts about Vestal being a killer, but this was a man in a hurry. What was in Vestal's office that was so important and did it pertain to the homicide?

Or did it connect Vestal to some other crime or scandal? Leo Lyons had more than once told Jake that while people in education were some of the best; there were many who had secrets in their lives that were as black as the dark side of the moon.

"Would you like some coffee?" Jake asked, more to delay things rather than be gracious.

"No thank you," Vestal said and looked at his watch.

"You won't mind if I refill mine?" Jake had already downed two cups himself.

Vestal mouth pursed but said, "No, that's fine."

Jake rose from his chair, walked to the coffee machine and poured coffee into his cup. Then, he opened a box of pastry, pretended to consider one, changed his mind and returned to his seat. Once at his seat, Jake took a sip of coffee.

"I probably drink too much coffee," Jake said. "I'm drinking more of it since I stopped smoking. Man, there's a habit hard to kick. Were you ever a smoker?"

"No," Vestal said. "It's a filthy habit." The man's jawline was taut and his lips were drawn up in a thin line. Jake noted the reaction and tried not to smile.

Jake continued, gesturing with his coffee cup. "Boy, I tried and tried but finally gave it up a few days ago. They say the first forty-eight hours is the hardest but I don't know, I'm past seventy-two hours and well...I gotta tell you, man, I'm drinking lots of coffee. I've tried candy bars and gum and that's about to—"

"Mr. Morgan," Vestal said, interrupting Jake. "Can we get on with it? Like I said, I have a lot of work to catch up on."

"I understand," Jake said. "That's why I'm hesitant to tell you I'm going to shutter your office for another day or so."

"This is ridiculous," Vestal said, his chin jutted forward. "There's nothing in my office pertinent to this case. You need to open this office at once."

"At once, huh?" Jake said, enjoying himself.

"Pardon me. At least open to me, please."

"I'll be glad to open up your office," Jake said. "Just as soon as you tell me what you're afraid I'm going to find in it." He lifted his coffee cup and looked over the rim at Vestal, who was struggling to maintain.

Vestal paled, chewed his lip, recovered and said, "I don't know what you're talking about."

Jake set his cup down, put his hands behind his neck, going folksy and said, "I'm just wondering about a school administrator who just had a valued employee murdered whose only thought is he has to get into his office. I've investigated homicides and most people want nothing to do with the crime scene. They may gawk and look once but most are shocked by violent death. It's like when someone gets a compound fracture, the bone sticking out, people tend to shy away from such things."

"Well…well, I was put off by it but…I guess in my grief my behavior may have seemed a little inappropriate."

"You tried a second time later that night. My posted deputy told me about it. What's in your office you don't want seen, Dr. Vestal?"

Vestal exploded from his chair. "What is this about? Am I a suspect?"

"Should you be? And sit down, please."

"I am not a suspect. I didn't…that is I didn't have anything to do with Martin's…passing."

"Hard to avoid the word isn't it? He was murdered."

"Next time we talk I will have a lawyer present."

"Why would you need a lawyer, Winston?" Using the man's first name now, changing gears on the man. "If you didn't kill him why the attorney? Do you know anyone who might wish to kill Saunders?"

Vestal stopped his theatrics, blinked his eyes and said, "What?"

Jake gestured with a hand in a downward motion and firmly now, said, "Sit down or get your lawyer, Kelton Sawyer, in here. I want to know if you have information about anyone who would want to harm Saunders or would benefit from his death."

Vestal looked deflated as he stood in his perfectly matched outfit. He sank slowly to his seat. "I'm emotionally worn out from this unfortunate situation. It's put everything in a turmoil."

"'Unfortunate' doesn't cover it. The man was brutally beaten and killed. I need names. You have any?"

Vestal looked off to the left, thinking about it. "I don't know. Everyone liked Martin. I liked him."

"Really?" Jake said. He leaned back and lifted his coffee cup up near his face but did not drink. "That's surprising? Nobody else does but you. What a humanitarian you must be."

"I know he had his faults but he was a good employee. It's just such a shock, you understand."

"I know what you mean," Jake said. "I have another question, Winston."

"Yes."

"Does your belt match your shoes?"

CHAPTER FIFTEEN

Police Chief Cal Bannister's phone intercom buzzed and it was Buster Mangold's voice. "Chief, Mayor Steinman is here and wants to talk with you."

Cal had a pretty good idea about what this was about. It was an election year and Steinman was being lit up by Felicia Jankowski who had an axe to grind with Jake. Jake didn't pull his punches and his whiplash sense of humor rubbed people the wrong way, but in his thirty years as a cop, Cal had never seen a better investigator. Once Jake got his teeth into something he would not stop even if it harmed him personally.

He remembered Jake's father, Alfred, who was the same type of tough individual who held on like a snapping turtle.

Paradise lucked out when Jake decided to return to his hometown despite rising in the ranks of the Texas Department of Safety, more famously known as The Texas Rangers. Jake had worked in the Special Response Team and later moved to 'Unsolved Crimes' which meant he handled Homicides and serial killers for the Rangers. Jake was one of the youngest men to make

Lieutenant in the Rangers but had drifted home during a "procedural leave" after he had gunned down two cartel soldiers and decided to stay in Paradise.

Cal also knew his daughter, Harper, had a lot to do with Jake's decision to take a pay cut and stay in Paradise.

"Send the mayor in, Buster."

The door opened immediately and Mayor Steinman walked in.

"I already did," Buster said.

Buster Mangold was beginning to annoy Cal.

* * *

Winston Vestal was boiling inside after his meeting with Jake Morgan. Vestal hated being treated like a clown by Morgan. Morgan's probing interest in Morgan's office was troubling and making him anxious.

Vestal decided to make a call he wished he didn't have to make but the situation demanded it. He should never have gotten involved with Felicia Jankowski who answered on the third ring.

"Well," Felicia said. "Look who is calling?"

"I noted that I missed a call from you, Felicia," Vestal said, chewing his lower lip after he said it.

"You liar, that was two days ago. Funny that you avoid me and now your teacher is dead. Did you kill him?"

"Of course not."

"Why not?"

"Felicia, I'm calling because we need to meet and talk about this situation. We have a mutual interest in seeing that Morgan finds the killer and ends his preoccupation with keeping my office sealed off."

"You can't get in?"

"No. Not until such time as he arrests someone."

"Are you telling me the...a...thing is still in your office?"

"How do you anticipate a homicide, Felicia? It was an unexpected coincidence."

"Maybe not such a coincidence. What if someone wanted attention focused on your office? Do you know any of the particulars about the murder?"

"Morgan won't let me in my office. This morning he interrogated me about possible suspects and then he intimated that perhaps I was hiding something in my office. He's an annoying person."

"He's a smug prick," she said.

"Well, where do we go from here?"

It was quiet on the line, long enough that Vestal wondered if she had hung up.

"Felicia? You there?"

"Yes, yes I am. How'd you fuck this up so badly? You should have removed that thing before now."

"Hindsight. I haven't had time to take it out of there. I was out of town at a Superintendent's meeting at the first of the week and then we had a board meeting Wednesday night and had to prepare for that. Felicia, I need you and the city council to put some pressure on Morgan and Cal Bannister to tell you what they have found out so far about Saunders'...well...death. That way we can perhaps move things along."

"Way ahead of you," Felicia said. "We will meet with the Chief and Morgan tomorrow and get an update. What about that Janitor in the hospital? Stanger?"

"What about him?"

"Maybe he makes a good fall guy."

"That's going too far, Felicia. I won't be a—"

"You won't be what, Winston? You may not have a

choice here. You don't want them messing around in your office."

"There is a strong possibility they may not know what it is when they see it. It's got—"

"We have to deal with possibilities not probabilities. I want Morgan's head on a pike for putting my husband in prison so I'll push it at a special city council meeting. Steinman is afraid I'll run against him in the fall and it is useful. Anything else?"

"Can I see you sometime?"

"I'm sorry, Winston," Felicia said. "The convenience store is closed. I guess you'll just have to use the self-service pump."

CHAPTER SIXTEEN

Jake looked at the wall clock that read 10:25. Rowdy was late. Kids, huh? Sometimes you just had to teach them the same lesson over and over. Jake grabbed handcuffs, his Sig Sauer .357, and a PPD hat. Jake didn't like hats but it was better than wearing the badge.

Jake picked up a flyer on a missing child, tri-folded it, and placed it in his police unit. Arriving at Rowdy's address, Jake stepped out of his unit and walked to the main building.

Rowdy lived in an older apartment complex, the kind with last-century wrought-iron entryways, dented mail-boxes and hallways that smelled of despair. There was a wall of addresses with scotch-taped paper inserts with names and apartment numbers typed in. 'Manners' was listed as 107 which put him on the bottom floor of the three-level complex.

Inside, Jake pressed the intercom button and heard Rowdy stir around and then say, "Who the fuck is it? It's the middle of the night. Told you guys I'd see you later."

Jake did not reply. He knew if he replied Rowdy would bolt to avoid him. Jake hurried down the hallway and knocked on the cheap door which rattled on its hinges.

"Who is it?"

"UPS," Jake said. "I've got a package needs your signature."

"All right. Hang on, huh?"

Shuffle of feet and then a hand on the doorknob. Rowdy opened the door and Jake said: "I meant to say, 'Police officer' not UPS. It just slipped out."

Rowdy smelled of stale beer, last night's cigarettes and marijuana. He yawned and scratched at his buttocks. A tattoo of a naked woman peeked through his robe. He started to shut the door but Jake placed a hand on the door, stopping him.

"C'mon, that's not friendly, Rowdy."

"Fuck you, I don't have to let you in."

"I believe I'm going to have to disagree, Mr. Manners," Jake said. "You didn't show for your appointment so as a caring public safety officer I said to myself, 'Gee, I hope Rowdy is all right and not suffering from alcohol poisoning or terminal stupidity' so I decided to make a 'Wellness check'."

"What bullshit. You set that appointment too…I don't fucking get up this early for anyone."

"But I'm not anyone, I'm the quality control director of Paradise County, and most of the world that doesn't sell drugs to children is awake. I'm coming in and if you resist or touch me, I will charge you."

Rowdy's eyes were furtive, looking back to his room. "Well, just give me a minute so I can straighten up, okay?"

"No."

"C'mon, man, I just got up. I gotta take a dump and I need a cup of coffee and a cigarette."

"Go have a sit, I'll wait. I have coffee in my office. And

please spray some air freshener. In fact, do that before you use the bathroom, you smell like cattle afterbirth."

"Do you have a warrant?"

Jake smiled broadly and held up the tri-fold missing person flyer. "As a matter of fact, I do. But if I use it then procedure will require that I handcuff you. And then because you didn't show on time and messed up my event calendar, I'll have to put you in a holding cell until I work on more pressing items than dealing with tough talking asswipes that miss appointments. It also means no shower for you."

He looked at Jake with bloodshot eyes and a slack mouth, looking for mercy. "C'mon, Morgan. Shit, man."

"You're making this too hard, Rowdy. I have no interest in your drugs today or if you have an underage girl hidden in your bedroom. Wait, do you have an underage girl in your bedroom? I may have to look. Wait here, while I do that."

Rowdy held up a hand. "Hang on. What do you think I did?"

"I just want you to help me as a material witness in a little matter I'm working on."

"I don't know nothing about the Saunders' thing,"

"How do you know it's about the homicide?" Jake shook the faux warrant papers. "Let's see, what else can we look for in your apartment? I'll take 'controlled substances' for six months in County, Alex."

Rowdy squeezed his eyes shut, took a deep breath and said, "A'right, I'll come down after I get dressed."

"Too late for that," Jake said. "You ever take a ride in a real police car? It's an experience. Wait, of course you have. Quick shower and get dressed. Ten minutes is all I'm giving you. If you take ten minutes and one heartbeat, I'll drag you out and you go in bracelets."

"Wait, is S.S. down there?"

"S.S.? You mean that three-hundred-pound sack of stupid with you last night? You were going to sic him on me but he wasn't up to the task. Yeah, he's in a holding cell and you know, he's kinda mad at you for not bailing him out. Keeps saying things like 'kill the muh-fugger', yeah he says it like that probably because he's less smart than even you are."

"Man, why you always fucking with me?"

"Because you're an idiot. Nine minutes and forty seconds to go. You're burning clock."

"All right, all right." Rowdy hurried back into his apartment. "Hold on. Shit."

"And use some kind of body spray. You're melting my olfactories and I just cleaned my vehicle."

* * *

Rowdy plopped down in a chair across from Jake's desk and said, "Well now we're here. You happy? What is it you want and why couldn't we talk about this in your car?"

"You said you wanted coffee and I didn't have any in the unit."

"Un-fucking-believable," Rowdy said. He squeezed his eyes shut, opened them and shook his head like a wet dog. "Shit you're recording this or something. Dammit, I'm never up at this time of the morning."

"So you say."

"How about coffee?"

Jake nodded at the coffee machine.

"I need a cigarette," Rowdy said.

"No."

Rowdy looked at the ashtray on Jake's desk which contained three spent cigarettes. He pointed at the ashtray and said, "Then what is that?"

"Want to see the blood trail of the person who smoked those? You light up and I'll have to quell you some."

"Quell?" Rowdy screwed up his face and said, "Who talks like that? You can't do that."

"Oh Rowdy," Jake said. "You're a funny kid. Of course, I can. I've got a badge, a gun, and the scales of justice tipped in my favor. You have to do what I say."

"I still haven't seen a badge."

Jake slid open a drawer, produced his badge and held it up.

"Why don't you wear it?" Rowdy said.

"It pokes holes in my shirt."

"It's a clip-on."

Jake made a show of examining his badge as if the first time he'd seen it. "Well, look at that. It *is* a clip-on."

"How about it with the lame-O comedy. You're not funny. I got things to do, too."

"I'm sure hanging around dimwits with bad breath is pressing work but you need a lesson about punctuality and becoming a productive member of society."

"A what?"

"Martin Saunders was killed in the superintendent's office. You were a former student of his, right?"

"Yeah, everybody knows about it. I was in one of the plays, so what? I'm getting coffee."

Jake sat and waited for Rowdy to pour himself some coffee. Rowdy poured half a shaker of sugar into the cup, spotted the donuts, pointed at the box and Jake nodded. Rowdy selected a long John and returned to his seat. He took a big bite of his pastry, chewed on it, sipped coffee and then another bite of the pastry, some of it crumbling down into his wispy beard. Jake waited some more, looking at Rowdy.

After a long moment, Jake chuckled and while still chewing, Rowdy said, "What?"

"I was just wondering if you want a ramrod to facilitate the feeding frenzy."

"Ha, ha, you're fucking killing me."

"I got a tip from a good source that tells me you have information about the Saunders' homicide," Jake said, turning serious. "You can buy yourself some good will if you help me on this."

"I ain't gonna be a snitch. I'm stand-up."

"Good for you, Rowdy. I am proud to work with someone of your integrity. I get so few lowlife dirthags in here who ascribe to such scrupulous honor. I almost regret having to serve you with a warrant to search your apartment, your car, give you an anal probe..."

Rowdy held up both hands with his head down. "All right. I get it. But I give you something, you tear up the warrant?"

"If it's good enough."

"How about a get-out-of-jail-free card next time I get a traffic stop."

"No."

"C'mon."

"No. Let's hear it."

Rowdy looked around the office as if invisible cameras were recording what he was saying. Which, of course, they were.

Rowdy leaned forward in his chair. "Pete Stanger and that's all I'm gonna say."

CHAPTER SEVENTEEN

"Mayor Steinman was here while you were talking to Rowdy," Cal said. Cal sat in a worn padded swivel chair behind a steel Army surplus desk. There was an American flag and a Missouri state flag behind him and between the flagpoles was painted the words, 'Paradise Police, Paradise, MO est. 1936'. On the walls were photos of past Police Chiefs, some local dignitaries along with a photo of Henry Fonda from "My Darling Clementine", the one where Fonda, as Wyatt Earp, seated in a wooden chair, has his boots up on a horse hitch, balancing himself.

"I'm sorry I missed him. He's a great guy."

"He's a weasel all right," Cal said. "But basically he's a good citizen with a tough job without the guts to handle the Felicia Jankowskis of the world. He says people are coming into his store to complain about your investigation rather than buying appliances. They're frightened that a murderer may be their next-door neighbor or even their kid's teacher. People are coming by his house, calling him, even his own family is bitching at him. He's just a small-town shop owner dumb enough to run for mayor."

Jake shrugged. "It's one of the things that happen in a homicide investigation. People get nuts. Besides this murder was personal. Probably the killer's first time, though it beats me how he pulled it off so slick."

"Well, the town's not the Norman Rockwell community it used to be. Mostly, my officers wrote speeding tickets and I had weekly meetings about somebody throwing trash on the street. The good old days. I notice Dr. Zeke hasn't made a determination as to the cause of death. What's going on, Jake? What does Rowdy Manners have to with this?"

Jake recounted his talks with Dr. Zeke and getting the M.E. to delay on his final determination. Also his talk with Rowdy.

"He said it was Pete Stanger who killed Saunders?" Cal asked.

"No, he just mentioned the name and said that's all he would tell me. He just wanted out of my office before we released his buddy, Frye, so I think there's more but that's all I could get for now. I have no reason to hold him. But, he'll screw up at some point and I'll press the matter."

"You didn't pull that fake search warrant thing again, Jake?"

Jake rubbed the back of his neck and said, "Why that would be deceitful. I am hurt you would ask such a thing."

"Of course you are. Do you have anybody you see as a possible suspect?"

"Nearly everybody I talk to. Tompkins and Sutherland had reason because of their affair, Eb Eberhard has reason because of a boundary dispute and an old problem with his son, Ransom, and that's just for starters. I'm beginning to dislike Saunders and I didn't know him. And then, there's Winston Vestal who I believe is hiding something in his office that may or may not have something to do with Saunders' death."

"I was afraid it was going to be like this from the start. Right on school property. Hard to be a worse place for it. On another front, I'm getting pressure from the FBI to let them run things."

"Because the school takes federal funds?"

"Yeah."

"They have resources we don't. You want to do that?"

"No. No, I don't. This is our problem, and we need to show we're capable of handling it. Besides their over-bearing attitudes and expensive suits annoy me. They come around they'll blow things up in the media."

"Already happening. I ran off one TV reporter."

"Yeah, Melissa Vanderbilt mentioned you last night on KCKS. Called you 'uncooperative'. Buster let her in, right?"

Jake nodded. "He's a tiresome man."

"You want to fire him?"

"Not my job."

Cal rubbed his forehead and then reached in a drawer and pulled out a bent pipe and pouch of tobacco. Jake gave him a look and Cal said, "It's not a cigarette."

"Is that an equivocation?"

"No, it's a rationalization. Rationalizations are the key to living with our faults." Cal placed the pipe stem between his teeth, packed the tobacco, and fired up the pipe with a butane lighter. That done, he pulled in some smoke and exhaled a blue-grey cloud at the ceiling. "Like I'm going to now rationalize away Buster Mangold's screw-ups because finding people who want to work long hours for little pay is not easy and Buster is a big body who used to be a reliable officer and besides, he looks good in his uniform."

Jake smiled and nodded. "Yes, he does."

"He was more reliable before his divorce. He went through a bad stretch during and afterwards, drank too much and seems to be in perpetual rut since that time. He'll do about anything for a pretty girl."

Jake didn't say anything.

Cal saying now, "You think he's a screw-up, don't you?"

"He's your call, Cal, not mine. But that crap with the apple compromised the crime scene."

Cal nodded and said, "It did. Mayor Steinman wants an update. Wants to know who your suspects are."

"I figured that," Jake said and sat quietly.

"But you're not going to do that, are you?"

Jake shook his head. "Can't."

"They'll want to know about who you have interviewed so far and what you learned from them."

"I had a thirty-year man in the Rangers give me good advice about interviewing witnesses. He told me 'the key to interviewing witnesses is to find out what everyone knew, heard, experienced or saw.' He didn't mention be sure and tell the mayor and the city council what they said."

"They want you to appear at an emergency council meeting."

"That should be fun."

"Yeah," Cal said, as he looked into his pipe bowl before tamping the ashes. "I'm really looking forward to it."

"What would you do if you were me?" Jake asked.

"The very same thing except with more tact. You can't even spell the word."

"If you knew that, why did you ask me?"

Cal took a puff on his pipe, settled back in his chair and said, "Because I'm the Chief and Harper's father. Figure I have you coming and going."

"What if I mess the thing up with Harper?"

"I'll have to shoot you. I won't enjoy it but she is the apple of my eye."

"What if it's not my fault?"

"Then I'll just shoot you in the leg or something."

Jake nodded. "That seems fair."

"Fair don't enter into it, boy," Cal said, a big smile behind the pipe between his teeth. "Fair don't live here."

CHAPTER EIGHTEEN

Jake entered Hank's bar on the main drag of Old Town Paradise where he was going to meet Leo the Lion after work. Hank's was the definition of small-town honky-tonk and a landmark of the former village that sat along the town square. Small town Paradise had exploded in new businesses, population and fragmented into different demographic groups. The farmers and third-generation citizens frequented Hank's and took their breakfasts and lunch at the Dinner Bell while the commuters and newbies hit the motel bars and franchise restaurants off the interstate.

Jake scraped a chair across the wooden floorboards and took a seat while he waited for Leo to show up.

Hank walked over to the table and said, "I am honored to have such an esteemed pillar of society enter my lounge."

"It's a bar, Hank," Jake said, correcting him.

"Don't interrupt," Hank said. "We have a delightful selection of Whiskeys and various wines to augment our pate' and caviar."

"Johnny Walker black on the rocks. And don't water it down."

"Anything you say. Oh thank you for coming in, I will now be able to send my grandchildren through college. So, who killed Saunders?"

Outside of Leo the Lion, Hank was Paradise County's most colorful personality. Hank's sarcasm and gruff manner was the draw for his regular customers. Leo and Hank had a long-running love/hate affair that started back in high school when Hank suspected teen-aged Leo of pilfering a case of beer from the back storeroom. Over the years since that time Hank had grown fond of Leo and vice versa but if you didn't know them you would think otherwise.

"You killed him," Jake said. "I figure he ate some of your food, staggered back up to school and expired."

"Well, I had reason. I didn't like him."

Jake nodded and said, "Nobody did."

Hank saying now, "Will the football coach with the stupid-looking facial hair be joining you?"

Leo the Lion styled a Three Musketeers type mustache and beard which made him look less like the successful football coach that he was. It was his trademark besides being the smartest person in town along with Dr. Zeke Montooth.

"Any minute, Hank."

"You'd think he'd spend his time winning football games instead of hanging around my bar."

"Runner-up state champs last year."

"Still can't win the big one, right?" The bar door opened and Leo Lyon entered, the sunlight framing his lumberjack shoulders. "And there he is. I've got to do something about those doors. It's getting where every turd in town thinks they're welcome."

Hank motioned at Anna Armstrong, his server, and

then pointed at the table. Anna was familiar with the tradition, so she poured a beer and placed it on the table for Leo. She smiled and shook her head at Jake, both enjoying the inside joke.

"Beer again," Leo said. "Hank, how do you know I didn't want a magnum of champagne?"

"Because you have no class."

"If I had any class I wouldn't come in here."

"What a loss if you didn't." Hank walked away and over his shoulder, said, "And, by the way I pissed in it."

Leo looked at Jake and held both hands out in Hank's direction. "What do you do with that guy? So, how is the investigation going?"

"That's what I wanted to talk to you about."

"I don't see how I can help."

"I don't either but I'm getting desperate enough to confide in you. Leo, do you remember Ronald Manners."

"Rowdy? Yeah, I do. He's a cull. Hang on." Leo took a long draw from his beer. "There, needed that. My first year at PHS Rowdy came out for football and could've helped us being he had some talent which we were deficient in but would rather smoke dope with the local forever-shitheads so I turned him loose."

"Do you remember him being in the school play?"

"Yeah, I was surprised he would do something like that. He had as much school spirit as a hog. You got something there?"

"What was the name of the play, if you remember?"

"Sure. It was 'Failure can be Deadly'."

Leo's recall still amazed Jake. "Do you remember who else was in the cast?"

Leo thought a moment and then said, "Let's see, Betty Crain was the victim's wife, Eddie Hammer was the victim, Rowdy ironically, played the police officer."

"Who was the killer?"

"It was Ransom Eberhard and wow...Pete Stanger."

"Both have reasons to dislike Saunders. There was a commemorative plaque at the murder scene that mentioned 'Failure Can be Deadly'. What does that suggest to you?"

"Like somebody sending a message."

"Could be a red herring to get me to chase rabbits."

"Over the years, Martin has been on a mission to run the school from the speech and drama department," Leo said. "He's good at what he does but his modus operandi is to be abrasive and demeaning. He stayed clear of me as I spray on asshole repellant every day." He gave Jake an appraising look and continued saying, "Must be wearing off. Anyway, he gets good performances out of his students but his style intimidates the introverts and eventually ticks off the better students yet he manages to get a good performance out of students like Rowdy Manners who otherwise would never get on the stage. Martin is an anomaly as an educator and as a human being. Pissing people off never seemed to matter to him."

Leo paused to sip his beer, set the glass down and stroked his beard before continuing:

"Check school records for the cast members and see if any of them failed Saunders' class. Rowdy wouldn't care so it could be meaningless and check all student school records to see how many students flunked Saunders' class."

Jake nodded and said, "I'll see if I can borrow Bailey for that. Do you remember any students who complained about Saunders?" Jake said. "You know, a student who had a legitimate reason."

"I know one that was a big deal?"

"Who was that?"

"Brenda Sutherland's stepson, Clay. There was a big row about it, you know fireworks, physical threats and gnashing of teeth, and her husband, a school board member got it changed."

"Did Brenda like the stepson?"

"I don't think she dislikes Clay, that's Knox Sutherland's boy from his first marriage, but she never treated him badly."

"Knox is on the school board, along with Forrest Taylor, who as you know…"

"Both men are Martin Saunders' uncle," Jake said, finishing the thought. "Small towns, huh? Apparently, those people overlooked Saunders' downside and moved him up ahead of Brenda Sutherland."

"She and Knox were separated at that time. It got pretty nasty."

"So," Jake said, twirling his Scotch glass on the table. "Knox took out a little revenge on Brenda. Why did they separate?"

"Knox supposedly was screwing around with Felicia Jankowski."

Jake shook his head. "You're kidding? Felicia Jankowski. Now there's a woman to reckon with. I met her last year and it was…She sort of dislikes me a lot. Small-town politics and small-town affairs. They seem to go hand-in-hand."

"And everybody knows about these affairs, everybody whispers about them and the people in the sin-banging business think they're getting away with it. Talk about living in denial. Knox is big enough, wealthy enough to absorb the fallout, and Felicia doesn't care, but it hurt Brenda. She was very professional and even a bit on the shy side before being passed over and the divorce damaged her. I liked her because she was a solid teacher, but you could see the change."

"And now the thing with Tompkins."

"Right. But we have hope that our local investigator,

formerly the useless and worthless, Jake Morgan, can ride to the rescue, find the killer so we, the fine people of Paradise can return to watching reality shows and gossiping about sexual affairs. By the way, have you managed to screw up your budding romance with Harper Bannister, who though comely and winsome, seems to have bad taste in men?"

"Her ex-husband, Tommy, is in prison."

"Where you put him. Some say you did so in order to have a shot at Harper."

"Do you blame me?"

"No," Leo said. "Good move on your part but I'm not sure if you're really an upgrade from Tommy."

"Neither am I. But I'm taking supper at her place before the City Council meeting tonight."

"Brenda Sutherland was briefly a nurse before she became a teacher."

"And a good one, be my guess," Leo said.

"I would think she got a good settlement in the divorce from Dr. Sutherland when you consider the reasons."

"She did," Leo said. "She hit Doc Sutherland hard, got the house, the cars and a pretty good monthly alimony check. She teaches because she likes it."

"So, you like her?"

"I like anyone who does their job right. I make an exception for you."

"Can you get me a copy of the playbook for Failure Can be Deadly?"

"I'll see what I can do, but first you have to buy the second round."

"I already paid for the first round."

"Law enforcement is expensive work, isn't it?"

"By the way have I told you lately that you are an insufferable poseur masquerading as a football coach?"

"And you are the love child of Barney Fife and Rosie O'Donnell." Leo raised his glass to Jake.

Jake raised his Scotch glass and said, "Up and over the top."

Leo drank, slammed down his empty beer mug and said, "Hank, a menu for me and more whisky for the horse's ass."

CHAPTER NINETEEN

When Jake walked through the door of Harper's cute two-bedroom home, he was met by Bandit, Harper's salt-and-pepper miniature Schnauzer. Jake pulled a dog treat from his pocket and gave it to Bandit, who wagged his tail, snatched the treat from Jake's hand and found his spot on the floor where he began to crunch the treat. Jake liked Harper's tidy bungalow as it felt warm, clean, and safe to him.

The television set was on and KCKS news was on.

"You're spoiling him," Harper said. She had her hair pulled back in a pony-tail, and an oversized Paradise Pirates football jersey over dark yoga pants that accented her shape.

"He's already spoiled," Jake said.

"No, he's domesticated, you're spoiled. Dinner's ready. Chicken fried steak, sweet potatoes, hot rolls, and green beans."

"Is that all?" Jake asked.

"Keep it up, Morgan," Harper said. "I have a rolling pin and I'm not afraid to use it."

Jake rose from his seat and asked, "What's for dessert?"

"Play your cards right, don't chew with your mouth open and maybe I'll let you hold my hand. Or...," She twirled around once and then put her arms out as if presenting herself.

"I've got a city council meeting tonight."

"I heard. What is it this time?"

"Felicia Jankowski worked her magic and scared Mayor Steinman into calling a special session where they—"

Harper waved him off and pointed at the television where the banner at the bottom of the screen read 'New development in Paradise killing'. Melissa Vanderbilt, her hair perfect, saying now, "According to a reliable source the Paradise police have a suspect in the weekend killing of—"

"You have a suspect?" Harper said, raising her eyebrows.

Jake shaking his head, said, "I've narrowed the list down to the Paradise phone book."

"We don't have phonebooks anymore."

"There, see my problem? Saunders torched his bridges at every opportunity. It's amazing he wasn't killed before now."

"So, who is the suspect she's talking about?"

"Ms. Vanderbilt is making it up. Maybe you can help me with something. You were in school when Saunders' put on a play called, 'Failure Can Be Deadly', right? Pete Stanger, Ransom Eberhard, and Rowdy Manners were in it. Ring a bell?"

She nodded her head. "It does. We couldn't believe Rowdy would participate in a school function."

"Did you take any classes with Saunders?"

"Yes, I was also in two of his productions."

Jake nodded at her. "Well?"

"He could teach. I ignored his insulting behavior towards some students."

"But not all students?"

"No, he had his favorites."

"Name some."

"Clay Sutherland, for one."

"Really?" Jake said. "That's interesting."

"So, you know about the big blow-up between them. Saunders was petty and vindictive. Whenever one of his darlings failed to please him or refused to act in one of the plays, Saunders would turn on them."

"Jealousy?"

"Yeah, like that," Harper said. "But it wasn't as if it was a homosexual thing. Saunders looked at drama students as if they were his personal playthings, like Barbie and Ken dolls. Even had the same kind of thing with Ranse Eberhard. Ranse thought Saunders was gay for him but learned the hard way that wasn't true."

"What about Pete Stanger? You remember much about him when he was in school. Did he have problems with Saunders back then?"

"Is Pete Stanger a suspect?"

"He doesn't stand out as one." But Jake remembered Rowdy's tip. But, Rowdy could be misdirecting him. Rowdy Manners was not a solid person and he could not hang his hat on information from him. "I'm just gathering information at this point."

"How about Ransom and Rowdy?" Harper said.

"Same thing. Talking to people hoping something jumps out at me."

"Should you be telling me this?"

"Telling you what? I don't have anything to tell."

"Well, this is disappointing. What's the use of dating a

homicide investigator if there's no insider information? Where's the drama, where's the romance?"

Jake put his hands out and shrugged. "I don't know, either."

They moved to the dining room to eat. Harper had set the table with blue willow dinnerware. After they ate, Jake made the coffee and they talked some more.

Jake said, "Anything more on the coffee shop?"

"Sherry is excited about it and I think it would be fun."

"Would it make any money, you know, with Starbucks out on the highway?"

"Sherry has a good business plan and she has a good head for money. But, I don't know. I'm still working on my law degree and doing para work for Jessup. I hate to think about crowding up my schedule. I like being busy but that may a bit much."

"You and Sherry have been close for a long time."

"Since middle school," Harper said. She brushed hair behind one ear. "Volleyball camp, shared a locker things like that. She called me out on my little girl crush on you back then."

Harper picked up her coffee cup and looked over the rim at Jake. Jake said, "I like these cups you have. Kind of old-school."

"The one thing I have from my mother. They belonged to Grandma and I remember them from family dinners on the farm. Grandma handed them down to Mom and now mine by default when Mom took off. Grandma died leaving me as the last female in that line."

"Are you worried about going into business with your best friend for any other reason than the time element?"

Harper thought about it for a moment before she said,

"I don't want to lose her as a friend. Boyfriends and business break up a lot of friendships. I have other girlfriends but Sherry is special, just like Leo and Buddy are for you."

"Buddy and I work together."

"Different for men," Harper said. "Some women have a penchant for jealousy and drama; two things I don't understand. I have girlfriends but I'm more comfortable around you and your buddies."

"You're a woman but you tend to think like a man. Probably because you were raised by your father. It's why you don't understand the jealousy. Well, thanks for dinner, but I better get going."

As he stood, Harper said, "Jake."

"Yeah."

"Make an attempt at diplomacy tonight."

"You don't think I'm diplomatic?"

Harper grinned and said, "Do you?"

* * *

Deke Gower drove past Harper Bannister's house and watched Jake Morgan pull out of her driveway and head in the direction of Old Town.

"What's Morgan driving there?" Deke said. "Some kind of old Lincoln from before we were born. But sweet like he restored it."

"That's Harper Mitchell's house," Rowdy Manners said, from the passenger seat of Gower's Chevy Silverado pick-up. "That's some prime stuff right there, baby."

"She goes by her maiden name again, Bannister. Morgan's seeing Tommy Mitchell's ex?" Deke said.

"You didn't know that? That's why Tommy's inside at Jeff City 'cause Morgan set him up so he could get her."

"Bullshit," Deke said. "Tommy got himself sideways

with his family and then copped to get himself a reduced sentence. They were already divorced. By the way, what'd Morgan talk to you about, dragging you downtown?"

"He didn't drag me nowhere."

"No? You said you weren't going but when I came by you were gone with your truck and your bike still in the lot. I heard you had a heart-to-heart with Morgan. S.S. Frye is not happy about it. What did Morgan want? What did you tell him?"

"I didn't tell him shit. He wanted to roust me a little about drug traffic in Medfield, said he knew I had information and if I dumped on a couple guys he'd cut me a break on traffic violations but fuck him."

"He asked you about the killing up at the school didn't he?"

"He thought maybe I heard something but he got nothing from me. Sometime I'll get him alone and I'll shove that badge up his ass."

Deke made a face and said, "You sure you should call attention to us right now? We got things going and maybe we shouldn't—"

"Fuck you, Deke. I'll take care of things my own way, besides I've got the entire operation down to science. I am better than that guy on 'Breaking Bad'."

"I never saw that."

Rowdy flicked a disposal lighter to life and touched the flame to his cigarette. "We got it going on, ya know? We've got some big shots involved who can't talk about it."

"Who?"

"No way, baby." Rowdy tapped his temple. "Got it all up here in my head. Better that way. I see the future and you got questions. Have a little faith."

Deke nodded, turned left two blocks shy of Main

Street and then said, "You're right about Harper Bannister, though. I mean, shit, that girl's extra deadly."

"Yeah," Rowdy said. "Wouldn't mind some of that myself."

"Yeah, 'cept you're afraid Morgan might kick your ass."

"He don't knock me outta my socks. He's mostly bluff."

"You mean like the other night when he told us he'd 'shoot three' of us? You think that was a bluff? The man is a stone killer. He'll pull for sure, he says he will. I heard he killed two Mex cartel soldiers as a ranger and I know for sure he shot down old Sheriff Kennedy a couple years back."

"So what?"

"So best we don't fuck with his girlfriend right now with the way our business is going. I don't want nothing to do with that man. Morgan's a scary motherfucker."

"Yeah well we'll see about that. Right now I'm wondering how Morgan got on my ass like he did. Somebody snitched. See if you can find out about that, will ya, Deke?"

"I guess. I don't know how I'm gonna do that."

"Put Super-Size Frye on it. By the way, I need to borrow your pick-up again, Deke."

"Why this time?"

"Mine needs a fuel pump. Got it on order."

"Where'd you take it Thursday night, anyway? You know, the night they found Saunders?"

CHAPTER TWENTY

The Paradise City Council board room was little more than an old storefront building with ancient wood floors, older stamped ceiling panels and a large table. Felicia Jankowski was not taking any chances tonight. She had brought in a tray of mini-sandwiches and two fresh-baked pies from the Dinner Bell and there was coffee in an air pot and bottled water iced down in a low tray.

It was not a full house as three members were missing due to the sudden timing of the special session. In attendance were Beth Moreland, who ran a beauty parlor in Old Town, along with Knox Sutherland, and Forrest Taylor. Forrest Taylor being Martin Sanders' uncle was important to Felicia's plan.

Felicia served Mayor Steinman a sandwich and a slice of cherry pie and asked if he wanted coffee. Steinman was surprised by her uncustomary kindness.

"Why, thank you, Felicia," Steinman said. "Coffee would be nice."

"It's a big night," Felicia said. "We get a report on the

murder at the school, you know. I want to know what our police force is doing."

"Well," Steinman said, pausing before he said, "Felicia, it may not be like that you know? I talked to the Chief and well, this is a murder case under investigation and..."

"I don't want you to misunderstand me, Arthur," she said. "It is our job to have oversight on the police force and we should not allow Jake Morgan to keep this information from us. This is not a time for you to get wobbly."

Steinman's mouth worked before he said, "I just wouldn't get my expectations up..."

She cut him off. "I'll get your coffee."

Dr. Knox Sutherland was at the refreshment table and spoke to Felicia as she walked up. Felicia had prettied up the table with fresh cut flowers in a bowl and a stack of plastic, not Styrofoam, serving plates and flatware.

"Are you all right, Felicia?" Sutherland asked her. "You seem anxious."

"I'm fine," she said.

"Yes, you are," Sutherland said.

She smiled at him and made a phone out of her thumb to her ear. She pumped coffee from an air pot into a sleeved paper cup thinking that the problem with working a weak man like Arthur Steinman cut both ways. The mayor was intimidated by her but possibly feared standing up to Chief Bannister and the smug asshole Morgan.

She added a sugar substitute and powdered creamer into Steinman's cup thinking about a grown man who feared sugar. As she stirred the coffee, she watched Morgan and the Chief enter the council hall. Such a shame Morgan was such an attractive boy and still a smartass. She was thinking that when hot coffee sloshed over the cup and onto her hand.

"Dammit," she said, between clenched teeth. She changed the cup to her free hand and shook coffee off her hand. She checked her clothing for stains. Damn, a spot on her blouse. When she looked up she saw Jake Morgan smiling at her predicament.

God, how she despised him.

* * *

Jake sat next to Cal at the end of the council table. "The hot seat," said Mayor Steinman, and then laughed at his joke. As they began the meeting with the usual town business such as the proposed City Park improvements and chatter about their families and golf game while Jake studied the council members.

The other female member besides, Felicia Jankowski, was Beth Moreland, a lady who sang in the church choir and had two teen-aged boys who played football for Leo. She was a pleasant woman, smart and well-liked, which is why she was re-elected to this assemblage. Dr. Knox Sutherland was on staff at Paradise County Memorial. He had marquee looks, salt-and-pepper hair at his temples, a golf score in the low eighties and a reputation as a ladies man. The most interesting person to Jake was Martin Saunders' uncle, Forrest Taylor.

Taylor was an imposing man of Eastern Mediterranean heritage, dark hair, and thick mustache with piercing blue eyes. He had risen from day laborer to successful construction business owner and was built like a shot-putt athlete. Taylor ran the school board along with a large part of the community. Jake noted that the other members of the council deferred to him, smiling or leaning forward when he spoke.

Cal Bannister sat, composed, wearing an understated white dress shirt, blue tie with the name-plate 'Chief of Police' stitched into the chest pocket. In front of him Cal had a leather notebook which contained his calendar and notes. Jake wore his cobalt blue Paradise County Undersheriff long-sleeved dress shirt open at the collar, blue jeans and casual loafers, no socks.

Mayor Steinman offered refreshments to both Jake and Cal and they declined. The meeting started with Forrest Taylor addressing Cal and saying, "Cal, where are we with your investigation of my nephew's murder?"

"We are accumulating forensic evidence at this time. County M.E. Dr. Montooth has performed an autopsy to determine the cause of death and Jake here has been interviewing school personnel and assigning both city and county officers to canvas neighbors and anyone who may have information about the case. My office and Sheriff Johnson's office are cooperating with some assistance from the State Patrol."

Taylor turned his attention to Jake. "Mr. Morgan, what have you learned about this? This whole thing has been unsettling for my family. Where are you in your investigation?"

"I think the Chief said it all. Collecting evidence, talking to people, gathering information, studying the forensic evidence that might prove useful."

"That's not telling me much. Do you have a person of interest?"

"I'd rather not say."

"The members here and also the mayor are getting pressured about this incident so my question to you do you have a person or persons that warrant investigation and may possibly be the killer."

"I understand that there will be pressure in such a high interest affair, especially when it occurs in a school.

That affects the entire community. It's an ongoing investigation so any information regarding persons we may find with a motive need to remain confidential. Sorry."

"You work for us," Dr. Sutherland said.

"Also for the County," Jake said.

"Yes, I understand the arrangement. Still, you are the source of consternation in the community. People want to know what is going on and you're not forthcoming with information. So, my question is what you are doing?"

"We're knocking on doors, talking to people, examining evidence and eating the occasional donut."

"This isn't funny, Morgan."

"Wouldn't it be jolly if it were?" Jake asked. "Homicides stir-up emotion in a community, especially a small community like ours. No way around it. Doesn't matter that you want to know when I cannot tell you; only that I have to keep digging at things. Some of you here have ties to the school, like you Dr. Sutherland and also Mr. Taylor who is related to the victim. The suspect pool is large and information about the how and why have to be secure. We are not at liberty to make accusations that will further inflame the community."

"Instead, you're creating fear and people are drawing their own conclusions."

"Can't be helped at present."

Beth Moreland spoke up, saying, "What about the FBI? Can we access their expertise?"

"Yes, if I feel that it is beyond the capabilities of myself and our resources I will of course, bring them in. Right now, the Missouri State Highway Patrol has offered their assistance."

Sutherland nodded during Jake's statement and then he said, "Why did you interview my ex-wife?"

"Who is your ex-wife?" Jake said.

"Brenda Sutherland. Why did you interview her?"

"We interviewed all school personnel."

"Did you learn anything from her?"

"She liked a paper I did in high school."

Sutherland leaned back, blew air between his teeth and said, "This is getting us nowhere. What did you expect would happen at this meeting?"

Jake nodded. "This is what I expect anytime there is a murder. People want to know about it. It frightens people."

Jake heard Felicia Jankowski's fingernails, clicking on the table, noted her rising agitation. She broke in and said, "Maybe if you're not more cooperative you can be replaced."

"That's your prerogative and I won't spend time worrying about it. Either way I'm going to do the job as I was trained."

"The Texas Rangers?" Beth Moreland said. "Pretty good place to learn I would imagine."

"Do you know why you're here Mr. Morgan?" Felicia asked. "Because it seems you don't understand your position."

"I'm always willing to provide what information I can about our office, how we conduct it and any criminal arrests. I even wish I could give you more than I have. However, what you want from me is to help you with the illusion that this is about your civic pride and not about me arresting your husband."

Felicia sat upright as if by electric shock, addressed Cal, and said, "Are you going to allow him to speak to me in this manner?"

The usual unflappable Chief fixed his eyes on Felicia and flatly asked, "Was his statement inaccurate?"

Felicia now turned to Mayor Steinman and said, "Really, Arthur? Do I have to endure this disrespect?"

Beth Moreland leaned her arms on the table and very calmly said, "Felicia, you attacked the man's authority and position. What response were you expecting?"

"I demand respect from him."

"Then," Moreland said, placing her hands together on the table, "give him the respect his office deserves. He has a difficult job and since he has taken over his duties, he has done outstanding work, I think. He is a highly-trained investigator that few towns our size could attract, retain, or even afford."

"Investigator Morgan," Forrest Taylor said, breaking in now. "Have you made any progress in your investigation?"

"We have conducted several hours of interviews with yet more to conduct. As previously stated, we have accumulated forensic evidence. We will now have to determine which of that evidence is germane to the investigation."

"It was my understanding that my nephew was beaten to death. Is that true?"

Taylor was smart, posing the leading question to either affirm through acknowledgement or dismiss the blunt force verdict if Jake said that was not the result.

"I can't comment at present, that is, I cannot confirm or deny anything related to the cause of his death. I realize he was a family member, appreciate your loss, but I have to reserve any information about the cause or manner of his death for the time being."

Taylor nodded. "I understand. Do you have a timetable for when you will release Martins'…a…passing…so the family can make funeral arrangements?"

"That will be up to Dr. Montooth, the county Coroner and I think that will occur sooner rather than later."

"What about Pete Stanger?" Felicia said.

"He's comatose."

"I've heard he was a suspect."

"Do you have a source for that information?" Jake asked, interested that Felicia mentioned the name.

"I just heard it around town."

Just picked it out of the air, Jake was thinking.

She pressed in. "Many of my voters have remarked that Stanger did not like Martin Saunders and has a motive to kill him."

"If you have information pertinent to this investigation, we will be glad to hear it. Do we need to arrange an interview with you and why you brought up Stanger's name?"

"This is ridiculous," Felicia said. "I didn't kill anyone."

"That's your story," Jake said and then shrugged. "Go with that."

Beth Moreland hid a smile with her hand.

Felicia bored in, saying, "You know you're not very popular in some circles around town."

"Imagine my disappointment."

"You are a rude man and we are not making progress either here or in your investigation it seems. We might as well adjourn and eat sandwiches."

"I agree," Beth Moreland said. "He's told us he cannot give us any more information and I believe him. Anyone here disagree with my thoughts on that? No? Then, I move we adjourn and eat sandwiches and pie."

There was a second and the meeting was over.

Outside, media people and photogs had gathered to snap videos and photos of Jake leaving the meeting. Two young men and Melissa Vanderbilt stuck microphones in Jake's face, but he kept walking.

"What progress are you making in this murder investigation?" Vanderbilt asked. Jake pointed at Cal and kept walking. They turned their attention to the Chief who said, "No comment at this time. Mayor Steinman has additional information if you wish to talk with him."

Jake grinned and as the two men walked on, Jake said, "That was a mean thing to do to the mayor."

"Arthur likes to talk." Cal Bannister tugged on the bill of his Police Chief cap and said, to Jake, "God bless Beth Moreland."

CHAPTER TWENTY-ONE

"Okay, what do we have so far?" Cal asked the group which included County Sheriff Buddy Johnson, Deputy Grets Bailey, Corporal Fred Ridley of the State Patrol and dual jurisdictional investigator, Jake Morgan. They sat in the County Sheriff's office meeting room which was sound-proofed, adjoining the County lock-up. In front of each participant were yellow legal pads and folders and Jake had prepared crime scene photos for each in attendance.

Jake said, "Bailey tell them what you have so far?"

Deputy Bailey put down her pen and said, "I have gone through all of Mr. Saunders' files in his classroom office and theatre office. I don't have much. Jake and I will be traveling out to the Eberhard ranch today to talk to Eb and his son, Ransom. Both father and son have a long-standing resentment against the victim. Confusing the investigation is the fact that nearly everyone we've interviewed are not broken-hearted that Saunders is gone. I have petitioned the court for a warrant to examine the contents of the computers of Martin Saunders' home computer, along with Brenda Sutherland's and Bill Tompkins' school laptops. I am also seeking access to the School District mainframe. It is moving slowly due the rights-to-privacy issue as regards school personnel as well as student personnel. Several of us participated in interviewing staff and faculty and Jake has that information. I have canvassed Saunders' neighbors which led me to Eberhard and son. We are still going through Saunders' hard copy files along with his computer files."

She stopped there and looked to Jake.

Jake said, "Fingerprinting will probably prove worthless although Deputy Bailey checked some unique places. All the school personnel and half the town have been in the outer office of that building making fingerprints moot and could be argued in court and dismissed by a good defense attorney. However..." Jake paused for effect before saying, "Drum roll, Buddy."

Sheriff Buddy Johnson, rolled his eyes, turned to Trooper Ridley and said, "God, what I put up with to get a semi-competent investigator."

Jake said, "As a cause of death, Dr. Zeke, Bailey and I are looking into and considering the introduction of paralytics or poisoning as the cause of death. I know somebody tuned him up pretty good but Zeke is adamant that the assault was not the cause of death."

"How can that be?" Cal asked. "He was so badly beaten and only one cut on his inner lip which may have been caused by the commemorative apple. The leaf broke off and was under the victim."

"I trust Zeke on these things. He's a character but a fine M.E."

"What about fingerprints or DNA on the metal apple?" Ridley asked.

Jake looked to Cal who spoke up, saying, "One of my officers picked up the apple and contaminated it as possible evidence. We're considering hospital paralytics, horse tranqs, ethyl glycol, or anything that may have stopped Saunders' heart. Narrowing this down is a problem as some of the principals involved have contacts in the medical profession. Brenda Sutherland was formerly a nurse, her ex-husband Knox Sutherland is a Doctor, Bill Tompkins whose wife also works at County and of course, anyone who has an older container of anti-freeze."

"Have you considered the possibility that the body had been moved," Ridley said. "Was he killed in the office or dropped there?"

"That's a good point," Jake said. "As a possibility, I have considered that the body was dropped in the office and it was there that the introduction of a foreign chemical was introduced."

"It would take a very strong man to drag a body into the building," Buddy said.

"And he would have to have a key," Ridley said.

"Or," Jake said, "Two people carried him into the office after beating the living shit out of him. He could've taken Saunders' key from him. And, the person who administered the beating knew what he was doing and that brings up another variable. Tompkins is a strong athletic type and Pete Stanger did some intramural boxing in Junior College."

Buddy said, "Jackson Howard, the high school principal, was a boxer at one time. He did not reveal any animus towards Saunders though he admitted the guy had a way of pissing people off around him."

Jake nodded. "The problem is I can't seem to get a handle on the volume of information and those with a motive. I have a bumper crop of suspects with motive, skills and access to different types of drugs. We are swamped with suspects but as yet I don't know where to go with it. I can't see the forest for the trees."

The meeting broke up and Jake accompanied Ridley out to his Highway Patrol vehicle.

"You've got quite a mess to deal with, there, Tex."

"Yeah," Jake said.

Ridley said, "If I guess it was Buster Mangold who contaminated the crime scene do I get a prize?"

Jake stopped walking and looked at Ridley for a long moment.

Ridley nodded and said, "Yeah, I'm familiar with Mangold. He's an idiot, isn't he?"

* * *

In the intensive care ward of County Memorial Hospital, Zanda Robinson, a candy-striper nurse's aide, shrieked in surprise when coma patient Pete Stanger sat bolt upright and said, "Who was that?"

CHAPTER TWENTY-TWO

Dr. Winston Vestal drummed fingers on a makeshift desk in his temporary office situated on the stage of the elementary school multi-purpose room. School resumed Wednesday morning but Investigator Morgan produced a court order to seal off the Central office along with Martin Saunders' room and the theatre backstage area.

Vestal was sweating the reasons for such an order but hoped that even if Morgan found the item there was a good chance Morgan would not recognize its importance. Vestal had overplayed his desire to get into his office which raised suspicion in that over-zealous investigator's mind. He'd heard about Morgan but had written him off as just a cocky young man playing homicide detective.

But Morgan was turning out to be far more than that. Since Saunders' death, Vestal learned that Morgan had been trained by the Texas Rangers and was some kind of prodigy for that agency.

As for Felicia she had lately become dictatorial about their relationship which is why he hadn't been calling her. He wished he had never taken up with her and now she was cutting him off which should be a good thing but Vestal thought about her and wanted her during moments of stress.

His need for her was disquieting to a man such as Vestal who liked control and his need gave her the upper hand and Felicia Jankowski was the type who could sense weakness and was quick to seize and utilize every weapon that gained her an advantage. He thought of her as a romantic terrorist. Plus there was her growing obsession with wanting to get even, no, destroy, Jake Morgan. Now that he knew Morgan better he certainly understood why Felicia and many others in the community did not like Morgan.

Vestal looked at his watch. He had an appointment with Board President Forrest Taylor in fifteen minutes to go over the agenda for the next board meeting. Felicia had failed to get any information from the city council meeting but she still managed to turn things around as if it was Vestal's fault she could not break down the local police. Adding to his worries Vestal was sure Taylor would want to talk about his nephew and what Vestal knew about his death.

What would he tell him? Felicia had told him to push Pete Stanger as a possibility. "Stanger didn't like Martin and he's in a coma," she told him. "He can't argue the point."

What would happen if Taylor knew of his relationship with Felicia Jankowski knowing that Taylor did not like Felicia for reasons known only to Taylor himself? Further, even though it was the twenty-first century, Paradise was predominantly a religious community that frowned on sexual affairs even while they were indulging in the sin themselves.

"We have to talk, Winston," was all Taylor had said on the phone.

"That's fine, Forrest," Vestal had said. "What about?"

"Not over the phone."

They *had to talk and not over the phone*. Vestal more anxious by the minute.

* * *

The Circle E Ranch, owned by Barnard "Eb" Eberhard was a large rambling affair with a white rail fence, the real thing, not the vinyl fencing around the property. There was a modern ten-stall stable with the Circle E emblem emblazoned on the entrance. There was a tack room next to it and an older red-painted barn. Adult oak trees shaded the red-roofed ranch house that displayed an out-sized front porch.

Deputy Bailey had called ahead and asked if they could come talk with Eb and his son, Ransom.

"I see no reason not to," Eb said, over the phone. "Come on out and I'll have the coffee ready."

"At least he's friendly," Bailey said, to Jake, as the pair traveled the paved drive to the house where Eberhard, all six-feet-three inches of modern cowboy stood on the covered front deck to greet them.

"Now there's a guy looks like a rancher," Jake said. "Stetson on his head, lean and weather-beaten."

"You're so eloquent," Bailey said, looking straight ahead.

"Did I tell you Brenda Sutherland liked a paper I did back in high school?"

"Not yet, but I'm sure you're going to."

Bailey parked her County unit, which was a Ford Explorer like the one Jake had before Pete Stanger whacked it. They got out and shook hands with Eberhard.

"C'mon inside and rest yourself," Eberhard said. "I'll

call up to the tack house and get Ransom down here. You wanted to talk to him too, right? Neither of us is going to pretend that Saunders didn't get what he deserved though I don't like to see anyone killed like that."

"Like what?" Jake said.

"Beat him up, didn't they?"

"Mr. Eberhard," Bailey said. "We haven't released that information. The cause of death is only known to the task force assigned to the case."

"Well, that's what people around town are saying. I didn't mean to get ahead of you. And call me 'Eb', okay?"

Jake looked at Eberhard. Tall, knuckled hands, rangy limbs with knotted forearms used to hard work. He'd be tough enough to damage Saunders and strong enough to carry him, but Eberhard's demeanor was not that of someone who had something to hide. You couldn't always go on such at face value, but Jake trusted his instincts about such. Eberhard's face was lined with years of hard work in the sun, his body language was relaxed and open. This was not their killer but Jake wasn't ready to cross him off the list just yet.

"You know, Mr. Eberhard," Jake said. "I like horses and I've heard you have some fine mounts. Maybe I could walk up, find Ransom and let him show me around your stable, that is, if you don't mind."

"No, I don't mind," Eberhard said, sweeping an arm towards the stables. "Go, right ahead. Ranse can show you around while I talk to Miss Bailey here. But take a cup of coffee or some lemonade or...even a beer if you want, with you."

Jake walked through the back yard and on to the barn to locate Ransom Eberhard. As he neared the tack house, he picked up the pungent aromas of animal hide and dust and then heard grunting sounds along with thick thudding noise which made him wary. Jake quietly made his way to the tack room entrance and the sounds increased. As he looked through the entrance he saw a large young blond-headed man punching a heavy bag hanging from a rafter.

Thud...thud...left...right...and then Ransom threw a spin kick at the bag and landed with his feet in a fighter's stance. Jake's eyes adjusted to the low light of the room as sunlight filtered through the dust and he could see the sweat glisten on the young man's bare chest and arms. Ransom now worked on a practiced move, one Jake was familiar with from his own training.

Ransom threw a high kick at the bag, barely brushing it, dropped his right foot close to his left, appearing to be vulnerable, then launched a devastating side-kick that rocked the heavy bag. The young man did it well and practiced it two more times before Jake let him know he was there.

"Not bad," Jake said. Jake eyes were at Ransom's chin level. This was one big farm boy. "Tae Kwan do?"

"Yes." The young man grabbed a towel and wiped his face and chest with it before he said, "Also some Chuck Norris stuff."

"Chun Kuk Do?"

"You know about that stuff?" Ransom said. "You train?"

"A little."

"What style?"

"Krav Maga. Some boxing."

"Krav Maga? That Israeli commando stuff? Pretty aggressive."

"It's effective if you need to end things quickly. How long have you been training? You have a teacher?"

"I did but he packed up and left town. Couldn't make enough scratch in this area. I worked on my own after that and watched one of Norris' training films, studied his moves on youtube, you know, what else is there to do around this town except drink beer and chase poontang?"

Jake was learning that the son was a different person than dad.

"I think there's more than that to do," Jake said. "I'm here about Martin Saunders."

"I know," Ransom said. He spun around and kicked the heavy bag, landed and said, "Glad he's dead."

"Okay," Jake said. "How glad are you?"

Ransom lifted his chin slightly and looked down his nose at Jake. "I didn't kill the son-of-a-bitch. He was always eyeing me back in high school, pushing me to be in his theatre productions, I even did one and after that, well…shoulda knocked him out the time he put his hands on me back in school. Fucking weasel."

"Lot of people agree with you about him," Jake said. "He wasn't popular. You seem to have a lot of anger about him."

"So does Dad. But that's a moot point now, right?"

"Not if you killed him. You mentioned you were in a play. What was the name of it?"

"Don't remember. Something about 'failure'. 'Failure is bad' or something."

"Failure Can be Deadly?"

"That's it. You already knew the name of it."

"I did," Jake said. "You know Ronald Manners?"

"Rowdy? Hell yes I know him. He's kind of a rounder and a thug these days. Used to hang out with him but we had a falling out years ago."

"What was that about?"

"You sure ask a lot of questions."

"It's just about my whole job, asking questions. That is, besides drinking coffee and eating donuts. Once in a while I get to write a speeding ticket. I heard the play was a big success. Is that where you had your falling out with Rowdy?"

Pulling on a T-shirt now. It was a size too small and showed off Ransom's biceps and shoulders. Kid was proud of his body and his moves. This guy could carry a limp body and a sack of feed while eating an apple, plus he was harboring a truck-load of rage about Saunders. Could this be the man he was looking for?

"No, that was later, but that was the end of Rowdy and me doing any more plays with Saunders. He begged us to do more and told us how we were naturals. Shit, learning those lines was hard and I didn't really like it, felt like a pussy up there on the stage."

"Who gave him the trophy?"

Ransom turned his head slightly to one side as if confused by the question. "What trophy?"

"The one with the golden apple on it to congratulate Saunders on the success of 'Failure Can be Deadly'. You don't remember that?"

"Drawing a blank. The play was successful though. Everybody said it was but you know how it goes, your family and the teachers give you props for even trying but your friends? My buddies?" He smiled and chuckled to himself. "They ragged on me for weeks started calling me 'Barrymore'. I didn't even know what that meant. What happened later was that thing that pissed me off at Saunders."

"Which was."

"Me and Rowdy wouldn't do his Spring theatre thing so he flunked us in his English class. I never had an 'F' before and dad got mad at me and took my truck keys. I told Dad it was bullshit but Dad…well, he don't like excuses. I went to Saunders to tell him how he had screwed me over and he told me I screwed myself by turning down his offer for the Spring production telling me that 'little bitches miss opportunities' and that got right next to me and I kinda lost it and yelled at him and he pushed me."

"But you didn't retaliate."

"No. I was in enough trouble with Dad already. But after that Dad realized the guy had screwed me on purpose and he went to talk with Saunders. Saunders claimed Dad threatened to kill him and the cops came and handcuffed Dad and that really frosted the old man. It was one of the town cops, that Mangold guy that took him in. Mangold's kind of a dickhead, thinks he's tough. I'd like a shot at him myself."

Buster Mangold again.

"Buster's big enough all right," Jake said. Ransom had given Jake some things to think about so maybe take the tour, engage him about Rowdy some more. Something about Rowdy giving him Pete Stanger's name didn't sit well, knowing what a troublemaker Rowdy was with little reason to help him out. "You mind showing me around. Your dad said it was okay if you showed me some of your horses."

"Yeah." Nodding his head enthusiastically. "I'd like that, we got some of the best in the state."

"Some say in the entire country."

More nodding and a big smile. "That's right."

Ransom showed Jake the champion Fox-trotter, Gable's Charm, and a few other top-tier level horses including a Belgian Draft Horse named 'Hoss', a black Morgan, some quarter horses, and his dad's cutting horse named 'Tag'.

"Tag can cut a steer out of a hundred head and all dad has to do is point," Ransom said. "He doesn't even have to be mounted. Tag does it all by himself."

Jake thanked Ransom for the tour and said, "Well, I

better get back to work. Appreciate your cooperation. Do you own a pick-up?"

"Yeah, Got a Ford F-250. Two superchargers on it and some pipes sound like a monster."

Jake nodded and said, "Just so I can cross you off the list, you didn't happen to be out on Highway 27 last Friday night?"

CHAPTER TWENTY-THREE

On the way back to town Jake asked Deputy Bailey what, if anything, she had learned talking to "Gary Cooper's love child?"

"That he's a really nice man," Bailey said. "Very old-school with his manners. Removed his hat when he walked in his house, polite and straight-forward when he answered my questions, wasn't guarded and had nothing to hide."

Jake looked out the passenger window and nodded. "Yeah, that's what I figured. What's dad have to say about his son?"

"Proud of him," Bailey said. "But, disappointed in his attitude. Eb told me that Ransom's a man now and has to go his own way."

"Wow, that's old-school cowboy of him."

"Very John Wayne-like," Bailey said. "Dad wishes Ranse, calls him 'Ranse', would be more circumspect."

"He used the word, 'circumspect'?"

"Actually he said less reckless. Read a dictionary, Morgan. The boy is cocky to the point of over-confidence. Said he had to change his son's thinking once

Ransom turned eighteen, Ransom thinking he didn't have to do what Eb said, anymore."

"But Eb disabused him of that notion, correct?"

"Yes, he did. Eb's not our man, is he?" Bailey said.

"Nope."

"What about the son?"

"Ranse is rocketing up the charts. He's into martial arts, body-building, and you could strike a match on his ear lobes. This kid is wired tight and looking for someone to try him. I think he's eating steroids but can't be sure. He would be a lot to handle for anyone and he knows it."

"So, he gives you pause?"

"He does."

"Rumor is Jake Morgan fears no man," Bailey said, teasing him.

"Started that one myself."

"Anything else?"

"Yeah. He wants to take on Buster Mangold, owns a pick-up truck and was out on Highway 27 the night Pete Stanger had his wreck."

"Oh, that's another thing, came over the county radio while you were talking to Ransom. Bill Tompkins' wife filed for divorce and that's not even the big news."

Jake took a cigar out of his pocket, unraveled the wrapper, and said, "Well, what's the skinny?"

"You're not going to light that thing in my car," she said, adamant.

"I quit cigarettes. So, I'm weaning myself. You going to shoot me?"

"If it comes to that. But, after you die of lung cancer I'll make sure you're buried with a box of cigars." Enjoying herself.

"Okay, I won't light it," Jake said. "So what is the big news?"

"Pete Stanger came out of his coma."

Jake put the cigar back in his shirt pocket.

* * *

"You can't be a thoroughbred two hours a day. It's a full-time job. Do your classwork, do your part" read the placard on Coach Leo Lyons desk. It was positioned so everyone could read it when they entered his office.

Head Football Coach Leo Lyons was doing non-football work, that is, he was preparing lesson plans for his Algebra II class and getting the Advanced Math Topics team ready for the Conference Math Relays. They were looking to three-peat as conference Math champions and Leo put in as much time on his classes as he did preparing his football team.

Today, Leo was surprised by a visit from the administration in the person of Dr. Winston Vestal. Leo wondering who showed the man where the Football office was located? Vestal had never been there before, in fact, Vestal hadn't said more than a dozen words to Leo in the two years Vestal had been superintendent, a situation that suited Leo as he had little regard for the man.

Vestal knocked on the open door, peeked in and asked, "Do you have a minute, Mr. Lyons?"

Leo smiled to himself, extended an open hand and pointed at one of the chairs in front of his desk. Vestal sat.

Leo asked, "What can I do for you, Mr. Vestal?"

"Doctor."

Leo mimed a quizzical look, knowing full well Vestal loved the "Dr." in front of his name.

Vestal repeated his claim to fame, saying, "Dr. Vestal. I prefer it."

"Of course," Leo said, thinking okay, I'll play. Then Leo said nothing allowing dead air between them.

"Mr. Lyons…"

"I prefer Coach."

Leo watched the man's eyes flash for a nanosecond and his lips thinned to a narrow line. Leo smiled inwardly; relished making the guy flinch. Marvin Vestal liked being deferred to, not lampooned. Leo thinking, I'll bet Vestal's talk with Jake was torment for this guy. Jake Morgan could piss off a rock formation.

"Yes, of course, I'm sorry, Coach."

"No problem." Leo waited again.

"Coach, the reason I'm here is…well, you're friends with Jake Morgan, correct?"

Leo nodded. "That would be correct."

"What I need from you, Coach, is a small favor."

"I love doing favors." Leo waved an arm and nodded encouragingly. "Please, feel free to ask."

"I was hoping you could prevail upon Morgan to allow me to get into my office. I have some important material in there that I need. School business, that's all it is."

"I don't know," Leo said. "Jake can be pretty prickly about such things. That's a tall order."

"Well, coach, I know you're wanting a sprinkling system for your football field…"

Holy Moses with a Popsicle. The man was offering a bribe. A bald-faced Machiavellian offer of quid pro-quo. Leo wondered if he spat across his desk could he hit the man in his face? Might as well milk this a bit.

"I don't know. Doesn't seem enough. You know, the football locker-room could use a facelift."

"That can be arranged, Coach."

"Now we're getting somewhere. I'm guessing we would want to keep this information on the QT."

"The what?"

"The quietus, confidential, just between us buddies, right?"

"Yes, that would be excellent."

"I would also, if you don't mind me asking, that is, just between friends…?"

Vestal sat back, confident, a smile on his face. "Of course, Coach Lyons, just between friends."

"What would really seal the deal for me would be an autographed photo of Julius Caesar and have the Dallas Cowboy Cheerleaders perform at every game."

Vestal's face flushed and the smile ran away from his face.

"No wait," Leo said. "That's just ridiculous, isn't it? Okay, they would only have to attend home games. What do you think, ol' buddy?"

Vestal now giving Leo his full 'pissed-off' face complete with popping veins. "Do you think it's smart to mock your superior?"

"My superior? I'm not sure you're my equal."

Vestal rose from his chair and Leo could see the tension at his jaw. "Mr. Lyons, this is a mistake on your part. I will not forget this. I could've been a great help to your career and to your sustained tenure at Paradise High School. I've known coaches in your position that have attempted to disobey directives from central office that got black-balled and never worked again."

"Really? You know what, Winston, ol' buddy? We finished second in the state last year. First time in our school's history. I've outlasted some other poseurs in central office before so I think I'll take my chances against you, a guy I consider NFL, which sage philosopher, Jerry Glanville of the Houston Oilers once said stood for 'not for long' here at Paradise."

Vestal pointed at Leo and started to say, "I tell you—"

Leo interrupted Vestal saying, "Listen carefully to what I'm saying and don't mistake it. I don't like you and if you don't get out of my office in record time, I'm going to abandon my normal pacific demeanor and throw you through that window." Leo pointed at the large plate glass window that allowed him to observe the locker room.

"You wouldn't dare."

Leo stood and started around his desk.

Vestal fled the scene.

What a tool, Leo thought.

* * *

By the time Vestal returned to his temp office in the multi, he was on the cusp of hyperventilation. He chewed a handful of Tums and swallowed four aspirin. A football coach. That muscle bound cretin. Nobody talks to me that way. He was furious. He had never had a subordinate talk to him that way. 'He was not his equal', what gall that man had. He sat and tried to compose himself, plan a line of attack to remove Mr. Lyons, no matter what his football record was.

Call Knox Sutherland and Forrest Taylor, get going on this thing.

As if things weren't bad enough Vestal had developed an itch in his private parts. He had been working out some at the local gym. Wondering about jock itch. Burning now.

He picked up the phone and called the doctor's office and made an appointment to have it checked out.

CHAPTER TWENTY-FOUR

Jake took the call from Sheriff Buddy Johnson.

"Jake, you got anything on right now?"

"I was going to drive over to County Memorial and interview Pete Stanger. It's possible he has something to do with this murder thing. I'm still wondering what his hurry was and maybe he can tell me."

"Pete's conscious? Good. I got a call from Bass Arnold about some damage to his grain dryer. Could you check on that?"

"No problem. I'll head that way now. Be good to see Bass anyway, he's always got a good story to tell."

Jake figured there was no hurry on Pete Stanger. Even though the man had come out of the coma they would keep him for observation so Jake drove out to see Bass Arnold, an old friend of the family, at his farm north of Paradise. Bass was a character; a man who always looked on the bright side of things and one of the many good people around Paradise that made Jake glad he had returned home. Bass met him with a can of beer in hand, offering one to Jake.

"I'm on the clock, Bass," Jake said. "But, I'll take a rain check. What's going on with your grain dryer?"

"Those asshole druggies stealing my copper wire," Bass said. Bass was a slender man, with a narrow face and a ready grin, accented by the smile lines at the corners of his mouth. "I'm thinking about running a hidden back-up power source so when they steal it next time they'll get the joy ride of their life."

"Bass, I would appreciate it if you didn't do that."

"It'd damn sure break them of stealing things."

Jake looked at Bass for a long moment and Bass said, "Or just some birdshot through their windshield."

Another pause before Bass laughed and said, "Don't look at me like that. I'm just kidding but dammit, this's a bunch of shit."

"Do you have anyone in mind for this?"

"Yeah, I'm thinking it's Rowdy Manners and that bunch a shitheads. Caught him out here once." Bass pointed east. "Down that road runs behind my place, just sitting there in a truck. Asked him what he was doing and he told me it was none of my fucking business. Damn kids these days. Anyway, I told him I catch him out here again I'd kick a mud hole in his ass and stomp it dry."

"You were always a colorful individual, Bass." Jake said.

"Can you do anything about this?"

"Not a lot but I'll run him down and ask where he was last night. He'll lie about it but it will put him on notice. I would like to catch him though. You might want to get one of those trail cams, you know cameras that video movement."

"Way ahead of you. Ordered one today."

"Anything else I can do for you while I'm here?"

"Where are you on that teacher killing? Or can't you

say? I know, I know…I watch Law and Order. But, maybe I can help you out some."

Jake knew that although Bass liked to bullshit, the man was no bullshitter.

Jake nodded and said, "Okay, how?"

"One of the people out there with Rowdy that day surprised me. It was Eberhard's kid, Ranse. He used to be a pretty good boy, hard worker, but he's changed, Jake. I thought he was better than to hang out with that bunch but they were out there on that road drinking beer and smoking weed. Not the first time I seen Ranse Eberhard out on an abandoned road. I think he's seeing someone."

"Well, he's at the age for that," Jake said.

"This'd be somebody's wife."

"You have a name?"

"I do, but not sure enough to say and I don't want to carry tales but I think if you'll wait an hour, drink a beer with me, I can probably tell you where they'll be. They don't know I saw them. I think you'll be surprised who he's seeing, not that I blame him. She's got some miles on her but she's still a dandy and he has information you want."

"Already talked to the young man."

Bass drained his beer, crushed the can in his hand and said, "You won't be sorry you waited."

Jake looked at his watch, thinking he could wait to interview Pete Stanger. If Bass thought he had something worth seeing, Jake would honor that. Bass didn't say things out of school, much.

"All right, Bass," Jake said. "I do enjoy your company. I'll have a coke, if you have any on hand."

* * *

Harper Bannister was back home after a meeting with her friend, Sherry Hammersmith, a meeting that had gone south, quickly.

Sherry had come to Harper's office at Jessup & Jessup, attorney's-at-law where Harper worked as a para-legal. The long-time friends were to discuss plans to open the coffee bar Sherry had mentioned earlier. Harper was interested and it might be a fun thing but had her doubts about its viability as a successful venture. Still, Sherry was a good friend and she was willing to listen to what Sherry had in mind. Sherry was a go-getter and a hard worker but had a penchant for running ahead of herself.

"That's why we're a good team," Sherry said, arguing the point. "I'm passionate and full steam ahead while you're measured and possess a ton of good sense. I talked to the bank about a business loan and also checked other lenders. I can swing this alone and it might be a strain on my night life, but together we could make this work. And, as I said earlier, I can manage it while you finish up your degree."

"It sounds good," Harper said. She picked up a folder she had prepared and handed it to Sherry. "I have done some research and crunched numbers and I think it's going to run you more than you may think. There's business licenses, taxes, inventory expense and Sherry, start-up businesses seldom make money initially. In fact, most lose money for an extended period of time. Do you have enough money put away to sustain losses?"

"Did you ask Jake Morgan about buying in?"

Harper had been dreading that question. Sherry was headstrong and once she got up a good head of steam she was hard to dissuade.

"I am not comfortable asking Jake to do that."

"Why? You're engaged to him so why be afraid to ask

him to help you get a business off the ground? What's that about? He has the money to leverage a loan. That farm of his for one thing."

Harper didn't like the direction of the conversation. "If we do this thing, open up a coffee bar, I want it to be you and me, and not access Jake's money, which is not as considerable as you might think."

Jake was comfortably fixed but not wealthy, having been left land and a stock portfolio from his father despite the fact father and son were estranged for the last few years of his dad's life. Harper loved Jake but worried about being married to a man like Jake Morgan. For one thing he held a dangerous job as an investigator. He'd already been shot at more than once. And if that wasn't enough, Jake Morgan didn't care who or where he made enemies. Jake didn't like blurred lines. You were either with him or against him and Jake liked to draw the battle lines himself regardless of repercussions.

Still, she had never in her life met or known a better man. He was straight up honest and good to her.

"So you're not even going to try?" Sherry said.

"I'm not going to use Jake as a cash register."

Sherry screwed up the side of his lips and said, "So, all Jake is good for then is breaking up marriages."

This was a side of Sherry she had never seen. Harper turned a hand over and made a face.

"What is that supposed to mean?" Harper said.

"My cousin is going to divorce Coach Tompkins."

"Val Tompkins is your cousin? I didn't know that. How is that Jake's fault?"

"For one thing, he brought in Bill for questioning and made him a suspect. That blew open Val's suspicions about Bill and Brenda Sutherland. For Val that was the last straw."

"So, as you see it, the problem is that Jake is running

an investigation rather than the fact that Bill can't keep his pants zipped. And you think half the people in town didn't know about that, already? You know how small towns are."

"Well, if Jake would do his job and arrest Pete Stanger none of this would've happened."

Harper made a puzzled face and then asked, "Sherry, where are you getting that Pete Stanger killed Mr. Saunders?"

"Well, like you said, *half* the town knows about it." Sherry bit off the sentence like spitting out seeds.

Harper raised a hand and gave her friend a sidelong look before she said, "This is a very strange conversation, Sherry. It's getting too personal. Maybe we would be better served if we re-visit this another time."

"Don't lawyer talk me, Harper Bannister," Sherry said, leaning forward in her seat. "I *know* you better than anyone and know how you think. You're not so lily white. Who was it married that idiot Tommy Mitchell."

"Yes, that was a mistake. But, you know, Sherry, right now this discussion, to utilize what you call lawyer-speak...this discussion has degenerated to a point where nothing is to be gained by continuing. Why don't you leave and when you have composed yourself we can try this again without the catty comments."

"Catty? I'm not the bitch in the room. Somebody else is holding that title."

Harper leaned back and frowned. "Sherry, this is why friends should not go into business together. Already we're having problems and we haven't even started."

"Guess you can blame your boyfriend for that. He needs to do his job. The whole town is scared to death that there's a murderer loose and wondering who is next. Felicia Jankowski says that Jake is dragging his feet and protecting Pete. I'd think your dad would be smarter than—"

"Felicia Jankowski? That's your source? If she had as many sticking out of her as she's had stuck in her she'd look like a porcupine." Harper put her hands out. "I am not believing this conversation. You're better than this but we're done here, Sherry. You're just spitting out accusations to get a rise and you probably need to leave."

"That's fine with me," Sherry said. "Good-bye."

After Sherry left, Harper sat and stared at her desktop. She sighed deeply and brushed back hair from her face.

"I believe in you Jake," she said aloud. "But, get this done before I run out of friends."

CHAPTER TWENTY-FIVE

It was twilight when Jake drove out to the place Bass Arnold had said Ransom Eberhard and his "lover" met for romantic trysts. Though Jake was uncomfortable with this type of thing he knew Bass had reason to share it with him. Bass was not the type to meddle in other people's business which was a characteristic of most men from his generation.

The site of the rendezvous was a dead end lane off county road NN. The road had been rendered obsolete when the state re-routed the highway and now isolated from traffic. Jake parked his unit two hundred yards west of the site, kept the setting sun at his back as he crossed over a sagging barb wire fence and quietly picked his way along the fence line.

The fading light filtered through the brush and trees, casting shadows on the abandoned farmland. Jake could make out a spark of sunlight on the red Ford F-250 that had 'two superchargers and pipes that sound like monsters'. Ranse should've stuck to working out rather than take up with married women.

Jake heard the rocking and squeaking from the pick-up. He approached from an angle where he would not be seen from either the side or rearview mirrors. Ardent yelps from the back-seat. He wished he was anywhere else but you go where the work led. Jake owned a Ford F-150 and knew the vehicle had a large back seat. He also figured the backseats would be in the upright position and the two lovers would be on the floor.

Jake did not enjoy this; feeling like a voyeur. Police work was ever like this—catching people at their worst. He shook his head, took in a breath and knocked on the door panel. Ransom Eberhard's head popped up and he said, "Somebody's getting an ass-kicking."

"County Undersheriff Morgan here. Ranse Eberhard, you rogue, you," Jake said. "I'll give you a couple minutes to cover up before we either talk or you kick my ass."

"Get back in your car and get the fuck outta here, Morgan."

This kid, huh?

"I don't think so. Get dressed and we'll talk. That is, I'll talk, you'll listen, Ranse. If it doesn't go that way then we'll go with indecent exposure."

There was movement inside as someone tried to open the back door of the four-door pick-up.

"Don't let him see me, Ranse," a flinty female voice said from within the pick-up. It was a voice Jake recognized.

"That you, Mrs. Jankowski?" Jake said, smiling big as he said it. "Beautiful evening for an assignation, isn't it?

"Fuck you, Morgan."

"Too late, Ranse beat me to it."

"You can't talk to her like that." Ransom said. "I won't put up with it."

"You're in no position to dictate, Ranse. Both of you get your clothes on—"

Ransom Eberhard burst from the truck, wearing only

underwear and intent on closing the distance between himself and Jake. God, the kid was big. Jake didn't want to fight Ransom but it looked like there was going to be no choice.

Ransom threw an ineffective high kick that Jake blocked and moved back. It was the same move Jake had watched Ransom work on back in the barn. Jake feinted forward and when Ransom delivered the sidekick Jake used his left arm to sweep away the sidekick, followed by a hard kick with his right foot to the kid's groin.

Ransom barked loudly in pain and went down in the scrub weeds where he curled up in the fetal position, his hands on his crotch. "Oh shit, what the hell did—it fucking hurts."

"Stay down, Ranse," Jake said. "You come at me again, I'll mace you."

"That's not fair," Ransom said.

"You're too big for fair," Jake said. "Soon as you recover I'm going to cuff you."

"Can I dress first?"

"I'll throw your pants to you and we'll talk about it. Anything else and it gets even uglier."

A pair of jeans came flying out of the backseat but as yet Felicia had not made an appearance. Jake picked up the pants and threw them at Ransom and they landed on the man's legs. Jake walked to the pick-up and said, "Are you decent, Mrs. Jankowski?"

"What do you care?"

"I want you to maintain what little dignity you have left, Mrs. Jankowski."

"What if I don't come out?"

"Then I'll look anyway."

"What if I'm naked?"

"Then I'll have nightmares for a week."

"You smartass…"

"You have ten seconds to cover-up but I'm going to open that door." Jake started counting but when he got to 'nine' the door opened and there was Mrs. Felicia Jankowski, her clothes rumpled, hair disheveled.

"Here I am. Are you happy now?"

"Conjugal visits not working for you, Felicia?"

"I'll have your badge for this."

"You don't have anything to pin it on right now."

"I ought to kill you."

"That sounds like menacing a law enforcement officer, which is a felony. Should I read your rights and cuff you, too?"

Felicia set her teeth in a line and looked off to one side. "No."

"Then dial it down, lady."

Jake cuffed Ransom and placed him and Felicia in the back seat of his County vehicle. He let them suffer for a few moments while he decided how he wanted to deal with them. He could use the incident to leverage information from them or he could book them. As he was deciding, he got a call from Leo the Lion.

"What's up, Leo?"

"Where are you?"

"Couple kids are out on NN playing push-push. I may have to run them in."

"For parking?"

"Long story. I'll tell you later."

Leo saying, "I had a meeting with Winston Vestal today that you need to hear about."

"What was said?"

"I'm still in my office. I'll meet you at Hank's, later when you're available."

Jake thinking he really needed to see Pete Stanger but

it could wait if Leo thought it important. "Okay, let me take care of this first. I'll call you after I decide what to do with them."

* * *

Dr. Knox Sutherland checked Pete Stanger's chart and asked Pete how he was feeling.

"Getting better," Pete said. He was eating orange Jell-O and washing it down with iced tea. "Still a little foggy but don't know how I got here."

"Well," Sutherland said. "Looks like you're doing well. Your vitals are good and you're young and strong. Maybe we can release you in the morning."

"That would be great," Pete said, though he wasn't quite himself yet.

"Pete, you have been in a coma for a few days and a lot has happened. Martin Saunders was murdered. Did you know anything about that?"

Did he? Stanger couldn't focus on the question. For some reason he had a vague recall of Jake Morgan but he didn't know why. There was a hazy memory of being at the school and something terrible happening.

But, what was it?

"No. I...a...didn't...that is...I'm sorry but I'm not myself yet."

"Well, if you think of something I'd be glad to talk to you about it. Meanwhile, get some rest. There are some meds I will prescribe for you and have some food brought in to you later this afternoon."

After Dr. Sutherland left Stanger worked to clear his head. Saunders *was* dead, that Stanger knew from seeing him, but now he was having trouble remembering other things and why was Sutherland releasing him when Pete didn't feel ready yet?

But, Sutherland was a doctor so who was he to question it. Starting to remember more things now, things roaring back to him like a snake, fangs bared.

CHAPTER TWENTY-SIX

Jake turned Felicia loose even though the way she was looking at him suggested she would love to stab Jake in the eye with a fork. He let her off with a written warning regarding indecent exposure and menacing telling her he could come back on that at any time. As for Ransom, Jake took him into town after securing the kid's truck and dropping Felicia at her car which was parked a mile away at an abandoned missile site. Jake called a tow for the pick-up of Felicia's Mercedes SUV.

"It's embarrassing to get caught out like that," Ransom said.

"Diddling married women carries some baggage."

"Not that, you taking me down so easily. How'd you do that?"

"A real fight with no rules is not the same as kicking a bag that doesn't fight back. That move you tried? Seen it before. From the size of you, I'd guess you've not had many real fights in your life."

"Yeah, you're right, in fact I never had one before today. Thought I could take you but, man...I learned something from it, though." He snapped his fingers.

"Damn, you watched me work out the other day. You saw that move and waited on it."

"Like an O-2 fastball."

"Are you going to book me?"

"You mean arrest you?" Jake said, smiling at the 'book me'. "Thinking I should. Had you laid a hand on me you would be looking at assaulting a law officer and booking some jail time. Think about that. I don't know, though, maybe you can help me out with something. Do you know anything about somebody messing with Bass Arnold's grain dryer?"

Ransom lifted his chin, nodded, and said, "I tell you something, do I get off the, you know, assault thing? And especially about the deal with her? No arrest?"

"Give me a name, if it's good and get off the 'roids. You don't need them and they're messing up your head. Your Father doesn't know but that doesn't mean I won't hold it over you if needed."

Ranse dropped his head a bit and said, "I don't...okay."

Jake nodded. "It's a deal."

"Thanks. Here's what's going on. Rowdy's got it in for Bass because Bass ran us off when we were partying on a back road so Rowdy fucked around with Bass' grain dryer, taking the wire, he also stole some tools."

"Will you testify to that?"

"Sure. Piss on Rowdy. Maybe you could just tell Bass and let him beat it out of Rowdy, that'd teach Rowdy something."

"Not a terrible idea," Jake said, "but then I'd have to arrest an old friend. Bass is creased about the grain dryer and that man is a tough knot. I don't turn people loose as vigilantes. No, I'll need your testimony. You understand it'll make Rowdy mad at you."

"Manners and his little gang of wannabes don't buckle my knees. Yeah, I'll stand up."

"Why are you hanging out with Rowdy anyway? Thought you guys had a falling out."

"Same reason I got caught with Felicia and then tried to kick you. You're right, it's the steroids. Sometimes I do stupid things."

Jake smiled and said, "Most people do stupid things, some more often than others. What's the rest of it? Does Rowdy get your steroids for you?"

"Rowdy told me he could get anything I needed. I wanted to bulk up and he said he could supply at a cheap price."

"You're right, that is stupid. You're big enough already. So, Rowdy said he could get anything you needed? Does that include things like Coke, heroin—"

"I don't use that shit, you know, just the 'roids."

"How about pharmaceuticals? Pain-killers, Oxy, Molly?"

"Molly?"

"It's bath salts, you may know it as ecstasy." Jake thinking about Saunders' cause of death.

"I guess so. I'm scared of that stuff, but I've heard things, like he has a source at the hospital."

Jake gave that some thought. "Did he mention the source?"

"No, never has, it's just scuttlebutt."

Jake ran a thumb along his jaw and then said, "Is Rowdy and his gang of wannabes, as you call them, doing a lot of trafficking?"

"They seem to be branching out. He's got a couple of new guys with him. Big guys."

"Okay, Ranse, I'm going to cut you loose contingent upon your testimony and you get clean. No statement, no get out of jail free card."

"You're not going to tell dad, are you?"

"I haven't any interest in talking about you and Felicia engaged in Skanko-Roman wrestling on a dirt road. Seems beneath me, somehow. That's your job and it depends on what kind of man you want to be."

Ranse nodded slowly. "You sound just like him."

"I hope that's a compliment."

"It is." He was quiet for a moment and then said, "What's an assignation?"

"You sparking Mrs. Jankowski."

"Oh." He made a face. "Right now I don't feel so good about that. Hey, you ever have...you know, VD? What would that feel like?"

* * *

Jake drove home, changed clothes, switched out the borrowed County SUV for his F-150, leaving the vintage Lincoln in the garage. He called in to see if Buddy or Bailey could go out to the hospital and check on Pete Stanger, but the dispatcher told him Bailey had a night class and the Sheriff was speaking at the Country Club. Jake worried it in his head but decided to see what Leo had to say about Winston Vestal so he drove to town and parked in front of Hank's and found his best friend, Leo the Lion, back at a corner table, working on a frosted mug of beer.

Jake nodded at the server, pointed at Leo's beer and then back at his chest. The server got the message and brought Jake a beer.

"What's this about two kids out on NN?" Leo said. "So you've finally sunk to busting teenagers engaged in coital embrace."

"They were somewhat older than that," Jake said.

"Felicia Jankowski was teaching Ranse Eberhard the joys of sex with an older woman."

Leo raised an index fever and said, "I only have one thing to say about that. Ick. And you can quote me. Eb will shred that kid's hide."

"Yeah, it seemed to be Ranse's number one concern. Felicia sure gets around."

"You don't know about Felicia?"

Jake shrugged.

Leo saying now, "You were gone for ten years, Jake. Felicia and her husband, the guy you put behind bars, had somewhat of an open relationship, you know, key parties and other things that Mrs. Lyons might strenuously object to providing you with another homicide to investigate. Felicia knows how to use her body and how to leverage that information to further her agenda. You see, Felicia doesn't care if her affairs are talked about so when you jump her bones she owns you."

Jake thought about it. He took a sip of beer, set the glass down and said, "So, who are some names associated with her."

Leo named a few names that meant little to Jake but there were three that interested him.

"Knox Sutherland, Forrest Taylor, Martin Saunders—"

"Hang on, Leo. Martin Saunders?"

Leo nodded. "That's not even the best one."

"Who?"

Cecil Holtzmeyer appeared, beer in hand and said, "What're you boys up to? Hello officer Jake. Coach Lyons you're having a great season, can I buy you a beer?" He turned and waved the server over and held up two fingers, then pointed at Jake and Leo. "On my tab, okay." He looked up at the TV monitor and said, "Looks like the

Royals are losing another one. To be a Royals fan is to have your heart broke on a daily basis."

"How're you doing, Cecil," Leo said.

"Doing good, Coach," Cecil said. He patted Jake on the shoulder. "This man here is an ace human bein'. Cut me a break and got me home the other night. That's just between us three though, right boys?"

"That's right, Cecil," Jake said.

"You know, Jake, my boy, I'm thinking I may have recognized that pick-up that drove past us so fast."

This could be good, Jake thought. "Yeah? Well, tell me."

"Well, I'm not sure," Cecil said. He raised his head to look at the ceiling as if lost in thought, though more likely lost in barley malt musings. "I almost remember it and then…I need to do some more…investigation on the subject."

"Cecil, either you know or you don't."

"I'm very glad to help out. I'll leave you boys to talk amongst yourselves." He looked up at the TV again and said, "Aw, dammit. They're down four runs in the eighth. Well, see you two around."

Cecil walked back to the table to join his friends.

"Cecil means well," Leo said.

"I need him to decide if he knows what he's talking about, but he was drinking that night. I feel like I'm chasing my tail. Everybody has a motive to harm Saunders."

"Getting frustrated by this killing?"

"My sun sets to rise again."

"Now you're a poet?"

"At least Browning is."

"Who would ever figure you for a fan of English Lit?"

Jake put both hands around his beer glass and said,

"I'll sift through all this and find what I'm looking for. Who's this other guy you were going to tell me about?"

Leo took a long pull on his beer and said, "And now for your consideration…" Leo mimicked a drum roll on the table before he said, "Winston Vestal."

"You're kidding?"

"Are you surprised?"

"Stunned." Jake had another thread to pull on. Vestal goes right back into the suspect list. Gotta love Leo the Lion.

CHAPTER TWENTY-SEVEN

Melissa Vanderbilt of KCKS brushed the hair back from her face and Buster Mangold caught a wisp of Chanel No. 5. This lady smelled like a promise.

Buster was on his second Jack and Coke while Miss Hotty sipped at a white wine. Man, he was feeling good and lucky sitting here with this info-babe. He knew she was pumping him for information, and he wasn't above keeping her on the hook promising to get some for her.

"So," Vanderbilt said. "What have you got for me?"

"Whatever you want," Buster said.

"I don't know if we're on the same page, Buster."

"Tell me what page you're on and I'll try to catch up."

Vanderbilt sucked in her lower lip and then said, "The homicide of Martin Saunders. Do you have any information?"

"Couple things in mind," Buster said. "You sure are pretty."

"That's sweet of you," she said. "You're not hard on the eyes yourself. Do you lift weights? You have big shoulders."

"Played linebacker in high school," he said. "Played two years at UCM but I quit. College wasn't my thing."

"How well do you know Investigator Morgan?"

"I just work with him."

"Is he always an asshole?"

"Pretty much," Buster said. "He's got some mouth on him, too. Blew into town a couple years ago, thinks because he was a Texas Ranger he's God's gift to law enforcement. But this murder thing has him running in circles. I've got some ideas of my own about how it happened and who did it?"

"Really?" Vanderbilt said, leaning forward, her chin on a hand. "Who do you think is the killer?"

"Not yet, but I'm getting closer to the truth. I've done my own investigation, gathered some information from good sources."

"What are you close on?" she said. "Tell me more."

"I'm waiting on something. One of my informants tells me that a certain person of interest could become a factor." He didn't have any informants but all's fair in love and sex, right?

Vanderbilt stroked Buster's arm with the back of her fingers and said, "Well, tell me about it, Buster."

Buster wagged a finger. "Now, now, be patient. Can't say yet. I should have something for you tomorrow." And more if things work out, he thought.

* * *

Jake and Leo finished their second beers and Jake watched Cecil Holtzmeyer walk out of the bar, Jake wondering if he should make sure the man didn't drive. Cecil lived two blocks away and often walked to Hank's. The weather was warm for October so Jake figured Cecil would be fine.

"You're telling me Winston Vestal tried to bribe you?" Jake said.

"I was so embarrassed," Leo said.

"You've never been embarrassed in your life."

"True, but I did pass up a new locker room and a sprinkler system. Being a man of impeccable integrity and inner fortitude I resisted temptation."

"You already have a sprinkler system."

"Yeah, but Vestal doesn't know that."

Jake gave his friend a half-smile and said, "Maybe you should've asked for some coaching lessons."

"I give those, Inspector Clouseau. You want to know what I think or just insult my myriad talents?"

"All of that if possible," Jake said. "Go ahead and dazzle me with your blinding insight."

"That's better," Leo said, nodding. He held up a hand to get the server's attention and held up two fingers. Leo shared his conversation with Vestal and Jake asked for his friend's thoughts on the subject.

"Winston Vestal and Felicia Yank-a-zipper as a thing is so Mr. Peanut meets The Happy Hooker that it staggers the imagination. It is an abomination that assaults the senses. But there has to be a reason they are coupling. Either Felicia wants something from Vestal besides his shriveled joystick or Vestal wants...skip that, it makes me doubt whether the species can continue to evolve. It has to be something Felicia wants, something of a political nature or something that can be used to give her more of whatever she is seeking."

"That's not bad, Leo."

"They don't call me 'The Professor' for nothing. The rumor mill is churning like a riverboat on a muddy bank. Old friend, you're being roasted over a fire in the community. I'm hearing some nasty things about you, lately."

"I've heard them, too and not second hand," Jake said. "I'm almost as popular as Martin Saunders is."

"Was," Leo said, correcting Saunders' state.

"Vestal has something in his office he doesn't want revealed. I've been through the place and I can't find anything incriminating or anything that ties him to the Saunders' homicide. What does your head tell you?"

"First, you're a cop, and you think like one. You're focused on the homicide and criminal acts and aren't familiar with school politics and the paranoia of central office personnel. School Superintendents are weird creatures who went into education and then ascended to a non-educational position. What an over-educated boob like Vestal is worried about doesn't have to be something earth-shattering or even criminal and may be something as simple as a mistake in his budget proposals to the school board or a rift between Vestal and a staff member who happens to be a local. Local people love to work at the school they graduated from—"

"Like you."

"The perfect example. Like me, however, some work at their local school because they want to re-experience the feel of their youth or because they fear leaving Paradise for a strange situation. School secretary jobs are fraught with peril for administrators and even board members when several local women apply. They are sought after and the campaigning often gets serious."

"So, you think it's something political and school related."

"Just floating the alternative."

Jake looked at the foam drying on his empty beer glass for a long moment before he said, "My court order restricting access to Vestal's office ends at midnight tonight. How about going to school with me and you take a look around Vestal's office and maybe you can see what I am not."

"I often see things you don't. It's like a rule. You know this could backfire on both of us. We don't find anything then you've shut Vestal down for no reason and if it is known that I went through employee files that is a big-time breach of confidentiality and a violation of the rights to privacy rule. The rest of the faculty could begin to eye me askance if they even imagine I have seen their personnel file."

"All right then we won't look at their files. Bailey went through the personnel files anyway and I trust her nose for detail. Just come with me and give it a shot."

"All right, I'm in," Leo said. "Just remember 'When you strike at the King you must kill him'."

"Meaning you could get fired."

"More than likely."

"Wow, a bonus. I get what I want and PHS gets a real football coach. So, let's go."

"I'm waiting on applause for the Emerson quote. How'd you like it?" Leo said as he buffed his fingernails on his shirt.

"A nice touch," Jake said, as they stood. "You get a cookie."

CHAPTER TWENTY-EIGHT

Forrest Taylor and Dr. Knox Sutherland cornered Chief Bannister and Sheriff Buddy Johnson in the PPD office telling the two law enforcement heads they wanted a few minutes to dialogue about Jake Morgan. Cal knew when Forrest Taylor said he wanted to talk what it meant is he wanted to talk at you. Buddy Johnson knew Dr. Sutherland was of the same state-of-mind. Both men drew a lot of water in Paradise County. Big fat fish in a murky pond was part of the occupational hazards of small-town law enforcement. Over the years Cal had handled such things with his settled disposition of tolerance and stubbornness.

"We cannot share anymore about suspects and cause of death, Forrest," Cal said. "You know that already."

Forrest held up a hand and said, "I got that, what I'm concerned about though is the way the young man conducts himself with people."

"Meaning?"

"He is very pointed and fails to consider who it is he is addressing."

"Like Felicia Jankowski?" Buddy said.

"Not just her," Dr. Sutherland said. "He was pushy with my ex-wife, asking questions that have nothing to do with his investigation."

"Dr. Sutherland," Cal said, "There is no such thing as 'questions that have nothing to do' with any police investigation. Jake Morgan is the most talented investigator I have ever worked with. He has an ear to hear what is not being said and an eye for what matters and what doesn't."

"The man has no sense of propriety. He fails to understand his position in the community as a public figure and who he is talking to."

"Doesn't know his place?" Buddy said. "I have some experience with that way of thinking."

"Don't put words in my mouth, Sheriff" Sutherland said.

"I don't think I have to," Buddy said. "I'm not going to pretend you're crusading for justice."

"You're not going to listen to reason?"

"I am listening, you're just not saying anything," Buddy said. "And I'm not going to react because Felicia Jankowski put a bug in your ear."

Cal put hands up, interrupting and said, "Listen, Jake goes where the facts lead him. In a murder investigation when you're gathering information one does not initially know what things will become germane and even crucial to the investigation. A word, a thought, an event that may seem trivial, even to the person being interviewed may turn the investigation in the right direction. This is not Jake's first rodeo. He is tough, fair and do not be fooled by his age, Jake has a lot of experience in these things."

"I think, Cal," Forrest said, "Is that we would like for Morgan to be more discreet and courteous. Yes, he appears to be a talented law enforcement officer but that doesn't mean he has step on toes in every inquiry."

"As I said, he has to go where the facts and evidence take him. Forrest, you of all people, should appreciate his determination and skill. It is your nephew's killing he's looking into."

Sutherland leaned back in a chair and slapped his knees. "I don't think you understand, Cal. Morgan works for us and is endangering his—"

"No," Buddy said, standing to his full six-and-a-half foot. "Jake does not work for you, he works for the people of the county and community."

"Calm down, Sheriff," Sutherland said. "You're getting your back up because you're his best friend. And Cal, Morgan is engaged to your daughter."

"Yes, he is and I like Jake," Cal said. "More than that, I trust him and have faith in his law enforcement abilities. Having Jake Morgan as an investigator is like having a Division I Quarterback playing for our high school team."

"Still, Cal," Forrest saying now, "wouldn't it be better if we brought in the FBI? They have resources neither you nor the Highway Patrol can bring to bear on this and it is the consensus of the City Council and the School board—"

"The School Board?" Buddy asked.

"…that we would like you to bring in the FBI and take Morgan off the case."

Cal shook his head. "I'll not do that."

"If you don't," Sutherland said, cutting in. "We will suspend Morgan."

"He'll still be working for me," Buddy said. "And I'll lend him back to the city."

Cal glared at Sutherland for a long moment. He

pulled up his pipe, stuck it between his teeth, removed it and said, "Why not just suspend me instead of Jake?"

Forrest saying now, "Cal, we've known you for many years. And we know of Morgan's, well, his past history. You remember what he was like when he was younger. And his parents? His father was an alcoholic and his mother—"

"Be careful of your words, Forrest."

Forrest put up hands and said, "Jake's known for his temper and his, well, he was a handful back in high school and you know that yourself. So do you, Sheriff."

Buddy looked down at both men before he said, "What I know is that Jake Morgan does what he says he will do. He is honest, some say, he is honest to a fault and pays no deference to class or color, which if you're going to have character flaws, I like those. Jake will not be intimidated, and he is resolute and meticulous in an investigation."

"He's also a grown man now and as solid as any man in this room." Cal paused to look at both men. "Probably more so."

"You're taking this wrong, Cal," Sutherland said.

"I take them as I see them."

Forrest said, "We'll give Morgan twenty-four hours to come up with something."

"Come up with what?"

"Make an arrest," Sutherland said. "And he should start looking hard at Pete Stanger."

"Why are you obsessed with Pete Stanger?" Cal said. "He was in a coma and it is doubtful we will get much from him. And so there is no confusion, Forrest, I won't be held to a timetable."

Forrest and Sutherland stood to leave. When they reached the doorway, Forrest Taylor turned and said, "Your choice. 48 hours."

"Bullshit," Buddy said, as the two men left. "All my life people like those two have been keeping people down and I don't mean just because of my color. You heard them about Jake. His background? Jake's not good enough because his father wasn't one of them."

"It's that way in every community, every job, BJ," Cal said. "No matter the size of the place, there's always those who believe they are a cut above everyone else. This place is no exception."

"You going to tell Jake about the ultimatum?"

"Oh no," Cal said, laughing. "You know how he is."

Buddy smiled and then laughed. "Yes. Yes, I do."

* * *

Brenda Sutherland poured tea into an icy glass and added a lemon slice. She stepped out on her front porch as the dark clouds overheard swelled with rain. She considered how she had managed to mess up her life so badly. She loved the teaching profession and liked her life, more or less, so why did she involve herself with the young baseball coach.

She brushed hair back from her face and thought about whether to have her beautician touch up the burgeoning grey around her temples or just let it go. She watched as a red-throated hummingbird fluttered near by the bird feeder she'd set out for the little birds. She loved birds. Cardinals, Gold Finches, Mourning Doves, and sparrows. Enjoyed their songs early in the morning.

Blue Jays were beautiful blue birds but they were predators, raiding nests and spoiling the eggs. She watched as a large Jay flew into an oak tree searching for prey. She searched the ground for a pebble to shoo it away and that's when her ex-husband, Dr. Knox Sutherland, the known bastard, pulled his red Cadillac into her drive.

Knox unfolded from the vehicle. He was still a handsome man who knew how to wear a suit. Today it was his dark blue power suit, set off by a perfectly knotted tie at his throat. Square jawline, dark blue eyes and his salt-and-pepper hair rivaled George Clooney's. Knox had been a tremendous athlete in his day and stayed in shape. Knox weighed within five pounds of his college weight when he played baseball at UCM. Remembering now why she was first attracted to Knox, but learned the hard way that he was an expensively designed suit on the clearance sale rack.

And he had cheated on her, multiple times and she didn't see it until too late. She disliked herself for the affair with Bill Tompkins. It was unlike her. She had flirted a bit with the investigator, Jake Morgan, and he had ignored it. Why was she doing that? Was it because she was past forty and feeling it? Maybe it was time to find another school in another town far away from Knox and Bill and this town so inappropriately named.

Knox raised a hand in salutation and said, "Hello, Brenda. How are you doing?"

Like you care, she thought. "What do you want, Knox?"

"I'd like a word with you, if that's possible."

"We've had enough words between us. There's nothing else to say."

"I want to ask you about your interview with Jake Morgan. It's City Council business."

Brenda shifted her feet and rattled the ice in her glass. "It's also none of your business, Knox. He interviewed me and told me to keep the information confidential and I will do that. Some people keep their word."

Knox looked around as if there were ghosts with

recording devices. "May I come inside and, you know, avoid the neighbors staring."

Brenda laughed. "Oh, Knox. Of course you can't come in and they all remember when you used to come in late at night after one of your little episodes."

"Brenda, I just want to know if Morgan asked about you or...myself?"

"You're wasting your time. Speaking of time, you're overdue for your maintenance payment. Please remit this at your earliest—"

"Dammit, Brenda. This is important."

"It must be for you to show up. Just like you to appear only when you need something."

"You know this cuts both ways, Bren. Maybe he doesn't know about your little love interest at the school."

"He knows," Brenda said. "I think you'd be surprised by Jake Morgan. I know I am. He's very thorough and not just another local cop with a big belly. He's highly intelligent for a Paradise High School grad. Don't let his Levi's and off-hand personality fool you. He's smarter than you and articulate. And don't call me 'Bren', that doesn't work anymore."

"We have to talk, Brenda."

Knox started to ascend the steps but Brenda put a hand out. "Stop right there. You're not welcome here and I'm not going to tell you anything regarding my statement."

"I heard Tompkins wife is divorcing Bill."

"I've heard that, too," Brenda said, seeing Knox as a Blue Jay come to spoil her nest.

"So are you and that kid going to hook up and play 'house'?"

"Oh, Knox," Brenda said. She sighed, took a sip of her

tea and then said, "For someone with a medical degree you are so dim."

"You shouldn't cross me, Brenda. I'd think you'd know better."

"Are you going to go out and screw one of your patients in your office to get back at me? Yes, I know about that, she came to me crying, but as yet I have not mentioned that. I wonder what the state certification board would think of that."

Sutherland's eyes narrowed and he bared his teeth. "I'm warning you, Brenda, and don't forget this. If you fuck with me, I will take steps to see you run out of town, one way or another. You're going to regret this moment."

As Sutherland slammed his car door, Brenda dropped her eye and quietly said to herself, "I already regret many things."

* * *

It was 12:37 AM when Winston Vestal drove to his office. The deadline to open his office was midnight and he did not wait until morning. As he pulled into the parking lot he saw a vintage Lincoln Mark IV leave. From the driver's seat, Jake Morgan waved to him.

"Son of a bitch," Vestal said out loud. Vestal seldom used profanity.

CHAPTER TWENTY-NINE

Jake woke to the sounds of rain pattering against the roof and the smell of bacon. The bacon aroma was a surprise so he pulled on his jeans and slipped into his moccasins and walked into his art deco kitchen.

"Good morning, sleepy head," Harper Bannister said.

Jake rubbed his face and eyes. "What are you doing here?" Jake asked.

"It looks like I'm cooking breakfast, what do you think?"

"I appreciate it. When did you get here?"

"I've been here over an hour. You were snoring. Late night?"

"Yeah, it was." He blinked his eyes and said, "What time is it?"

"Almost ten. I didn't know people slept this late. Also you need a haircut. You look like you slept standing on your head."

"I gotta get going," Jake said. "I need to talk to Pete Stanger. I put it off too long. He's been comatose and I don't know what or even *if* he knows anything helpful."

"You sit right there, Jake. You are going to eat a real breakfast instead of coffee and cigarettes."

"I quit smoking."

"Again?"

"But not coffee." He poured himself a cup from the coffee machine and gave Harper a kiss on her cheek. She smelled of apple blossom lotion, Estee Lauder, and sunshine. He could just eat her up. You're a lucky man, Jake. "I was up at school looking for something Dr. Vestal didn't want me to find. I took Leo with me. How's it going with the business venture? You know, the coffee shop?"

Thunder rolled and rattled kitchen windows of the house which was built twenty years before Jake was born. He was too busy to farm so he leased out the land to a couple of local farmers. The money came in steadily to him and the farm retained its vibrancy.

Harper cracked two eggs, dropped them into a bowl and beat them with a fork. "Not well," she said. "It's pretty much a dead issue. Sherry blew up at me."

"About what?"

"You."

Jake leaned back and close one eye. "How was I part of it?"

"Bill Tompkins' wife is her cousin. Small towns, huh? They're getting divorced and somehow she thinks it's your fault for uncovering the...uh...the affair. You'd think she'd blame Coach Tompkins for running around but there it is. People are so...Jake, the whole town is worked up. I'm hearing things about your investigation, not good things, and by that I mean people are frightened and it's making them suspicious of everyone and... mean. They don't know you like I do. I have information they don't have so they make it up. Some of them, the jerks, are blaming you."

"I'm hearing it too."

"So, did you find it?"

"Find what?"

"The thing in Vestal's office?"

"Leo did." Jake scraped one of the mid-century retro chairs across the floor and sat. "I should've used him earlier. It took quite a while to find and I was up against a midnight deadline. If I hadn't taken Leo, I would've missed it."

"So what was it he found?"

"The most interesting thing was that we met Vestal pulling into the parking lot as we were leaving."

"He knew the court order expired."

"Yep."

"Well?"

"Well what?"

She gave him a look and said, "You know what."

Jake smiled and said, "Oh yeah, I almost forgot. Better sit down. You're going to love this."

* * *

Jake arrived at Paradise County Memorial Hospital and was told that Pete Stanger had been released. Jake wondering how that could be possible.

"Who released him?" Jake asked the information person, a woman in her late sixties with copper hair turning white. The lady clicked up some information on her computer screen.

"Dr. Sutherland released him," she said. "Two hours ago."

Jake left and drove to Stanger's home, a blue-grey ranch on Midland Drive in the southeast part of town. A nice neighborhood of last century homes well-kept and festooned with mature trees and one car garages. Jake rang the bell but there was no answer. Concerned Jake walked around to the rear of the home and knocked on the back door.

No answer.

Jake was now debating whether to make a 'wellness' entry as Stanger was recovering from brain trauma when Stanger's next door neighbor, Sally Juarez, the wife of the County Highway Department Supervisor, Reye Juarez, and a person he knew, called out to him.

"Jake," Sally said, over a chain link fence separating the properties. "Pete isn't home. Reye took him to the grocery store. Pete is on medication and did not want to drive himself."

Jake thanked her, gave her his card and asked if she would have Pete call when he returned. Sally agreed to do so. On his way back to his office, as if to punctuate Harper's words, Jake stopped at a C-store for gas and a cup of coffee at a C-store, and three different people asked what "he was doing to find the killer". They were polite for most part but Jake knew they were disappointed in his progress. He didn't blame them.

One of them even mentioned Pete Stanger's name as a possibility. Tying Stanger to the killing seemed to be the word-of-mouth number one suspect and that could be dangerous for Stanger and potentially a red herring for the actual killer. Someone was stirring the soup for Stanger and he had candidates for spreading the word.

Law enforcement was a profession with various legs of authority. In Jake's case, he had many bosses—Sheriff Buddy Kennedy, Police Chief Cal Bannister and Prosecutor, Darcy Hillman along with a few Judges. P.A. Hillman was a straight shooter who was also aware of the political ramifications of law enforcement. As Jake was returning to his office he received the call from Hillman's assistant, Samantha Jones.

192 | W. L. RIPLEY

"Darcy would like to see you," Samantha said.

"I've got a couple things to do first, Sam." One of those being he needed to talk to Pete Stanger and get that off his plate.

"She used the word 'immediately'."

"Was there any profanity or the prefix, 'that asshole' in her demand?"

"Funny you should mention that."

"I'll be right there," Jake said.

Now what?

* * *

Samantha Jones stepped into the Prosecutor's office and said, "He's on his way, Darcy."

"Without argument?" Darcy said. "That's a first."

She cleared her desk and straightened the line on her jacket. Talking to Jake Morgan was always an event in her office. Her assistant, Samantha Jones, thought Morgan, 'is so cute' and while Darcy would agree she was more impressed by his police talents. However, Morgan's style as a law enforcement professional often created problems for Darcy. Jake Morgan had no use for PR and little patience with fools, which as Mark Twain would say, 'H'aint we got all the fools in town on our side and ain't that a majority most places?'

Jake Morgan walked into her office, no hat, no badge, wearing a polo shirt, Levi's and Alligator skin Boots; his service weapon clipped to his belt. Jake's swagger and confidence often walked in the room with him. It wasn't that he thought about those things they were just a part of him.

"Jake, I just had quite a discussion with Foster Taylor and Dr. Winston Vestal."

Jake sat in a vinyl padded chair, leaned to one side

and said, "Did they swing by to tell you what a stellar job I'm doing?"

"It didn't come up," Darcy said. "Taylor tried to pump me about the progress of your investigation. I told him you have been professional and even prescient with warrants and subpoenas which makes my job easier. I appreciate that, Jake, and I always have confidence that you are proceeding in a proper course even when no one else does. However, once again, your propensity to treat the puffed up community leaders like perps creates waves. Is there any way we can work on that aspect of your style?"

"I treat everyone the same."

"That's what they don't like."

"You know how the song goes, 'can't please everybody so I just please myself'."

"Taylor has campaigned for me during the last two elections and is my biggest contributor. That is a reality and a reason to listen to what I'm going to say next."

"Darcy, I know you don't let politics affect your job but in between the lines I'm hearing a request for a favor."

Darcy thinking, this guy is scary intuitive.

"Well, Jake," she said. "It's a bit much but it won't affect your investigation, in fact, it might even work out to be a benefit."

"Fire away."

Darcy traced a finger across her desk calendar and said, "How do I put this? I'll just say it straight out." She chuckled, and put her hands out to her side. "Foster has been in contact with a certain individual and is offering up a…aw hell…he has this lady he says has ESP and wants you to use her."

"In a sexual way? As you know I am affianced to—"

"Stop that. Just humor Foster for my sake. Who knows, maybe she will come up with something."

"I can do that," Jake said. "If it'll help you out. She gets in the way, no promises."

"That's not all," Darcy said. "Would you like a cup of coffee, maybe a latte?"

Jake smiled at the offer. Something was up. "I'm waiting for the other shoe to drop."

Darcy set her teeth in a line as if in pain. "Vestal was worked up. Did you take Leo Lyon into Vestal's office right before the deadline?"

Jake lifted one hand and said, "Funny you should ask."

"Well?"

"You sure you want to know?"

Darcy made a face and asked, "Off the record did you take a citizen into the superintendent's office to search for something?"

"I did."

"Dammit, Jake. Why?"

"This citizen understands school politics and the kind of thing Vestal might be hiding. Vestal has been antsy about getting back into his office and his anxiety made be suspicious."

"Did you think he was the killer?"

"At first, but no, he doesn't have the guts to kill and that's just a guess based upon observation. However, I found something, well, that is Leo...pardon me, an expert on school functions assisted me in my investigation and I was able to locate something interesting."

"Which was?"

"I don't know whether or not it is somehow connected to Saunders' death but it's another piece of the puzzle."

"Are you going to tell me or not?"

"Not." Big smile on his tanned face.

Darcy narrowed her eyes and said, "Dammit, Morgan, are you teasing me with this?"

"Yes. Gives you plausible deniability. Always looking out for you, Darcy."

Darcy liked Jake but he was often the most infuriating person she knew. How did Harper Bannister put up with this man?

"I'm a woman and we don't like not knowing, Jake. At least I don't like it."

Jake said, "May I smoke?"

"Of course not."

"That's good because I quit anyway."

Talking to Jake Morgan was courting a headache.

"How about it with the dizzying asides?" Darcy said.

"Listen, Darcy, I wondered why he wanted in his office so badly. Vestal and Felicia have something going on. You mentioned Pete Stanger, who I will be interviewing as a person of interest or as a witness. Everyone keeps bring up his name and it makes me wonder if the killer wants to circulate that suspicion. Pete was in a big hurry the night he wrecked his car. Hopefully he will tell me why. Was Pete the killer or was he running from the killer? The other possibility is none of the above. Understand, and this is new information, Martin Saunders was not assaulted where we found him."

"Why do you say that?" Darcy leaned forward.

"Martin Saunders weighs over two hundred pounds whereas Vestal goes about on-sixty and probably hasn't lifted anything heavier than his TV remote in years. There were no drag marks in the hallway so that meant someone strong enough to carry Saunders. I think someone tossed the office to make it look like a struggle but didn't do much, meaning they were hurried. Whoever assaulted Saunders was a strong man, which eliminates females suspects like Brenda Sutherland and Felicia Jankowski."

"Felicia Jankowski?"

"Yes, again I doubt she would kill anyone, well that is other than me, who can understand that, right? She is involved in the periphery of this thing due to her connections to a few of the men we're looking at."

"On the periphery?"

"She's knocking boots with some of them."

"Some?" Darcy lifted her chin and slowly nodded her head. "I see. I know Felicia and not surprised."

"Several of the male suspects—Bill Tompkins, the Eberhards, and even Principal Howard—are big enough and athletically inclined enough to administer the assault."

"The principal?"

"Golden Glove boxer."

"Good God, Jake."

"There's more," Jake said. "The killer, who could be one of those mentioned, administered a foreign agent which caused the death."

"Such as?"

"Ethyl glycol which is antifreeze, arsenic found in rat poisons or a range of anesthetics used in surgery like succinylcholine or even a synthetic cathinone like bath salts."

"Sounds like someone with knowledge of such things," Darcy said.

"Like Dr. Sutherland."

"Not Knox."

"Or a drug dealer like Rowdy Manners. Why not Knox?"

Darcy turned over a hand and then said, "Well...it just boggles the mind. He doesn't strike me as a killer.

What would be his motivation? Isn't he related to Saunders?"

"He is, but Martin Saunders is an equal opportunity irritant. And murderers come in all sizes and shapes without regard to class, family, or financial status. In Texas I arrested a guy, his name was Monroe Axel Cross, why they always have three names I'll never know. Monroe, who always enunciated his first name like it was two words couldn't wait to hear his name on television as the killer. Biggest moment of his life. Conversely, one of the richest women in Waco, Texas, did in her extramarital lover with her husband's .44 magnum Kodiak Revolver, runs about four grand in an unusual caliber, and left the weapon on the scene hoping to kill her lover and implicate her husband. Thing is, she should've taken some practice shots first. A .44 magnum kicks like a buffalo and broke her thumb. She thought she had pulled it off but forgot about paraffin tests and the fact that her husband was surrounded by alibi witnesses at the moment she was breaking her thumb on Romeo. There are all kinds of killers and the one thing they share in common is they make mistakes. Killing another human being is a dirty thing, and it clings to the killer like tar. They can't sleep, their mind roils and the anxiety builds. They dread any knock on the door, fearing somebody like me will be there when they answer. Our guy will make a mistake. Count on it."

"I hope so for your sake," Darcy said. "You're hanging out here and the natives are restless. When I get people like Knox Taylor and Dr. Sutherland visiting my office, I know things are popping in the community. Buddy Johnson is worried about you. There's a good man. Cal and Buddy are taking a lot of heat. You're lucky to have them on your side, but even they won't be able to hold back the push to bring in the feds if you don't arrest someone."

Jake Shrugged. "Yeats says, 'The best lack all conviction, while the worst are full of passionate intensity'."

"Well, listen to him. What did you find in Vestal's office?"

Jake made a show of looking at his wrist and said. "Nice talk, gotta run."

As he left the room Darcy picked up a pen and threw it at him. When he left, she laughed out loud.

Jake wasn't wearing a watch.

CHAPTER THIRTY

Rowdy Manners followed Harper Bannister through town and right up to the law offices of Jessup and Jessup, Attorneys-at-Law. He parked across the street and watched her walk toward the office. Nice legs, cute butt. He remembered her from school when she was a skinny thing until her junior year when she became a stone hottie that treated Rowdy like he was fish bait when he'd flirt with her.

Time to see if things had changed.

Rowdy got out of Deke's truck and intercepted her just outside the door of the law offices.

"Hey, there," Rowdy said. "Remember me?"

"It's a small town, Ronnie," she said, eyeing him below her eye lids. "We aren't afforded the gift of forgetfulness."

"They call me 'Rowdy' now." Rowdy eyed her up and down before he said, "You're looking extra-deadly these days, Harper. How about you and me getting together some evening."

She furrowed her brows, gave him an amused look he didn't like and then she said, "Excuse me. Are you asking me out?" She held up her left hand and showed him the engagement ring.

Rowdy shrugged and lifted his chin. "That don't mean nothing."

"It does to me. And I think it does to him. Give that some thought."

She started to walk around him and he stepped in front of him.

"Ronnie," Harper said, cutting her eyes at him, a nasty look. This wasn't working out like he thought. "Your lame John Travolta pose isn't working for you. Maybe go practice your act with a mirror and you'll see what I mean."

"Who's John Travolta? You know, I know a lot of girls would take your place."

"Good, go find one. Me? I don't date outside my species." She put a fist on her hip now, being a tough girl, and said, "If you don't get out of my way I am so going to punch your face."

He brightened at her response, "Well, look at this. I like my ladies a little sassy. Are you going to sic your little boyfriend on me?"

"You think you're the first creep who ever hit on me. I don't need Jake for guys like you."

He reached out with a hand to touch her face, saying, "Give me a chance—"

That's when she lashed out and popped him full on the nose. His eyes closed involuntarily and he felt the sharp pain of the punch. He put his hands to his face and quickly put them back down. He started to hit her back, but stopped himself.

"Yeah," she said. "Hit me and see what that gets you."

"You shouldn't have hit me. Wait, that's assault isn't it?"

"Oh, Ronnie, you are still such a moron. Get help."
With that, Harper walked past him and into the building.

* * *

Jake finally caught up with Pete Stanger. Sally Juarez
called and told him Pete was back home. When Jake
arrived Pete greeted him like a man shipwrecked at sea
and Jake was the pilot of the rescue boat.

"Oh, Jake," Pete said. "I am glad to see you."

"You're in the minority."

Pete invited him in and they sat. Pete offered coffee
or beer and Jake shook his head.

"You care if I have a beer?" Pete said. His eyes were
glazed and his speech cadence was off.

"It's your house but aren't you on meds. Maybe not
the best idea."

"Yeah, that's right isn't it? It's my house." He left the room
and returned with a red-and-white can of beer. He popped
the ring and it made that happy 'cussshhh' sound they used
in their commercials. Pete sat down and took a long pull on
the beer and a little of it spilled down the side of his mouth.

The man's left cheek was purple and yellow from the
wreck and he walked with a pronounced limp. There
was another fading bruise on his forehead and his left
hand was bandaged. "What were we talking about?"

"Are you all right, Pete?" Jake said.

"The drugs make me a little foggy, but I'm okay. Tell
me what's going on, Jake. Reye Juarez told me a lot of
things I hadn't heard."

"Like what?"

"He told me, well…Come to think of it I already
knew it."

"Knew what?"

"About Martin Saunders getting dead...killed, I mean?"

"It was the night you had your wreck. Do you remember hitting my vehicle and crashing through Aaron Yoder's fence. Do remember Cecil Hotzmeyer's pick-up?"

Stanger looked at Jake like he was trying to focus his eyes. "Cecil?" He chewed his lower lip and said, "No, I don't."

"Why were you driving so fast?"

"I was?"

"Yeah, like someone was chasing you. Was someone chasing you?"

"Yeah." He rubbed a hand across his face, closed one eye. "Yeah...well maybe. I don't know. I'm still having problems remembering much. Are you going to give me a ticket?"

"No, Pete, I'm not going to give you a ticket. Do you know anything about what happened to Martin Saunders."

"Yeah, he's dead, right?"

"Yes," Jake said, and waited.

"I knew that. You want a beer?"

"Pete, you didn't like Saunders much, did you?"

"No." Stanger hesitated again. He screwed up his face like a kid who was trying to remember the answer to a test question. "No, I didn't like the sonuvabitch." Slurring his words now. Jake concerned about his intake of painkillers.

"Pete, what did the doctor prescribe for your pain?"

"Something. Why? Is it time for me to take one?"

"No, Pete," Jake said. Something was really wrong here, Jake wondering why they had released Stanger from the hospital. "I want to know what you're taking."

"Oh. Something." Stanger fumbled around in his

pocket and produced an orange-tinted pill vial. "Here." He handed the pills to Jake.

Jake read the label and said, "Oxycontin? They have you on Oxy?"

"Yeah, yeah that's right. Is that illegal?"

Jake had questions about prescribing Oxy for a recovering coma patient. No wonder the man's responses were hazy.

"How did you know Saunders was dead, Pete?"

"I did. I saw him."

"Where?"

"At the school. He was laying on the floor and then somebody..." Stanger's voice trailed off before he said, "There was someone else there...I think."

"Someone else? Did you recognize the person?"

Stanger closed his eyes tightly and then opened them. "I can almost see them and then I can't. I think it is, it is someone I know."

"Did they kill Saunders?"

Stanger thought about it, took another sip of beer, which drooled off the side of his mouth again. He absently wiped a sleeved forearm across his mouth. "Sorry. Can't say. I remember being, you know, frightened."

"Like the killer was after you?"

"I think so or..." His face changed and he said. "Or, did I kill him? Did I kill him, Jake?"

It was a good question. Did he? How well did he know Pete Stanger? From experience Jake had learned that murderers were from all walks of life—from politicians to celebrities to small town grandmas. Rich or poor, Men killed their wives, wives killed their husbands, criminals and churchgoers killed friends, family and strangers. He'd seen too much of it. The reasons? Money, jealousy, pride, fear and even because, like Ted Bundy and Rex Heuermann, they liked it.

Pete Stanger didn't seem right as the killer and in fact, Stanger felt one hundred percent wrong for it. Stanger was on pain-killers and a recovering coma patient. Jake had never interviewed a recovering coma sufferer but something seemed out-of-whack. Stanger's eyes were shining with a drugged light and his mouth was slack-jawed. Why was he released? What was going on here?

"Pete, are you taking any other drugs besides the Oxy?"

Stanger looked sidelong at Jake. "Maybe. Oh yeah, these." Another pill bottle.

Jake examined the vial. Zolpidem. Generic Ambien.

"Did he tell you what it was?"

The man shook his head slowly. "No. It makes me sleepy and when I wake up it feels like…like…I'm swimming inside my head."

"Maybe you should lay off the meds for today. Maybe quit the Zolpidem."

"Doctor said it was important for me to stay ahead… of the pain. To keep taking them until they were gone."

"Are you in a lot of pain?"

Dopey smile on Stanger's face. He chuckled absently and said, "No, I feel…good." He took another sip of beer, more slid down the side of his mouth and on to his shirt. "This my second one. I gotta piss. Okay?"

Jake nodded and opened a hand towards the bathroom. "Sure."

When Stanger left, Jake picked up both vials and shook one of each into his hand and then into his pocket, for Dr. Zeke to check them out. If something was wrong the pills would be inadmissible in court according to the rules of evidence.

There was also a Taurus handgun on an end table by Stanger's chair. Jake removed the magazine and hid it in a sofa cushion. He did not want to leave a loaded weapon where Stanger could lay hands on it.

Something was wrong here and Jake wanted to know what it was.

* * *

Buster Mangold was conducting his own investigation. The Chief and Morgan were not going to shut him out, no sir. He was tired of being kept on the bench. He had his own suspicions, his own hunches, and besides he was looking to get over on a leggy media babe. Can't overlook that. Part of his investigation was following Jake Morgan and watching him pull into Pete Stanger's driveway.

Well, well, well, look at this. He's at Pete Stanger's house; the guy had the wreck Morgan worked and was in a coma. He'd heard Stanger's name talked up around by some important people and now he had a line. Couldn't hurt to get in on the ground floor.

He watched the house, waited until Morgan left, and then went in to interview Stanger himself. What could be wrong with that?

CHAPTER THIRTY-ONE

Leaving Stanger's house, Jake called Harper and asked if she wanted to meet him at the Dinner Bell for supper.

"That would be nice," Harper said. "But, I've got a test coming up in a class and I'm editing some arraignment material Jessup needs in the morning. Some other time, Jake."

Jake decided he needed a beer and one of Hank's cheeseburgers so he called Leo Lyon and then Buddy Johnson. Buddy said he'd be a little late but would join them. Leo said he'd eaten but would be happy to drink a free beer as part of his C.I. work.

Jake arrived at Hank's ahead of Leo, ordered a Cheeseburger, fries, and a Tank 7, which was a Kansas City beer with a kick. Leo arrived and ordered the same. Jake told the server to put it on his bill.

Leo said, "Well, once again, the PHS Pirates are poised for another winning season, with a world-class coach and the power to crush all opposition with the piston-like thrust of our ground game and a lightning air attack to strafe enemy lines. The Pirates will rape and pillage through the campaign." He looked at his friend for a long moment before saying, "Okay, Jake, you didn't put up much fight about buying a round so what's up? Did Harper finally give you the boot you so richly deserve or is it this murder thing?"

"The latter."

Leo looked at him like a guidance counselor would look at a depressed high school freshman. "What, no comeback? Wow, getting to you, isn't it?"

"Not as an anxiety, more as frustration." Jake pushed around a salt shaker in a circular motion. "Hell of a start for a school year, isn't it? Too many suspects all who dislike, no hate, Saunders. I just talked to Pete Stanger and it was like talking to a cast member of 'The Walking Dead'. I don't think he even knows where he is or why he was released from the hospital. You know Stanger better than I do, Leo. Your thoughts?"

"I don't see Pete as a killer, even though Saunders treated Pete's sister like garbage. Pete's a solid guy. If he went after Saunders he'd be more direct and in Saunders' face. I can see him beating the shit out of the guy but delivering the coup de grace with a needle? Naw, he's not your guy."

"But he could've assaulted Saunders."

"Definitely," Leo said, "and with impunity."

Jake picked up his beer and then set it back on the table without drinking from it. "Leo, I've got a theory, not really a working theory, but it strikes me that there may be more than one killer or, and this could be crazy thinking, this homicide could be a killing of opportunity."

"What does that mean?"

"The killer took advantage of the assault to finish off Saunders after the fact of the assault."

Leo looked at Jake for a moment before he said, "Yeah, that's crazy. Don't go with that one."

"You don't like it?"

"I will, if you will," Leo said. "But if you're wrong, they'll crucify you in this town. But, no worries, I'll be there with torch and pitchfork."

Jake nodded. "Well, you're probably right. If they hang me, invite friends. I like a big crowd."

Jake finished off his cheeseburger and pushed the plate away. He looked up at one of the TV monitors Hank had installed. There were two of them. One was tuned to the NFL channel and the other to KCKS news.

Leo saying now, "Hank finally decided to update the place a bit. Bet he still has the juke filled with songs from the Jurassic age."

"Of course he does. And still spinning CDs when the whole music world is digitized. Hank is the one constant in a changing world."

"Yes, he's an atavistic jackass and that's why we love him." Leo turned and lifted his beer bottle in Hank's direction, toasting the bar owner. Hank lifted his chin and threw out his hands as if drinking it in. Leo turned back and said, "What about what we found in Vestal's office?"

"Could be nothing."

"What do you mean nothing?"

Buddy Johnson entered the bar and hollered at Hank, campaigned a bit with some of the customers and then joined his friends. Leo motioned to the server who bustled over and took Buddy's order. Leo said, "Put it on Morgan's tab."

"Thank you, Jake," Buddy said.

"I guess," Jake said.

"Just think, Buddy," Leo said. "A hundred years ago they wouldn't have served your kind in here."

"My kind?" Buddy said, screwing up his face. "Because I'm black?"

"No, because you're ugly."

Buddy looked to Jake and indicated Leo with an upturned hand. Jake shook his head and shrugged.

"Heard you're getting ESP help, Jake," Buddy said.

"Yeah, we're done with forensics and gathering information and dusting for prints. We're going full Dungeons and Dragons. We're going to hold séances and run around naked in our driveways drinking animal blood from fruit jars. I believe this will be the coming..." He stopped when he saw Melissa Vanderbilt on the TV with a chyron scrolling beneath her which read, "Paradise Police reveal a witness and a suspect in teacher killing."

Quietly, almost a whisper, Jaked said, "Son of a bitch."

"You have a suspect?" Leo said.

"Not even sure I have a witness."

"Then how?"

"Mangold, right?" Buddy said.

Jake nodded. "I'm gonna break his neck."

CHAPTER THIRTY-TWO

Paradise High School Principal, Dr. Jackson Howard, head felt so bad his hair hurt. It had been years since he'd done that and now he remembered the lesson about mixing Tequila and Bourbon.

His wife was out of town visiting her mother and Howard was watching MMA fighting, a good card tonight, and lost track of time and how much he was drinking. Lately he had taken to self-medication to assuage a growing apprehension about the Martin Saunders 'thing'. He called it a 'thing' to avoid having to admit it was a murder.

The teachers talked about it, the students asked questions about it in class, and classroom instruction time was getting pushed aside to talk about the 'thing'. That bothered him.

He swallowed three extra-strength Tums, four aspirin, washing it down with a large glass of water. He felt the rumblings of reverse peristalsis, but fought it off, his hands on his knees over the stainless steel wastebasket. Cold sweat on his forehead as he steadied himself against the counter.

Coffee, he needed coffee. He usually drank his with plenty of sugar and half-and-half but decided that was not the best idea, so he drank it black, sipping at it gingerly. After he emptied half the cup he started to feel semi-human.

He remembered his boxing days and hanging out after with his buddies. In those days he could drink it down with no remorse. Never had a hangover like this. Getting older.

The landline rang. Howard checked the read-out. Winston Vestal. He answered it.

"This is Dr. Vestal," the voice said

It was never Winston with this asshole, thought Howard. Always formal, always throwing his PHD at people like a gauntlet. Howard also had his doctorate but preferred to be called Howard or Mr. Howard. Among friends he liked Jackson or J.H.

But Winston Vestal was never going to be a regular guy or be his friend. Howard was okay with that. The man was not likable and Howard had survived three 'Supes' before him and he would outlast this one also.

"What's up?"

Vestal said, "Meet me and Dr. Sutherland at his office. We have things to talk about."

Howard agreed, hung up the phone, stuck his fingers down his throat and threw up in the kitchen sink.

* * *

Jake Morgan sat in his Ford F-150 pick-up, and took a sip from a steel travel mug. He was parked on a chewed up black-top road, a bygone avenue of a rural 1940's highway crumbling away. There was a chill in the air, breaking the Indian summer weather of September. Soon the nights would cool and trees would burst into fire. Jake loved autumn, the cool mornings. He really wanted to be in his office confronting Buster Mangold, the total ass, for giving out false information to Melissa Vanderbilt.

Better to let his anger cool before seeing Mangold. Last night he'd thought about knocking on his Mangold's apartment door, and shoving his head in the toilet, and realized that could be construed as the best move.

Cops like Buster Mangold who let their junk dictate their actions were annoying and unprofessional. Mangold was a loud-mouthed fool who let his divorce get inside his head and now inside his pants. This was going to cause problems, that is, unless it flushed out the killer.

Jake hoping it could work to his advantage. Maybe the killer would see the report, believe it and make a mistake. But things like that never happened in real life; at least not in his law enforcement experience.

He picked up his Bushnell Binoculars and scanned through the trees and leaves, across the scrub pasture, and zeroed-in on the dilapidated porch. A large bearded man stepped out on the porch and took a long pull on a tall-boy beer can. Jake winced at the thought of an early morning beer slapping his throat. Jake suspected the man had pulled an all-nighter. He recognized the big man as the second ZZ-Top guy with Rowdy Manners at Road Hogg. One of Rowdy's recruits. Was Rowdy cooking meth? Jake didn't doubt it but would need evidence that Rowdy was connected to the house and that would require probable cause and a search warrant.

He would work on that. He pulled up his camera, the one with the long range lens and snapped a few pictures. Jake started up his truck and headed to town.

A law enforcement officer is not just one thing; especially one dually employed by both the county and PPD. During his years as a Texas Ranger and the past two in Paradise, Jake had investigated several homicides, broken up fights, written speeding tickets, refereed domestic disputes, exchanged fire with criminals and killed drug cartel soldiers.

And now he was looking at a new situation when the dispatcher told him he was wanted at school.

"What's up?"

"A kid named Eddie Oswald called and said he needed to talk to you. Not 'wanted', 'needed' to talk to you, Jake."

"I know the kid. On my way."

Jake arrived at school, where he was met in the parking lot by Buddy Johnson's sister-in-law, LaToya Johnson, who was also the guidance counselor. She was standing with her arms crossed hugging her chest. She was a slender woman, coffee mocha complexion, hair cropped short with eyes that could make you smile or warn you off.

"Come with me, Jake," LaToya said. "Eddie doesn't want anyone to see him talking to you."

Jake got out of his pick-up, clipped on his Sig-Sauer pistol and said, "What's up, LaToya?"

"It's not good. Eddie is a tough little guy but he's scared. He's being threatened."

"By who?"

"I'll let him tell you," LaToya said. "Go around to the back so no one sees you."

"I've got a better idea," Jake said. "I'll just walk into the front office and tell Howard I need to check something related to the homicide. By now, they are used to me showing up."

"Okay, he's in my office. Dr. Jackson is not here this morning. He was called away by Dr. Vestal for some unknown reason. Let me get in ahead of you to keep everyone else out of my office. I'll tell the office I have to run home for a moment so they won't send anyone down."

Jake checked in, picked up a visitor pass, and walked down to LaToya's office. Jake checked the halls to make sure no one would see him enter. He knocked and LaToya opened the door. Eddie was sitting in a chair in her office. He looked smaller than before as if he had shrunk up within himself.

"Hello, Eddie," Jake said.

Eddie lifted a hand without looking up. Jake pulled up a chair and sat across from the teenager. Eddie was a small kid for his age, freckles, shock of reddish gold hair wearing hand-me-down clothes.

"Eddie," Jake said. "Mrs. Johnson tells me that you're having some trouble but you don't want them to know you're talking to me. Is that right?"

'Yeah, they said I talk to you again they're going to put a contract out on me."

Jake looked at LaToya who cocked her head and nodded at Jake.

"A contract? This is not the mob, Eddie. Who was this?"

"It was a big guy. Bigger than you. Almost big as Mrs. Johnson's brother."

"Almost as big as Sheriff Johnson, right?" Feeding it back to him.

"Yeah."

"This guy have a beard."

"Yeah." Eddie brightening a bit.

"A beard like one of those ZZ-Top guys?"

"Who?" Eddie said.

"He means long and full like your Uncle Yearly," LaToya said.

Eddie nodded. "Yeah, like that."

"Was he ugly and stupid-looking?" Jake said, thinking this was S.S. Frye.

First sign of smile tugged at Eddie's lips. "Yeah, he was ugly."

"And stupid." Jake said, nodding at the kid. "Did he have a bit of a limp?"

Eddie lifted his head and looked at Jake in surprise. "How'd you know that?"

"I'm a cop, I know everything. Tell me all of it."

Eddie telling Jake that the man came up to him downtown while Eddie was getting a soda and telling him, 'You got a big mouth, kid. You talk to the man again and we'll send couple of senior boys we know to straighten you out, get it? We'll put a contract out on you'. Jake listened and didn't interrupt until Eddie finished.

Jake reached into his pocket where he kept his badge, handed it to Eddie and said, "Eddie, nobody, I mean nobody is ever going to bother you again. You put my badge in your pocket and if you get threatened again you pull out my badge, show it and tell them, 'If you hassle me or even look at me, Jake Morgan says he's coming for you'. Can you do that?"

Eddie looked at Jake's badge like it was made of pure gold and said. "Yeah, I can do that."

"I'll go look this guy up and you won't have to worry about him again. Got it? After I share the facts of life with ugly and stupid, you give me back the badge, okay?"

"Okay." Eddie lifted his head and smiled through glistening eyes. "Thanks."

"You'd better get back to class, Eddie," LaToya said.

"I hate English class, can't I stay here a little longer."

"No, you can't." LaToya signed Eddie's pass and handed it back to him. "Now get."

Eddie left and LaToya sat down and said, "Thanks, Jake. High school is tough for a kid like Eddie and I can't believe you gave him your badge."

"I don't use it that much anyway. I have two of them, anyway."

"Still, that was quite a concession. How are you going to 'straighten out' this guy, like you told Eddie?"

"Modern Police strategies and tactics."

LaToya looked askance at Jake. "You're going to threaten the man."

"Who, me? They call me Morgan, the bighearted lawman."

"No they don't," She said, and smiled at Jake. "Apparently you know this creep. How did you know he had a limp?"

"Because I gave it to him," Jake said.

"Using modern police strategies and tactics?" LaToya said.

"One hundred percent."

"Jake Morgan, you are more full of shit than anyone I know."

"I've heard that, you know…around."

CHAPTER THIRTY-THREE

When Jake took the call from Dr. Zeke Montooth what Jake heard was, "It sucks."

"Always whining," Jake said. "What sucks this time?"

"Open your ears, dummy," Zeke said. "I didn't say anything sucks, I said, 'it was Sux', I'm telling you the killing agent was succinylcholine."

"Why didn't you just say that?"

"Because that's what we— Shut up, would you, and come to my office."

"Well, since you asked so nice and all…"

Jake entered Zeke's clinic where there were patients waiting, patiently.

"Dr. Montooth said to go on in, Jake," said the receptionist.

Jake entered and Zeke said, "Come in, come in, I got things to tell you."

Jake looked at Zeke who was wearing a weathered St. Louis Cardinals baseball cap like a crown on top of his thick unkempt hair, camo scrubs, a Seinfeld T-shirt under his doctor's smock, and a Camel cigarette stuck behind his left ear.

"That's a bad outfit, Zeke," Jake said. "I'm sure it inspires confidence for your patients regarding your expertise."

"It's casual day and screw you, Morgan. You don't even wear your badge half the time. And, where is it this time?"

"A kid stole it from me. I've got a BOLO out on him now. What is it you wanted to tell me?"

"Sit down, man," Zeke said. Jake took a seat. Despite Zeke's eclectic attire, the office was spotless and smelled of pumpkin spice. "Here's the deal. Like I said, the coup de grace was succinylcholine. The reason the lab didn't catch it was they didn't screen for it. It is very difficult to detect and I couldn't find a needle mark on the body."

"So how do you know it was Sux?"

"See? Sux. You're getting the hang of the lingo. They didn't find it, I deduced it by myself."

"I'll make you a deal, Zeke. You don't do any detective work and I won't perform open heart surgery."

"This is how you are. Cynical and egotistical. It's how you've always been and those are your best characteristics. It's downhill after that. Do you want to know how I know it is Sux, or not?"

Jake raised a hand. "All right, Hercule, I'm listening."

Zeke made a face. "Hercule?"

"Hercule Poirot. Read a book. How do you know Sux is the agent?"

Zeke opened a desk drawer and pulled out a photo. He handed it to Jake and said, "Take a look. This is the wound in the mouth of Saunders that we thought was caused by the apple trophy."

"It wasn't caused by the apple?"

"It was. It was also the point where the hypo was inserted. Had to be. He was struck with the apple either before or after the anesthesia was administered. I would guess afterwards due to the lack of bleeding and how quick the drug would act."

"How fast?"

"It would paralyze the victim immediately. A quick needle jab into the injured lip and then paralysis, breathing activity would halt and—"

Jake finished the thought with, "It would mimic heart failure."

Zeke nodded. "Exactly."

"How do you know it was succinylcholine?"

"I don't have proof."

Jake shaking his head now, said, "That's special of you."

"This is where you come in. Succinylcholine supplies are strictly regulated and documented. There has to be a record of whoever signed them out for use. All you have to do is check inventory documents to see if any is missing, check the sign-out lists to find out who has used any prior to Saunders death and perhaps even look to see if any of the supplies have been diluted."

"Watered down?"

"Yes."

"How many hospitals in this county have supplies of Succis…I mean, Sux? I see why you use the abbreviation."

"There are five. County regional here and four other facilities. You've got your work cut out for you, Jake."

"Five? Plus check the supplies and lab work for diluted mixes? I'd need an army of deputies for that. But, it's the best lead I've had so far. Thanks." Jake reached into his pocket and produced the pills he'd pilfered from Pete Stanger and handed them to Dr. Zeke. "Here, can run these and see if they are what was printed on the labels. Zolpidem and Oxy. I got these from Pete. He's taking Oxy and these pills and he is completely out of it.

He talks like he has a head full of mush. I want to know if the dosage matches the label also"

Jake read off the dosages. Stanger took the pills from Jake and turned them over in his hand. "I'll take a look and run a few tests."

"Thanks."

"Oh, I got your blood test results back."

"What blood test?"

"Who's the doctor here? The results tell me you need to quit smoking."

Jake pointed at Zeke's ear and said, "What's that behind your ear?"

"I'm a doctor, therefore immune. As your doctor I must inform you that you are a healthy thirty-year-old asshole that nobody likes. Now get out of here and run down this incredible lead I've granted you which should keep you busy."

"You were right in the first place, Zeke. It sucks."

CHAPTER THIRTY-FOUR

Chief Cal Bannister picked up his pipe, started to pack it with tobacco and changed his mind. He looked at some budget items but put them away. Buddy Johnson had called earlier and warned him about the KCKS report that PPD had a suspect and Jake's reaction could possibly result in confrontation, so Cal was keeping Buster Mangold busy. He'd already sent him out on patrol, then to the post office to pick up the mail but now Mangold was back...

And Jake Morgan just walked through the door.

Jake saw Mangold and started in that direction. Chief Bannister hollered at Jake, saying, "Jake, you got a minute. I need to ask you about something."

Jake looked in Cal's direction, then back to Mangold, and returned to Cal. The young investigator hesitated a moment, gave Mangold one more look, and then walked into Cal's office.

Cal was relieved. He trusted Jake's professionalism but also knew about the Morgan temper Jake had inherited from his father. Alfred Morgan had cleared out a couple of local bars more than once when they were younger and Jake was tougher than his old man, yet more controlled. Fortunately, Jake also carried some of his mother's ability to keep a cool head in tough situations. Jake's mother had fought cancer, tolerated Alfred's drinking, and was there every Sunday morning at Church with her son beside her. A good woman.

Jake had many of his mother's traits but Mangold was a loose cannon, a big man who used his size and strength to back off many men and was carrying around a twenty pound rock of bitterness about his divorce. Jake wouldn't start anything but Mangold did not possess the ability to keep his mouth shut. Jake might give up thirty pounds to the bigger man but Mangold could find himself in ER and Cal would then have a scandal on his hands.

He could not afford that with all the community pressure coming down on his office; most of which was directed at Jake. For his part, Cal knew Jake didn't give a damn about pressure or what people thought. Jake's disregard for pressure was one of his biggest assets and ironically one of his biggest problems. Once Jake Morgan had hold of something nothing or on one could dissuade him from moving ahead.

So far, the only person Cal knew that could head off Jake was Harper. Cal was pleased that his daughter had settled on Jake, but knew she was as stubborn as Jake and he wasn't sure Jake understood that yet. But Jake treated her well and saw the same things in Harper that Cal did.

Love conquers all.

Now, what to do about Jake and Buster Mangold.

* * *

Jake walked into the PPD HQ looking for Buster Mangold, telling himself, 'Take it easy, Jake. Smacking

Buster around, while satisfying, will not advance the investigation. You will confront him if he was the source that KCKS mentioned and you will dial back your attitude. Just let time cool things off. You can do this, Morgan'.

Pep talk over and that's what he was telling himself but the moment he saw Mangold he felt the burning behind his ears. That's also when Cal Bannister called out to him.

"Jake, you got a minute. I need to ask you about something."

Jake gave Mangold another look, realized that Cal knew Jake would be gunning for Mangold, and walked into Cal's office.

Cal Bannister was one sharp old lawman.

"Sit down, Jake," Cal said.

"I'm wise to you, Cal," Jake said. "You know about the news report last night. You don't want me to brace Mangold right now."

"I think it best that not happen, don't you? There's a lot of pressure coming from high places. They want to call in the FBI and I backed them off for 48 hours. Now, Jake, I need you to take some advice from an old campaigner. Just because you see a skunk in the middle of a forty acre field, why cross the ditch, jump the fence, chase it down and choke it with your bare hands because you end up smelling like—"

Jake threw up a hand, and then said, "Okay, I got it. I won't shoot Buster today. You're right."

"Of course I'm right. I'm the Chief. I'm always right. I'll talk to Buster and you let it alone. Also stay away from my daughter."

"Can't help you with that one, Skipper."

"Now you know I don't like to be called 'Skipper'?"

"Yes, I do," Jake said, and shot Cal with his finger. "How about 'Dad'?"

Cal made a face and shook his head. "I'll think on it. By the way, there is someone coming by this afternoon to talk to you." Cal started laughing.

"The Fortune-teller?"

"I believe the term is 'clairvoyant'." Cal started laughed again. "I'll tell you what, Jake. I'll saddle Mangold with her and you won't have to deal with it. How does that sound?"

Jake nodded and said, "Sounds good to me."

* * *

Jake ran the plates on the late model Chevrolet pick-up, located the vehicle and then hit the colored lights to stop the dark blue truck driven by one S.S. Frye, AKA Super-Size Frye. Once he got the truck stopped, Jake called in, checked for any outstanding warrants or traffic violations and bingo.

Suspended license. Probable cause.

Thunder storm moving in from the southwest as Jake rapped on Frye's window with his handcuffs. Frye turned his buffalo head and glared at Jake. Jake made a rolling gesture with a hand and Frye lowered the glass.

"Good afternoon, Mr. Frye," Jake said.

"What'd you stop me for? You gotta have reason, you know, like what's it called?"

"Reasonable suspicion. License and proof of insurance, oh wait I forgot, you don't have a license. This is not your vehicle and you're driving on a suspended license."

In the distance thunder crackled and rolled.

"This is chickenshit," Frye said. "I don't have insurance."

"That's really a shame because now I have to write you a ticket for the insurance and the suspended license. Do you have anything in the vehicle that could be considered illegal? Drugs, illegal weapons, explosives?"

"I ain't got any that shit."

"Then you won't mind me searching the truck?" Jake held out his hand and said, "Hand me your key fob please, sir."

"No. You can't search without my permission."

Jake shaking his head, saying now, "You disappoint me, Plus-Size. The suspended license is probable cause to search the vehicle for other violations. Step out of the vehicle and hand me the key, please."

"Can't you just write me a ticket?" Weakening now.

"It's the key fob or jail for a menacing complaint I have waiting for you. Plus whatever I'm going to find, which I'm sure will be drugs or weapons, because a guy like you, you're likely on parole and not allowed to have a weapon in your possession."

"Okay, okay." Frye produced the fob and handed it to Jake.

"Thank you, sir. Please step outside the vehicle. Your cooperation will be noted."

"What's this menacing thing?"

"Threatening little kids."

"I didn't threaten that kid."

"What kid?" Jake said.

"C'mon man. Look, I got a Glock under the passenger seat and a small, very tiny, amount of coke in the glove box. That'll violate me and I'll go back to prison."

"Aww. That's a shame. What is it they call you? Plus-Size? You've been inside, you know how to jail, right? I don't like you and I don't want you in my jurisdiction. Get down from there and walk back to my vehicle while I search the truck." It was a long-shot but he was hoping to find evidence that this was the truck that roared past him the night Pete Stanger wrecked his car.

Frye got out, walked back to Jake's Explorer and leaned against the hood. He fished a pack of Marlboros out of his pocket and started to light it.

"No smoking," Jake said.

Frye spread his arms and said, "You're shitting me. It's a public highway."

"It's a warning. Also no more bullying high school kids. You will promise me right here, right now, that you understand this condition."

"Or what?"

"Use your imagination oh wait, you don't have one."

"You don't have a club this time, shithead."

"Won't need it." Jake could see Frye's jaw working. "Don't bull-up on me and do something you'll regret. Think real hard, because this is not going to end as you imagine. What's it going to be? Tell me your chicken-hawking days are over or downtown eating jail food."

Thunder cracked and boomed, shaking the ground. The air was thick with ozone and approaching rain. Frye was used to people being in fear of his size and he wasn't in any kind of physical shape. Frye rolled his shoulders, pretended to be compliant but Jake knew the man was going to take a swing.

When Frye started to throw the haymaker, Jake feinted right, spun left and kicked Frye on the side of his knee. Frye bellowed, Jake followed up with an elbow to the side of Frye's head, slid behind the man, pulled his hair back, and gave Frye two quick jabs to the throat with the edge of his hand.

Frye sputtered, spit saliva, and sank to his knees. Jake quickly cuffed him. The big man coughed and wheezed, the side of his face against the asphalt.

Jake's breathing was accelerated and his blood was

pumping. "See, I'm not a little high school kid but thanks for the opportunity to give you what you so richly deserve."

Frye mumbled something indecipherable.

Jake saying now, "Mr. Frye, you are under arrest for resisting, assaulting an officer, menacing, possession of a firearm as a parole violation and being openly stupid. You have the right to remain stupid and silent..."

* * *

The Royals were playing an afternoon game. It was a make-up played before a regularly scheduled game. It was like a Christmas present for Cecil Holtzmeyer who settled in to watch the game on his seventy-five inch LG big screen. He had sixer of Tank 7 beer in a small cooler, by his side, and two hot dogs with mustard and relish on a paper plate. He sat down in his massaging recliner, took a bite of hot dog and washed it down with the beer.

Cecil thinking it doesn't get better than this. A perfect day. Bobby Witt was up for the Royals. The wind-up, the pitch, and Witt went yard with his swing.

Going, going...

Cecil didn't hear the glass break and never felt nor heard the shot that splattered his brains on the back of his massage chair.

Gone...

CHAPTER THIRTY-FIVE

"Fucking Jake Morgan just had my truck impounded," Deke Gower said. "The idiot got stopped and took a swing at Morgan."

"Well," Rowdy Manners said. "At least Morgan got his ass kicked."

"No he didn't. Just the opposite. I keep telling you not to fuck with that guy. I've heard things. Nussbaum drove by and watched Morgan put Super-Size down like he was a little kid. Said it would've been a lot worse if Morgan hadn't stopped. Nuss had to make a statement about what he saw and then called me. This is not good thing. Now my truck's in the tow lot. You fucking guys borrow my shit and…I don't know. Did you leave anything in it when you borrowed it?"

"Maybe some grass," Rowdy said. And some blow, but he didn't mention it because Deke was such a baby sometime. Morgan whipped S.S.? That wasn't good. He'd heard things about Morgan also but thought it was just talk. This cop was becoming a problem.

May need to do something about him. Something lasting.

* * *

Jake locked up Frye, then called Dr. Zeke to come down and tend to Frye's bruises and lacerations. Jake interviewed two witnesses to the altercation, had them write down in their own words what they saw. One of them was Wake Nassbaum, the big man with the ZZ Top beard, Jake had seen at the Road Hogg and again at the Meth house.

Jake was working on the arrest report when Dr. Zeke entered his office.

"You tuned him up pretty good," Zeke said.

Jake said. "Did Slats lock him up?" Slats Jacobs was the jailor. The city and county shared the jail and Slats, like Jake, worked for both.

"He did. Frye says he wants to talk to you."

"We talked and now he's locked up."

"Said he had some information for you."

Jake's desk phone rang and he answered it, saying, "Morgan."

It was Deputy Bailey. "Jake, I gotta a domestic, need your help."

"Who is involved?"

"The Tompkins. Coach Bill and his wife, Valerie. Also Sherry Hammersmith."

"Sherry?"

"Actually, Sherry created the domestic problem. I have her with me right now. It's a mess."

"On my way." Jake hung up the phone, clipped on his County badge as his city badge was with Eddie Oswald, turned to Dr. Zeke and said, "Tell Frye I'll talk to him when I get back."

"Trouble?" Zeke said.

"My middle name."

"I always heard it was dickhead."

"Good one, Zeke," Jake said, holstering his sidearm and grabbing a jacket. "Maybe you should give up this doctor gig and do stand-up."

* * *

When Jake arrived, Deputy Sheriff Bailey was standing beside her County Unit along with Harper's friend, Sherry Hammersmith. Sherry was in handcuffs.

Bailey intercepted Jake, giving him the lowdown.

"Well, this is a weird one," Bailey said.

"They usually are," Jake said. "What's up?"

"I get a call about some shouting and noise at the Bailey home. I get there, get it calmed down but apparently Val had called her cousin Sherry Hammersmith. Do you know Sherry?"

Jake nodded.

"Well, Sherry shows up and starts yelling at Bill and it all starts up again. I tell Sherry to knock it off but she just keeps talking which turned to screaming and then she assaulted Coach Tompkins by slapping his face."

Jake closed one eye and winced. What a day, huh?

"So, cuffed her. Coach Tompkins doesn't want to press charges. What do you want to do, Jake?"

"I'll talk to her, Grets."

Jake walked over to Sherry and said, "All right, Sherry, what is this about?"

"I'm sorry, Jake," she said. "I'm just a little emotional about Val. I was mad at Bill for the affair and I slapped him."

"He doesn't wish to press charges...so, if I uncuff you will you go home and stay away from them for a while? Like forever? You come back here I'll take you in and file you for the whole nine yards."

"None of this would've happened if you...well, if you would just arrest someone, anyone."

"Not the way it works. Can't arrest just 'anyone'."

"Well, a lot of people are bringing up Pete Stanger's name. He hated Mr. Saunders." Jake looked at her for a long moment. Jake had known Sherry years before but she was a kid then. Knew her better now through Harper. Jake saying now, "It's really not a good idea to accuse people without evidence."

Sherry pursed her lips and dropped her eyes. "I... shouldn't have said that. I should leave the police work to you, right?"

Jake smiled. "That would seem best."

He freed Sherry from the cuffs. She rubbed her wrists and said, "Did Harper tell you about our little fight?"

"She may have mentioned it."

"I owe her an apology, right?"

"I wouldn't worry about it. You guys have always been close. I figure it'll be all right."

"She's lucky to have you."

"I tell her that all the time."

Sherry smiled big and said, "I'll bet that goes over big."

Jake lifted his eyebrows. "Not really."

Jake let Sherry leave, nodded at Bailey, and then headed into the Tompkins home where he found Bill and Valerie Tompkins seated at the kitchen table, their eyes downcast. Their home was twenty-years old and the kitchen was tidy and warm, with mismatched appliances and flowers in the bay window. The kitchen furniture was second hand pottery barn with cloth placemats. Smell of potpourri and Lemon Pledge. There was a coffee carafe on the table.

"Hello, Jake," Valerie said. She had known Jake for many years. Bill had come to town three years ago and the couple met, dated and married soon after he took the job at Paradise High School. "This is not the way you want to see old friends."

"Happens," Jake said. "We okay here?"

"Yeah," Bill said. "We're trying to work it out."

"We *are* working it out, Bill," Valerie said. "This isn't an easy thing so it got a little emotional, I called Buddy and he sent Deputy Bailey and then just as things were settling down…well."

"Sherry showed up."

"Yes." Valerie smiled and nodded. "That's Sherry all right. Bill has something to tell you about the homicide. Maybe it will help." She nodded at her husband. "Go ahead, Bill."

Tompkins put his hands together and laced his fingers on the table. "Well, it's like this. I'm no cop and I know there has been a lot of pressure on you, lately, everybody knows how you should do your job. I get that as a baseball coach, you know, everybody has seen a baseball game and are experts."

"And everyone has seen cop shows. I get the same thing."

Tompkins smiled and relaxed. "The thing with…a… you know." He glanced at his wife, who nodded, encouragingly. "Is over. But, something she told me was that her ex, Dr. Sutherland, intensely disliked Saunders over something that happened with his son years ago."

"Did it have to do with a play?"

Tompkins seemed surprised. "Yeah. It did. Also, something to do with a grade he got from Saunders. Saunders used his grade book as leverage over kids, especially those he didn't like or would not be in his productions. Dr. Sutherland never got over it even though he is related to Saunders. Sutherland is not big on forgiveness, it seems."

"Did she mention specifics?"

"No, but maybe you could ask him about it. Dr. Sutherland is a violent man."

"Why do you say that?"

"He's threatened me over the thing with Brenda. It got a little hot between us and he threatened to get me fired, he's on the board you know, and I told him he did that I would see him and square that between us."

Jake mulled that over and then said, "He's upset about you seeing Brenda? His ex-wife. That doesn't make sense."

"He says she will always belong to him and nothing will change that. Brenda said he has threatened other men she dated."

"Good to know. Okay, here's what we'll do. You guys are working it out and I'm happy about that. No more fighting or yelling or I'll come back and somebody is going to jail, maybe everybody and that's a bad day for all of us. If you do have to fight, then it's Marquis of Queensbury rules, that is, no hitting below the belt about the affair, Val and," Jake pointed at Tompkins, "You, Coach, you will keep Val informed of your whereabouts at all times. Rebuild that trust. If you don't do that, I'll send Sherry back over here to slap you around, got it?"

The Tompkins chuckled softly. The tension left the room. As Jake started to leave, Bill Tompkins stopped him, his eyes hard, and said, "Morgan, I didn't kill Saunders."

Jake nodded and said, "I know."

CHAPTER THIRTY-SIX

Jake left the Tompkins and drove to Pete Stanger's home. He rang the doorbell, knocked on the door, then walked around behind the house and banged on a window. No answer. He looked through the window of the detached garage. Pete's car was gone. So, he was driving. Was he recovered enough to do that?

Getting concerned about Pete and what happened the night the man wrecked his car. Was he running from trouble or running from someone chasing him in a pick-up? Somebody assaulted Saunders before he was killed. *Before he was killed?* Assaulted and dragged to the super-intendent's office? Who would do that? Why the Apple commemorating a play that starred Rowdy Manners, Ranse Eberhard, and Clay Sutherland, the latter the son of Dr. Knox Sutherland. Leo the Lion had mentioned tension between the then-married Sutherlands and Martin Saunders.

Too many actors with motives, access to the school and even some people who were tough and athletic enough to both beat up Saunders and then drag the body into the office.

But, where had the assault taken place? And, regardless of the strength of the person who carried the victim into the office, dragging a limp body was no easy feat. Even two people carrying him was hard work.

Jake resented being reactive rather than reactive in his investigation. He was ping-ponging between leads and persons of interest rather than being proactive. His style was up close and confrontational.

Time to change that. Take the battle to the killer.

Or killers?

Jake got a break when his cell lit up and buzzed. It was Dr. Zeke.

Zeke saying, "Get ready to pat me on the back and get me an honorary Paradise police badge. I am for sure that Hercules guy you mentioned."

Jake rolled his eyes, though he knew Zeke couldn't see it. "Okay, what is it, Zeke? Skip the preamble and tell me."

"I checked with a couple of nurses worked with me on the autopsy. Remember we were checking for poisons or some other agent introduced into the victim? Well, these two ladies who you will now forever worship and adore, took urine samples from the victim and froze them. How about that?"

"You lost me, Zeke."

"Oh, I forgot you are of the uneducated in the world of higher medicine. Maybe I should be getting some kind of financial reward for this or just a key to the city."

"Dammit, Zeke. How does frozen urine help my problem?"

"It was Suxx, just like I said."

"You said it was undetectable."

"It dissipates quickly but I found a by-product of Succinylcholine in the urine. It is not enough as hard evidence but it suggests Suxx was administered. My guess is that the injection was administered to the lip of the victim where the blood issue was found."

"But it's just a guess?"

"Correct. However, I did some research. The by-product has been admitted as circumstantial evidence in at least two successful homicide convictions."

"Thanks, Zeke. You're a good resource. I don't know much but now at least I know how and that eliminates people. Your PPD badge is in the mail."

"But will you respect me in the morning?"

"Of course not."

* * *

Loose threads were tangled up in Jake's head. What part did the play, 'Failure Can be Deadly', have to do with the homicide? Or was that evidence planted to throw him off?

Deputy Bailey came through with a discipline file from Dr. Jackson Howard regarding Clay Sutherland and Rowdy Manners that resulted in suspension for both and removal from National Honor Society. She also scored a gem from Saunder's' email account regarding the production of "Failure Can be Deadly". Bailey had hacked into Saunders' email and obtained some helpful information. Bailey was handy to have around. Before Buddy Johnson became Sheriff she had been mostly utilized to make coffee and pick-up the mail.

How to put it all together was Jake's puzzle. Saunders seemed to delight in creating chaos in the lives of others. Why?

Jake called Pete Stanger. There was no answer. Jake had now had enough of that so he drove to Stangers' home, rang the bell and then banged on the door. Stanger was a recovering coma victim yet seldom home.

Worried now, Jake called in to dispatch to make a 'wellness check'.

"I'm going to knock on the door again and then I'm going to enter by force," Jake said. "Communicate this information to both the Chief and Sheriff Johnson."

"The Chief is right here, Jake."

Cal Bannister came on and said, "What've you got, Jake?"

"I have been unable to make contact with Pete Stanger more than once. I did talk to him earlier but he was semi-coherent. He is a recovering coma patient and I'm going to make entry into his home as a wellness check."

"Go ahead. I'll send some back-up and an ambulance if needed."

Jake tried the front door which was locked. He returned to his pick-up, retrieved a pry bar and then walked around the house to a pair of glass French doors. Unless there was a board in the runner he could easily jimmy the door. Inserting the short metal bar, Jake forced the locking latch to open.

"Jake Morgan, Paradise Police. Mr. Stanger are you here?"

No answer. Jake pulled his weapon and announced his presence again.

"Paradise Police Officer. Anyone home?"

Jake made mental notes of the condition of the home. Day-old food on the kitchen table, pots on the stove, and the smell of stale cigarettes. Also the scent of a cologne, a man's cologne, that Jake had smelled before but could not recall where.

He walked into the front room. With his hand, he felt the front door mat which was damp from the recent rains so someone had been there. He continued to call out.

"Pete, are you here? Anyone here?"

Jake found Stanger in his bedroom, fully-clothed, and unconscious. Stanger was listless, his pulse and breathing were shallow. Jake called for the ambulance.

While he waited Jake examined the premises and found a couple of interesting items.

One of the items was a suicide note. The other was a pharmaceutical bottle of OxyContin, the lid off and trailing pills. There was the handgun Jake had seen before meaning Pete had retrieved it but the magazine Jake had hidden was not attached. The new item was a Remington deer rifle. The pistol would've done the job, so Jake was glad he had disabled the weapon. It looked like Stanger had chosen pills.

Unless someone chose them for him.

That's when he decided to call Dr. Zeke 'The Sheik' Montooth and told him to "get here as quickly as possible."

The ambulance arrived and Jake asked the Emergency Med Techs to wait for Dr. Montooth. One of the EMTs was Yousef Marlon, a man Jake had used before. Yousef protested saying, "We need to revive the victim, Jake. Is it an overdose?"

Jake told him he would take responsibility. "The victim is stable and breathing. Good pulse," Jake said.

"Mr. Morgan, this is Pete's house," Marlon said.

"How do you know Pete?"

"He is one of us," Marlon said. "He is an EMT. Works with us part-time."

Dr. Zeke arrived soon after the ambulance and said, "Now what?"

"Back here," Jake said. "Attempted suicide but not a very good one."

Zeke checked Stanger's vitals, revived him and said,

"He'll be all right but I want to get him to the hospital for observation."

"Not the hospital," Jake said.

"Are you crazy," Zeke said. "Wait, I know you're crazy but you wouldn't say that without reason. What are you up to this time?"

"His life is in danger. Can you bus him to your office?"

Zeke took a cigarette from behind his ear, placed it between his lips, absently, then removed the cigarette and placed it back behind his ear. Zeke sighed and said, "You've got hold of something, don't you?"

Jake nodded. "I think so."

"Well, I've got a good rapport with the EMTs. But man, I hope you're right because I'm hanging out here if I don't report an attempted suicide."

"Both of us. Besides you are reporting it. To me. I'll take the hit if it comes to that."

"This is no time for bravery. I'll let you take the weight."

"Anything on the pills, Zeke?"

"Yeah," Zeke said. "They were a higher dosage than what you told me and that's why he looks this way."

CHAPTER THIRTY-SEVEN

Ned Robinson was ready to collect on a bet with Cecil Holtzmeyer. The bet was the over-under on the number of games the Royals would win this year. Cecil took the 'over', Ned had the 'under' for the night's tab at Hank's. With only a handful games on the schedule left the 'over' was no longer mathematically possible. Ned called Cecil twice to tell him, "They're not going to make it. You buy tonight, Cecil. Quit hiding out. I'll see you at Hank's. I'm on my way there now."

Ned drove to Hank's to wait on his friend, but an hour passed and no Cecil. Ned asked Hank had he seen Cecil, Hank telling Ned he didn't keep track of every knucklehead that came into the place. Go find him yourself.

"You're a sweet guy, Hank," Ned said.

"It's what attracts my clientele," Hank said.

So Ned went looking. He drove to Cecil's house and rang the doorbell. There was no response but Ned heard the television set blasting from the living room.

"C'mon, Cecil. You can't hide out. You lost. If you

can't cover I'll trust you for it. Don't Welch on me you fat turd."

Ned reached down and tried the door which was unlocked. He walked through the living room to the den, which Cecil called his 'man cave' and found Cecil, a beer in one hand, his remote in the other, bits of brain and blood on the wall. Ned sucked in a breath and said, "Oh shit. Aw no, Cecil. No."

* * *

Jake made a thorough search of the Stanger home, then told the EMTs to take Stanger to Dr. Montooth's office. That done he called Buddy and asked him to post a deputy at the Stanger house.

"What's up, Jake?" Buddy asked.

"I need a deputy to secure a crime scene." Jake explained what he had.

Buddy said, "This is PPD jurisdiction. Cal all right with this?"

"They're low on personnel and I don't want Buster Mangold to know what I'm doing."

"Have you got something?"

"I think so. I'll tell you later."

There was noise in the background as Buddy said, "Hang on, Jake. Something's coming in." It was quiet for a moment, and Jake heard an unintelligible electronic voice before Buddy came back on and said, "Jake, you're needed at Cecil Holtzmeyer's house, immediately."

"What's going on?"

"Cecil's been shot. He's dead, Jake. Kick the tires, light the fires, and get your cracker ass to Cecil's, Morgan. I'll bring Bailey and try to get there ahead of you."

Things were moving faster now. Jake jumped into his

truck, and the call came from PPD dispatch informing him of Cecil's killing. Jake told dispatch, "Tell them not to touch anything, not one thing, until I get there. And I don't want Buster Mangold within a mile of the crime scene. Not kidding."

Jake stuck the portable lights on top of the truck's cab, rang up the siren and ate concrete to Cecil's home.

* * *

Sheriff Buddy Johnson called Deputy G.K. Bailey to secure the Holtzmeyer crime scene. Bailey got there quickly, and Buddy saw her consoling a visually shaken, Ned Robinson.

Cecil Holtzmeyer's house was small and narrow with an add-on TV room at the back of the home. Buddy had made a cursory examination of the crime scene and walked back outside to honor Jake's request.

Mangold showed soon after Buddy arrived with a woman in tow. Probably the Fortune teller or whatever she was. What a Circus. Buddy stood on the front steps peering down on Mangold. Mangold wanted to pass by but Buddy shook his head slowly, arms crossed.

"It's not happening, Mangold," Buddy said. "Just chill until Jake gets here."

"Why I got to wait on him?"

"Because I said so."

"It's our jurisdiction."

"That's true."

"What if I come right by you?" Mangold said.

"Unless you've got some new superpowers I don't know about I would do that."

Mangold blustered and pursed his lips but he stepped off.

Standing on the steps to the Holtzmeyer home, Buddy heard the police siren growing closer, saw the lights dancing on homes, and then Jake's Ford F-150 slide into the curb with a screeching spray of chat. Buddy hoping Jake had his shit together and wouldn't start something with Buster Mangold. He knew Jake was simmering about Mangold's revelation to the media lady but he also knew Jake Morgan was a cool breeze in tight situations.

Jake emerged from the truck and hurried up the walk.

"I need to get inside, Sheriff," Mangold said.

"Nothing's changed, Buster," Buddy said.

Over Mangold's shoulder, Bailey saw Jake's approach.

Jake saying now, "We good here, Buddy? Buster, you keep the onlookers back."

"Don't boss me," Mangold said.

Buddy's eyes widened in disbelief. Was Mangold that stupid?

"It was a request, not an order. This is a homicide and I need to examine the crime scene without people disturbing it. So, pretty please with whipped cream on top, keep the fucking people off the premises."

"I want to see the crime scene," Mangold said.

"No."

"I've got my own theories about this thing."

"I know," Jake said. "And, they are all unauthorized. You shared your take on the homicide with Melissa Vanderbilt and it may be why Cecil is dead."

"Collateral damage is part of police work. I'm going in."

Buddy watched Jake's face change with the words, 'collateral damage'. Still, Jake held it together.

Jake saying now, "Vacate this scene or I will have

Sheriff Johnson detain and arrest you. I don't wish to embarrass you by doing that but don't try me and don't say 'collateral damage' again or you'll learn what it is. Does that connect for you?"

Mangold bellied up to Jake, in a challenging manner. Buddy thought it was going to happen. Inches from Jake's face, Mangold said, "Nobody's arresting me."

Jake averted his face and said, "Brush your teeth, huh? You ready, Buddy?"

"A stone pleasure, Jake."

Mangold gritted his teeth, looked at Buddy and said, "Back off, Johnson. This is PPD jurisdiction."

"I think we're done with this," Jake said, "Do it, Buddy."

Buddy smiled and said, "Buster Mangold, if you do not remove yourself from these premises you will be arrested and charged with adding and abetting and interfering in a homicide investigation."

"Maybe I won't go. What'll you do then?"

Buddy looked down at Mangold and said, "I think we can muster enough force to drag your sorry ass to the lock-up."

"I'm a cop, too, you know."

"I think we need a second opinion on that one," Jake said.

Mangold glared at Jake. Jake met the look full on. Mangold then looked up at Buddy who was unmoved. He rocked back and forth for a moment, chewed his lower lip and then cut his eyes back at Jake and said, "This ain't over, Morgan."

"I keep hearing that," Jake said.

"You think I'm blowing smoke?"

"I think you're galactically boring."

Mangold started to speak, then changed his mind. He stomped off, got into his police car, and roared off.

"Sometimes I wonder why Cal would hire a guy like Mangold," Buddy said.

"Me too," Jake said. "But don't he look good in his uniform?"

CHAPTER THIRTY-EIGHT

The Royals game played on the Cecil Holtzmeyer's big screen. It was the 7th inning stretch but Cecil wasn't going to stand for it.

There wasn't much for Jake in the way of forensics save that he found the spent .308 bullet imbedded in the wall behind Cecil's recliner. It had passed through Cecil's temple near his left eye, dislodging the eyeball, tore through his brain and exploded the back side of Cecil's head. After that, the bullet had barreled through the thick leather and foam of the recliner and ripped a hole in the sheetrock.

Jake looked at the beer clutched in the victim's hand, the remote in the other.

"Dammit, Cecil, I'm sorry I got here too late," Jake said. "At least you died doing something you enjoyed, buddy." He had always liked Cecil.

Dr. Zeke showed up and made the official determination of homicide by gunshot wound.

"Poor old Cecil," Zeke said, closing up his medical bag. "He was a nice guy. Can't imagine why anyone would want him dead. You think it has something to do with Saunders' death."

"Be a hell of a coincidence if it didn't." Jake was kneeling beside the recliner. He stood and said, "Cecil has no enemies and nothing to show in his background except a couple of DWI's. Cecil was harmless. Mangold caused this by leaking the 'eyewitness' information to the media babe. He wants to jump her bones. But I think it may have scared Saunders' killer and he took out Cecil to make sure. Are you ready to make a determination on Saunders, make it official?"

"Already did that," Zeke said.

"And you're just now telling me?"

Zeke threw his arms into the air and said, "Surprise."

"You're a seriously deranged individual, Zeke."

"So, what's your next move?"

"I'll try to locate the shooter's line of site, find where he took the shot, and see if I can scare something up that way. Then back to Pete Stanger's house and hope the rifle I saw there was not a .308 Remington."

"Something else," Zeke said. "I don't know how I forgot to ask you. Did you find any keys on Martin Saunders when you searched the body?"

Jake thought on it. "No, I didn't."

"I didn't find any when I did the autopsy. But Saunders was found in the building. How did he get in there?"

"Makes you wonder who has them, doesn't it?"

"It does," Jake said, nodding. "If you got this I'm going to see if I can find the location of the shooter. Hope I can recover a casing or footprints…something."

Jake lined up the hole in the window with the spot where it had shattered Cecil's head. Almost a perfect forty-five degree angle. A .308 caliber was a flat-shooting sniper cartridge, and it could've come from a good distance. Cecil's den backed up to the railroad tracks and an abandoned warehouse. The shot almost certainly came from that spot.

Jake met Buddy at the door speaking to a tall grey-haired woman dressed in loose fitting clothes and a veil-like shawl. It was the woman who had accompanied Buster Mangold. She introduced herself as 'Cynthia Wellstone'.

"I'm the Medium the District Attorney requested to assist you."

"Darcy's title is 'Prosecuting Attorney,' but you already knew that, right? You know with the psychic thing?" He smiled at her.

She raised her chin and an eyebrow, then said. "You doubt my skills."

"I'm afraid so." Remembering his promise, he said. "But willing to try anything at this point."

"I need to have access as quickly as possible," she said.

"Not yet."

"The sooner I get close to the victim the more intense the psychic vibrations. I can then lay out my cards—"

Jake interrupted her now, saying, "First, the M.E. finishes his examinations, then I will complete any forensic determinations including a possible location of the shooter, then when that is all satisfied you can go in and deal the cards and soak up vibrations like a tuning fork."

Shaking her head, Wellstone said, "So disappointing. This happens all the time. I'll have you know, investigator Morgan, I have solved two murders in my time."

"That's great," Jake said, as he walked away from her. "I've solved fourteen."

Jake left Madame Wellstone standing there without a word.

Buddy covered his smile with a hand and winked at Jake as he passed by.

* * *

Jake hiked it across the tracks and through the debris of the disheveled building. He made his way up rusted iron steps to a second story landing. Rats scurried ahead of him and some barn swallows stirred and flew out a broken window. In the grit of decades-old dust Jake found footprints which he photographed with his cell. He found the spot where the shooter had rested his elbows to fire. He would prevail upon the Highway Patrol to send some techs to fingerprint and look for fibers, from a shirt or jacket, on the windowsill. He doubted they would find anything as so far the killer had been careful about forensic information.

This killer was a careful, meticulous man and that eliminated some of the persons of interest. This one knew about such things or watched a lot of Investigation Discovery channel. Not only smart but no one turned in a reporting of a shot. Jake estimated the shot at 125 yards on a downhill slope through a window at a small opening. The shooter used a silencer, picked up his brass, and was confident in his marksmanship.

The killer wasn't an idiot and didn't leave much of a forensic trail, but he'd killed Cecil and that was his first mistake. Cecil had no idea who the killer was. Buster Mangold's big mouth had gotten Cecil killed.

A sniper killing of a harmless baseball fan, domestic squabbles, intertwined sexual affairs, and Psychic Mediums with tarot cards wanting to feel psychic vibrations.

Columbo never had to put up with this.

Thinking now about Mangold sitting in the superintendent's outer office, playing with the Apple trophy. About Winston Vestal wanting into the crime scene.

About his interviews and now about...Brenda Sutherland and a play called "Failure Can Be Deadly".

It was in there somewhere. Open up your head, Jake, he told himself. Don't try to make the evidence make sense; make sense of what the evidence is telling you.

Getting closer to it now. C'mon Jake, you can do this.

* * *

Buster Mangold watched Cynthia Wellstone close her eyes and put a hand to her forehead. With her free hand, she touched the chair where the deceased man had been sitting. Dr. Montooth had removed the body despite the protests of Mangold.

"She just needs to touch the corpse," Mangold said.

"No," Dr. Zeke said. He pulled the Camel cigarette from behind his ear and lighted it.

"You're not going to smoke that in my crime scene?"

"Why? You think it'll hurt the value of the home when it goes on the market?"

"I don't like it," Mangold said.

Zeke took a puff, looked down at the body bag that contained the remains of Cecil Holtzmeyer and said, "Well, it's not your house so let's ask Cecil. Cecil, can I smoke in your house? If it's okay don't say anything."

"Fucking smartass," Mangold said.

Madame Wellstone was spreading cards on a low coffee table.

"Hey, lady," Zeke said. "Don't get your nasty fingerprints all over everything."

"This is police business," Mangold said. "I'm in charge here and if you interfere, I'll arrest you."

Dr. Zeke looked at Mangold as if the man was wearing a fake nose. "That's right, arrest the Medical Examiner. I'm sure that won't be a problem. Are you as clueless as I've heard? I ask because what I've heard does not seem possible."

"She still needs to touch the body, Highpockets."

Zeke chuckled. "Highpockets, huh? You are special. Have you recently undergone shock treatment or fallen on your head? Listen, nobody touches anything once I have the cadaveribus pugnator."

"What does that mean?" Mangold said.

"Ask Morgan," Dr. Zeke said. "He knows and that's the difference."

CHAPTER THIRTY-NINE

Jake had allowed 'Madame' Wellstone to suck up psychic vibrations, put Zeke in charge. Deputy Bailey took Ned Robinson's statement. Poor guy just lost his best friend, for no good reason. Jake had Wiley take crime scene photos, while Bailey put up police tape and Cal showed up with a young uniform officer who would sit on the house overnight.

Jake had done all he could do for now. Something was tugging at him and it had started right after he had talked to the Tompkins. There were a lot of angry people involved and Sherry's outburst brought it to his attention. Revenge, of course, was the number one motive for Saunders' homicide. Revenge was triggered for being wronged and in some cases it lasted for years.

Jake knew he needed a resource for what was in his head and he asked Harper to meet him at Hank's.

Harper arrived at Hank's looking like a shampoo commercial wearing Capri's, white converse tennis shoes and a button front peasant blouse. She'd been outside and the sun had sprinkled a lovely spray of freckles across her face.

Jake ordered a cherry coke for both.

"Oh, goody," Hank said and rolled his eyes. "Soda pop. Does it say Hank's 'Malt Shop' on the door outside?"

"No, I don't think it did," Harper said. "Did you see that outside, Jake?"

"No, I didn't. Curious."

"I'll get it," Hank said. "And no smooching and goo-goo eyes or you're out of here."

Hank walked away.

"Okay," Jake said, to Harper. "First, I don't know much about women…"

Harper said, "Which goes without saying."

Jake made a face and said, "Point conceded. What do you know about jealousy?"

"Are we talking about men or women?"

"Both."

"Jealousy? Is this part of your investigation or are you wanting general information?"

"The investigation."

"Okay, be more specific."

"I've got a lot of people involved that are intertwined through divorce, cheating and general lust. How far does that go regarding both sexes as I have too many possibilities."

Harper tilted her head to one side and thought about it. "This is laymen terms but my experience is that men have a dilemma. Whether to blame the woman or go after the man creating the envy. By the same line of reasoning women want to curl up and die while some want revenge. Female revenge is far nastier than the male. Men are satisfied to beat up their rival and then they can go have a beer together. Women want the other woman to be disgraced, degraded and her appearance marred. Same goes for her straying male. Sometimes women, like black Widows, urge the male back into her web to extract revenge. If they have anything juicy that will foul the man's present relationship or marriage they will even make something up. It all depends upon the make-up of the person we're talking about. Most people regardless of gender, want to hide or at least disguise their jealousy. It's an ugly emotion. Is this about what you found in Vestal's office?"

"Maybe?"

She looked at him for a long moment. "Yes. Man or woman, the type of person you're talking about? That would be enough but it seems obscure, who are you looking at for this?"

Jake told her and she sucked in a breath. "Oh, Jake. It makes sense in context but it is still a bit of a stretch. Yes, I would talk to her again. Also, I think I'd better have a double bourbon now."

* * *

Harper went home to study and Jake drove back to Stanger's home. Once there, he pulled back police tape, walked into the home and examined the rifle he'd seen before. It was a .308 Remington. Recently fired. He would need a court order to seize the rifle as evidence but first he called Brenda Sutherland and asked if she had time to speak with him.

She said, "Are you going to grill me some more, disgrace me in the community and ruin the Tompkins' marriage?"

"The first," Jake said. "I think you beat me to the other two."

It was quiet for a long moment, long enough Jake thought Brenda had hung up.

"Touché," she said. "You are a worthy adversary. Why

would someone so intelligent and a lover of English literature become a policeman?"

"I lost a bet with God," Jake said.

"I'll put on some coffee," she said. "Come ahead, Inspector Dupin."

Jake arrived just as the last gurgle of the coffee machine emptied the black liquid into the carafe. Her kitchen was modern, matched stainless-steel appliances, glass for natural light, with the scent of Jasmine and Chanel in the air. She placed Amish glass coasters with coffee designs on the table in front of him. Jake's read 'Espresso'. Brenda's read, 'Cappuccino'

"Cream or sugar," Brenda Sutherland said, as Jake sat.

"Black."

"Of course. It could only be thus. Did you like the Dupin reference?"

"I like Poe."

"In *The Purloined Letter,* C. Augustine Dupin ignored the political consequences or his investigation. Sound familiar?"

"Dupin used intuition and wanted revenge, I'm stuck with facts and forensics. Revenge doesn't compute. I just want to arrest the killer."

She poured coffee for Jake and placed his cup precisely in the center of his glass coaster.

"Oh, you want more than that. You want justice, a righting of order in the universe. You enjoy tweaking the noses of those who consider themselves...do you realize most of the community's self-appointed 'important people' are aggravated with you? You're isolated perhaps even persona non grata."

"I have my baseball card collection for comfort."

Brenda threw back her head and laughed. "I wish I'd met you as a younger woman. You are delightful. Oh my.

I can't even be angry with you for your 'I think you beat me to the other two' comment."

"Sorry about that," Jake said. He sipped coffee. It was Hazelnut, which he hated, but said nothing.

"Don't be. I deserved it. You're not the type to resist the well-phrased comeback. You think I'm corrupt, don't you?"

"I want to ask you about your ex-husband, Dr. Sutherland."

She made a face. "Ugh. Why him?"

"His attitudes. You're divorced but my understanding is he keeps his eye on you. I don't wish to be indelicate but, again the bet I lost with God, what caused the divorce?"

She set her cup down dead center on her coaster. "I didn't think we should be dating outside our marriage vows." She stopped and stared past Jake, as if considering her words. "Ironic from me, isn't it?"

"What about jealousy?"

Brenda sat back two inches and chewed her bottom lip with her perfect teeth. "You've done your homework, haven't you? Yes, he's jealous but it goes beyond that. Are you familiar with the joke about the young bull and the older bull, sitting on a hill and looking down at the females? The younger bull says, 'let's go down and screw a cow. And the older bull says he has a better idea, let's go down and—"

"'Do them all'," Jake said, finishing it for her. "I've heard it. So, you're saying this is Knox's problem?"

"Knox is a selfish person and has an attitude about his maleness. He believes once he's had a woman, in his twisted psyche you're his exclusive property. Forever. It's almost like masturbation for his psyche." She looked at him.

"Did he ever act upon his jealousy?"

She nodded.

"An example?" Jake said.

"He fired a male nurse, a good looking young man, for flirting with me. I was flattered by the attention but it wasn't going anywhere but Knox didn't care. Another time he broke off a relationship with a golf-buddy who 'undressed me with his eyes' he called it. Men flirt with women. It happens."

"Did you ever return a flirtation?"

"Never. I was faithful, raised to marry once, marry forever, and endure whatever came with that. Now I've learned endurance doesn't bring happiness and Knox was a good teacher."

Jake took a finger and moved his cup ever-so-slightly on his coaster and said, "Did Martin Saunders ever, you know, come on to you or make romantic overtures?"

"Martin? Ick. I'd rather kiss a snail. Or, even Winston Vestal, another slimy individual."

So much for one theory, Jake was thinking. Now what?

"However," Brenda said. "Knox accused me of having an affair with Martin. I just laughed at the thought, but he was not convinced. 'I'll see that little shit fired for this,' he said."

"I thought Knox was Saunders' uncle."

"Distant and complicated. Martin was also the person who told me that Knox was cheating on me and with whom, including details. It wasn't for my benefit, Martin loved twisting the knife. He was a perverse little shit. Knox denied the affair and confronted Martin, who laughed at him, which was a mistake. Knox also thought Martin screwed his son, Clay."

"Did he?"

She nodded. "Martin was miffed at Clay because he and a couple of other boys in a play changed the lines and morphed the play into a comedy. Martin's fits of pique are sudden and nasty, or at least 'were'." She paused to place a finger to her lips as if shushing herself. "I'm concerned that the past tense gives me satisfaction. He failed all three boys and got two of them suspended for other things."

"Was the play, 'Failure Can Be Deadly'?"

"Why yes, it was. How do you know that?"

"Were the other two boys, Rowdy Manners and Ransom Eberhard?"

"Why…yes." She considered Jake's face for a long moment. "Who are you and where did you come from?"

"One more thing," Jake said. "Does Dr. Sutherland own a scoped hunting rifle?"

"Several."

"Can he shoot?"

"Gun club member. Along with Foster Taylor, Jackson Howard, and the mayor. They go out quite often. Foster is an ex-Marine as is Dr. Howard. Why do want to know that? Do you suspect Knox?"

Jake ignored her question. "Many people are happy Martin Saunders is dead. Even yourself. Therefore, I have several people to sift through, either to continue looking into their lives or to eliminate them as suspects."

"Here's another one, actually two," Brenda said. "The Eberhards, Eb and Ransom, are also gun club members."

"How do you know this?"

"Because," she said, giving him a Mona Lisa smile. "I am also a club member. And, I'm ranked third among members at the club."

CHAPTER FORTY

The court granted the warrant for Pete Stanger's home, including the .308 Remington along with a previous court order he had handed to Grets Bailey, telling her to look for a .308 Remington in another home on his list of persons of interest.

Jake told Bailey, "If you find a .308 then I can eliminate that person, if not they stay on the list." Jake had a third warrant to search the suspected Rowdy's meth house which he planned to personally serve.

Jake and Cal were called to a meeting with Prosecutor Darcy Hillman. Darcy was serving notice rather than coffee and Danish.

"Foster Taylor was here earlier," Darcy said, her eyes firmly on Jake. "What do you think he told me?"

"That Madame Butterfly threw some chicken blood in the air, creating a spirit epiphany and Pete Stanger did it. Case closed, Pentagrams all around."

"You think this is funny?"

"You don't?"

Darcy shuffled through some paper on her desk.

"Here it is. You removed a .308 Remington bolt action rifle from Stanger's home, correct?"

"Yes."

"And a .308 bullet killed Mr. Holtzmeyer?"

"Also true and the bullet matches."

Darcy slapped her desk and asked, "Then, why haven't you arrested Stanger?"

"Because he didn't do it."

Darcy threw her hands in the air, and cut her eyes at Cal Bannister. "Are you hearing this?"

"I am."

"Well?"

"Jake is in charge of the investigation."

"Not anymore," Darcy said. "I am issuing a warrant for the arrest of Pete Stanger. The charge is murder."

"Of Cecil Holtzmeyer?" Jake said. "Or, Martin Saunders?"

"First Holtzmeyer and then you will accumulate evidence that he also killed Martin Saunders. Jake, usually you are more clear-thinking about things but you're going over the falls and taking all of us with you. You cannot believe the pushback I'm getting. I can take the heat but I need a valid reason to do so. You have the weapon and you have the motive. Arrest him."

"Darcy, think about it. Pete Stanger, a recovering coma patient, positions himself to take a precision shot that few people can take, goes home and decides to commit suicide after, and this according to Madame Butterfly, Stanger has killed the quote 'eye witness' who could fit him for the killing of Martin Saunders? So he kills him, which takes him off the hook but says to himself, 'I can't go on' and instead of shooting himself he takes pills. Cecil Holtzmeyer could not have witnessed the death of Saunders because I can account for his whereabouts the night Saunders was murdered."

Darcy screwed up her face and sad, "You can?"

"I was detaining him for open container out on highway 27."

"I don't remember any charge for that coming across my desk."

Jake related the night he followed Cecil from the liquor store and stopped him, including Pete Stanger's wreck and the pick-up that barreled by after.

Darcy saying now, "You think the killer was chasing Pete Stanger and thinks Holtzmeyer can i.d. him?"

Jake nodded and said, "I do."

"You let Cecil go?"

"I did."

"Why?"

"I had bigger fish to fry."

"And now he's dead."

"And I hate that," Jake said. "I liked Cecil. As for Pete he has been in no condition to kill anybody. He can barely function as he has been on Oxy and generic Ambien that has kept him in a perpetual brain fog. No way he humps a rifle up a dark staircase, sights in and burns a bulls-eye through Cecil Holtzmeyer's head and then slips away to kill himself at his house."

Darcy touched a finger to her lips, tapped a nickel-plate Montblanc pen on her desk and was quiet for a long moment before saying, "What do you think, Cal?"

"What I said before. Jake's running the show."

More tapping, Darcy swiveled away from her desk, stood and walked to look out a window. Jake looked at Cal, Cal raised his eyebrows.

Finally, Darcy turned and said. "Doesn't matter. The clock is ticking."

"What's that mean?" Jake said. "This is a homicide investigation not a game show."

"The City Council wants a briefing from you, Jake.

Tomorrow evening at 6:00. You have to give them something. They want Sheriff Johnson there and also you, Cal. Arrest Pete Stanger and do it today."

"No," Jake said. "I'll have my resignation for you within the hour." He stood.

"Dammit, Jake, sit back down and stop being such an ass. I don't want your resignation, I want the murder solved and somebody locked up. You say Stanger is in a stupor? Placed him in protective medical custody at County Memorial and I'll hold the homicide charge until tomorrow after the city council meeting. There, will that make you happy?"

"I won't put him in county," Jake said. Darcy gave him a questioning look and Jake said, "I have my reasons."

Darcy blew air between her lips and then said, "Okay, put him with Dr. Montooth if that's what you want. Put him up at Disney World. Whatever. Please don't tell me why 'not County'. I'm sure I don't want to know."

"He's already with Zeke," Jake said.

Darcy squeezed her eyes shut and said, "Aw, shit. Pardon me. I should've known. What is it with you, Jake Morgan? You just do as you please. You are a pain in the ass." She waved him away with the back of her hand and said, "Leave me."

Jake pivoted to leave, but then looked back. "So. I guess," he said, "No hug?"

Darcy shook her head and chuckled in spite of herself and then said, "Shut up and get the hell out of my office before I remember what my job is."

* * *

Jake returned to his office to gather his warrant for the meth house. Gail Thurman, the dispatcher, told him that, "Mr. Frye want to talk to you."

"What does he want?"

"Said it's important and you will want to hear what he has to say."

"All right, tell the jailer to bring him to my office. Slats on-duty?"

"LaDonna Washington."

Jake smiled at the thought. LaDonna had competed in mixed-martial arts at one time. Jake was working towards making her a deputy sheriff or a uniform PPD officer. "I hope he resists arrest."

LaDonna Washington brought in a hand-cuffed S.S. Frye. Frye's shirt had a button missing, his hair was disheveled and he had a new bruise on his face. Jake had LaDonna remove Frye's cuffs and motioned for Frye to sit.

"Thank you, officer," Jake said and LaDonna gave Frye a hard look before she left. "Sit down, Frye."

Frye sat and said, "What the fuck's wrong with the black bitch? She went all fucking Kung Fu on me. She's lucky I don't hit women."

"Just little kids, huh? Her name is Officer Washington and you will remember that while you're here. Looks like you learned better than to ignore her instructions."

"She has a bad attitude."

"It gets worse you piss her off. She knows her job and she can handle two of you. Now, you said you needed to talk to me. Usually when people 'need' to talk it means they're looking at a parole violation. So, what do you have for me that'll make me forget you're a hemorrhoid with legs?"

"I want something in return."

"No." Jake shook his head. "It never ends with you guys. You got something you tell me and I'll decide its worth. You don't like that I'll send you back to your cell to await arraignment. I think they're serving broiled chicken and fried potatoes for supper."

"Wait," the big man said. "Why're you always such a hardass?"

"Because I don't like child molesters."

"I didn't molest him I threat—" Frye stopped himself too late.

Jake raised a hand and smiled. "Sounds like a confession."

"I get indicted, I go inside for five years, dude. I don't want that."

"The outlaw trail is a hard one. And I'm not your dude. What can you give me that cuts that down?"

"You gotta promise me," Frye said.

"I don't have to do anything except be smarter than you and pay taxes. I don't like you, I don't like your lifestyle and you have threatened to assault me twice. Pardon me, one assault and a butt thumping for you, which I enjoyed. Are you such a hopeless mental defective you don't see what's ahead? What am I saying, guys like you never see it. Okay, I'll go this far. Tell me something good and maybe, only maybe, will I forget out little dance and see if I can reduce the menacing charge to a misdemeanor, a reduction that, with your jacket, will be a hard pull."

"That's it?" Making a face now.

"That's it and it's going, going…"

"It's about something Rowdy told you."

"Okay, I'm listening."

"He told you about someone who killed that teacher, right?"

Jake nodded. Waited. He watched Frye struggling with it.

"Man," Frye said. "I ain't no snitch."

Jake just sat and looked at the man for a long moment

before saying, "You know, I've had you in the lock-up twice and you may not have noticed but I don't remember your buddy showing up with bail money. That's sort of Rowdy's m.o. He lets other people take the weight."

Frye's mouth worked before he said, "He lied to you. That guy, whoever it was, didn't do it?"

"What guy?"

"Stanger?"

Nod. "How does he know it wasn't Stanger?"

"Says he knows who did it? Said he was there."

That got Jake's attention. If this guy was shooting him straight, it was the cherry on top of the other information he had accumulated.

"He was there," Jake said. "Who was it?"

"He didn't give me a name," Frye said. "Rowdy likes secret information."

"We're getting close to forgetting the assault charge," Jake said. "I need something else. What about his meth operation outside of town? An old house in the middle of a field?"

"You know about that?"

"Wasn't sure until now," Jake said.

"Shit. Well, I gave you the information, are you cutting me loose?"

"Just as soon as you do me one more little favor."

CHAPTER FORTY-ONE

As requested, S.S. Frye called Rowdy while Jake listened in. Frye telling Rowdy that Sheriff Johnson, two troopers and some deputies were going to hit the meth house under cover of darkness.

"About four in the morning, Rowdy," Frye said.

"How do you know this?" Rowdy asked Frye. "Are cops listening in?"

"I'm in the lock-up and I overheard them talking about it. Man, I shouldn't tell your traitor ass shit. You flyweight, ho-helping shit head. You done nothin' for me, motherfucker. Twice they lock me up and I don't nothing from you. I hope they bag your ass."

"Look. Okay, I'm sorry about that. What phone are you on?"

"My bondsman is here and I'm waiting to bail out. I'm using the bail bondsman's cell." A lie as Frye was calling on one of the PPD lines so Jake could monitor the conversation. "You and the guys better get out there and do something with...you know. Shit, here comes that asshole, Morgan. Gotta go."

Jake took the phone back from Frye. Frye asking if that was good enough.

""That asshole Morgan'? You get the nomination but no Oscar yet," Jake said, "After I bring in Rowdy and the product you leave town, do not pass go, do not collect two hundred dollars."

* * *

Jake's county vehicle was still being repaired. There was a brand new Police Interceptor Utility badged with the Paradise County Sheriff's emblem that had just been cleared for duty. It had not been driven yet. Jake requested it.

Buddy said, "It hasn't been out yet."

"Just want to test drive it. I'm tired of borrowing other units and putting miles on my truck."

"Where are you going?"

"I'm going back over to Cecil's house to check on a few things."

"That's only a few blocks."

"Am I supposed to walk?" Jake said. "Don't be selfish."

"Why do I get the feeling you're working me?"

"Because you're basically a cynical person with trust issues."

"Not one damn scratch, Jake. I damn well mean it."

Jake gave him fake puppy dog eyes. "I'll treat it as if it were my very own."

"Knock it off. That's not convincing. You'll have to treat it better than that."

"So, Daddy can I have the keys?"

Buddy screwed up his face and said, "Piss on the day you came back to Paradise."

Jake clipped the .357 Sig-Sauer to his belt and picked

up the Police Interceptor at the motor pool. He even clipped on a badge. Time to go hunting.

The Police Interceptor was midnight blue, with a low sinister profile, and a motor that churned 400 horsepower and growled like a lion. Supposedly the fastest law enforcement vehicle made. Jake slipped into the seat, smelled the new and clicked on the police radio. He fired up the beast and headed north to bushwhack Rowdy Manners and his band of merry men.

Jake called Deputy Bailey and asked about the search warrant he had her working on. "You find the .308?"

"No," Bailey said. "But found something better. He kept good records of his arsenal. He had one, but it was missing. He has not reported it stolen. Something else, he wasn't there but his girlfriend was."

"Felicia Jankowski?" Jake said.

It was quiet on the other end. "Are you human? Yes, it was."

Outside the city limits, Jake buried the pedal and the interceptor nearly jumped out from under him.

"Easy there, big fella," Jake said, patting the dashboard and then in an appreciative monotone, he added, "Hi-yo, Silver."

* * *

The afternoon sun illuminated dust motes dancing in the air of the old house. Boots scuffed on board floors and the scent of marijuana was thick. Deke Gower wrapped crystal meth and fentanyl pills and put them in zip-lock bags, then shoving them into Folger's Coffee containers. He then covered the drugs with coffee grounds to fool the drug sniffing dogs. Deke was feeling pretty good. He never touched the meth, because he'd seen people on it— fucking zombies with impetigo and no teeth. He did like coke though and had taken a couple hits along with several slashes of Southern Comfort 100, even though Rowdy had told them to not to get loaded.

Deke was buzzed and happy in his work.

"Was Super-Size sure about his information?" Deke said, yelling back into the kitchen where Frankie Boy Degante was busy with a bucket filled with bleach and water, wiping out any drug residue where they had been cooking. Degante was wearing a cloth mask due to being worried about the bleach mixing with any fentanyl dust. Rowdy was overseeing the clean-up.

"Doesn't matter," Rowdy said. "We gotta move this stuff either way. Can't take the chance. I've got buyers for most of it and can move it right away. Just keep going and load up the truck."

"Somebody snitched," Frankie boy said, yelling it. He removed his mask, took a snort of coke, and wiped his nose. "Bet it was Eberhard."

Rowdy walked into the kitchen, "Stop snorting that shit. We're trying to clean this place up and we need to keep our heads. Ranse has gone all goodie-good on us, he doesn't know about this. At least I don't think he does. Who cares, we're outta here and then we'll do the deal and leave this town. Good-bye Paradise County, hello sunshine. Just keep packing shit. We gotta get outta here."

"I thought we were going to take Morgan out," Frankie Boy said.

"Delayed," Rowdy said. "Eventually though. We'll be back someday."

Gower heard the rumble of a vehicle, moved to a window and saw a dark vehicle blowing up the lane, spitting rocks and dust. Man, it looked like the Batmobile coming up the road. Gower yelled out, "Somebody's coming and, fuck me, it's a police car."

"Sonuvabitch," Rowdy said.

"What do you wanna do, Rowdy?" Degante said.

There was a holstered .45 Glock sitting on an old yellow vinyl and aluminum chair. Rowdy removed the weapon from the holster, shuffled the action and said, "He'll have to show us a warrant. Load up, and meet him outside. I'll keep moving the product and join you."

* * *

Approaching the lane that led up to the meth house, Jake got a call from Dispatch, telling him, "Sheriff Johnson wants to know your 10-20."

"Seven miles north on County road FF."

Buddy Johnson came on the radio and said, "What the hell, Jake. You said you were going to the Holtzmeyer location."

"Plan changed. Buddy, this thing runs like a sewing machine and boy howdy, when you step on it, I swear she wants to fly. You need to take a—"

"I talked to Darcy and she said you have a search warrant for a meth house. Are you serving it without back-up?"

"This is why you're the Sheriff, Buddy," Jake said. "Amazing powers of deduction."

"You wait until I get there with back-up, Jake."

"I'm already halfway up the lane. I'll wait if they allow it. Hurry up if you want in on the fun." Jake gave the 10-20 of the house and then signed off. "I'm out."

Jake banged up the long lane, engine snarling, tires crunching rocks and dirt. He stopped short of the house, to block the lane. He sat for a moment. Watched the ramshackle house. The house had cement blocks for steps and the sun-bleached porch was time worn. There was no movement from the house. A giveaway. They were watching him. Jake checked his sidearm, grabbed up the warrant, and stepped out of the interceptor. The interceptor was equipped with ballistic door panels that could absorb a 150 grain .308 bullet. Jake kept himself behind the door until he was sure what was up.

When Jake threw open the interceptor's door, Deke Gower and Frankie Boy Degante stepped out onto the porch. Both were armed. Degante had a semi-auto pistol with an extended magazine. Gower carried a short barreled tactical shotgun, one of those with the pistol grip, similar to the one in the boot of the interceptor which Jake wishes he had in his own hand.

Jake didn't like their body language.

"Jake Morgan, Paradise County Sheriff's office. I have a search warrant for these premises. Put your guns on the ground and step away."

Both men stood and considered him blankly as if they didn't hear him. Both were snuffling and their eyes were boggy with chemical abuse. Frankie Boy rubbed snot off his mustache with the back of his hand. They were smashed.

Not good. Frankie Boy and his 'load up and shoot all day' magazine wasn't the worry. He was too in the bag. He could aim at the ground and not kick up dirt. It was Gower's shotgun that concerned Jake.

"One more time," Jake said, pointing with his left hand while he slipped his right hand onto his Sig-Sauer. He released the safety as he removed the weapon out of their sight. "Weapons on the ground, faces in the dirt. Do it. Now."

Jake pulled his weapon, steadied it on the door just as Gower raised the shotgun. Jake yelled, "Don't", but Gower didn't stop and Jake put one in Gower's throat. Gower got off an errant blast from the shotgun that blistered the police car door. Frankie boy was pulling trigger as fast as he could and Jake's car pinged on impact, but Frankie Boy was only making noise. Jake aimed, sighted, and double tapped his .357, catching the shooter full in the chest.

Frankie Boy huffed in pain, swayed from bullet shock. The cocaine kept him upright. Frankie attempted to raise his pistol but it slipped from his fingers and onto the ground. He took two steps and face-planted into the dirt.

Practicing to qualify as a Texas Ranger, hundreds of hours at the shooting range and his farm paid off. He felt nothing for the two men he put down. That would come later with restless nights and bad dreams.

There was a roar of vehicle and a green pick-up burst from the side of the house and headed down onto the field. Jake fired off two shots and the rear window of the truck disappeared in a spray of glass. The truck bumped and slid down the hill and then pulled back onto the lane. No time to check on the two men he'd shot, he wanted Rowdy. Jake slid back into the Interceptor and fish-tailed down the lane after the Chevy.

* * *

Rowdy Manners loaded the last of the product into the over-the-hump truck toolbox, slammed the tailgate shut, when he heard a familiar voice say, "Jake Morgan, Paradise County Sheriff's office. I have a search warrant for these premises. Put your guns on the ground and step away."

Rowdy piled into the truck just as the first shots were fired. He put the truck in gear, buried the pedal, and swung out from behind the house tires spinning on the grass. He saw Frankie Boy pitch forward into the turf. He looked ahead and damn, the son-of-a-bitch had the lane blocked with his vehicle. He bounded across the field, past the police car, to swing back to the lane.

Two shots cracked through his rear window. One spidered his windshield and the other buried itself in the dashboard of the Silverado.

He yelled out, "SHIT!" and curled back onto the lane and down to the paved road. A quarter mile down the pavement he saw the nasty police vehicle swing onto the highway like a dark monster. Closing fast now. He couldn't outrun whatever it was Morgan was driving.

He decided to make a run for the old quarry and see if he could lose him on those cattle trails, cross the quarry backlot and hit the highway leading to the next county. Steal a car and head for Kansas City. He knew a couple guys would hide him out for a cut of the product.

His choices were freedom as a rich man, get caught and go to prison, or kill that fucking cop.

He was tired of Jake Morgan, and it was time to do something about it.

CHAPTER FORTY-TWO

When Jake hit pavement he called in. "Shots fired. Two men down at house location. Send ambulance. I am in pursuit of a dark green late model Chevy Silverado, license KJ5-734, driven by Rowdy Manners. We are westbound on county road FF. Redirect Sheriff Morgan."

Rowdy had a quarter mile lead. Jake fired up the siren, lit the lights and rammed his foot to the floorboard. The beast roared approval and chewed asphalt. After a mile, Jake was closing fast, his speedometer reading three figures. Rowdy turned off on Farm Road DD, heading northwest, which led to an abandoned rock quarry. Jake was familiar with the road and knew the old quarry was a dead end. An old spring that ran under the quarry had burst through the basin and washed out the quarry and also collapsed the roads leading into and away from the pit. It was now a swampy quagmire of snakes and frogs.

Apparently, Rowdy didn't know that.

Jake kept up the pressure, narrowly missing a coyote that wandered into his path. Ahead was a rise with a blind hairpin corner that dropped off suddenly. A few people, mostly kids, had slid off into the washed out quarry basin even before they closed it off. None who had done so were driving as fast as Rowdy was going. The Chevy drove right through the NO OUTLET sign and went over the rise at high speed. Jake lost visual contact.

But he knew what he would find.

Jake braked hard to a halt on the rise, called dispatch, gave his 10-20 and exited the interceptor, sidearm ready. Down below the green pick-up had rolled and settled into the murky waters of the abandoned quarry. Rowdy Manners was hanging half in and half out of the vehicle, pinned in the cab. The impact had ripped the undercarriage and caved the roof. Raw smell of gasoline was in the air. Rowdy's upper body was in the putrid water fouled by dead vegetation and moss. Rowdy had to push up to keep his face out of the rancid water and was whining in pain.

"I think my leg is broke."

Jake walked down in no particular hurry, put his hands on his hips and said, "Yeah, looks bad."

Rowdy raised up in the muck, yelped and said, "Get me out of here, Morgan."

"I don't know, Rowdy. You lied to me about Pete Stanger. So hurtful. Also I think you know who my killer is. I need you to verify it."

"I don't know shit."

"There's an understatement. But you will tell me what you 'don't know' or this is your new home. Lotta snakes around here," Jake shuddered in mock fear. "Some of those rattle-mouthed, copper-headed moccasins. Hate to be you."

"Man, get me an ambulance," Manners said.

"Information first," Jake said.

"I'll tell you what you want to know just get me out of here."

"I'm thinking about it."

"*Thinking* about it! I can barely hold myself out of the water and it stinks. There's gas everywhere. You can't leave me here, I'll die."

"Possibly. Want a cigarette?"

"Fuck no."

"Okay, I'll head back to town see if I can get somebody out here to help."

"You're a cop, you have to help me. There are rules."

"Ideally."

"What kinda cop are you, you mutha—"

Jake squatted near the water and gave Rowdy an appraising look. "You haven't heard about me, have you? I have authority issues, always in trouble with my superiors. Happened with the Texas Rangers, happening with the city council right now. Sort of a weakness. My girlfriend, you know her, yeah, you do and don't do that again. Anyway, she is on me to follow the rules, be more open to suggestion, but see, I can't seem to swing it. Turns out, I'm stubborn." Jake pointed at Rowdy. "As an officer of the law I've learned that shitheads such as yourself, poor bastard, you don't play by the rules and count on the good guys, like me, to follow the straight path, but I've adopted your playbook and use it against you. So, either give me what I want, which is a name, the name you witnessed leaving the scene of the Saunders' killing and I'll get you out of here. If not, I will leave you to drown and swell up with snake bites and a septic leg."

"They'll know you did that you bastard."

"I don't think so. Think you'll be missed? I'll report that you lost me during the chase. That Rowdy Manners? He's a slippery one. Another possibility is I charge you with the Saunders' homicide. Regardless of any one thing I choose I will go to Hank's tonight, have a beer with a couple of friends while you're sitting here in the dark screaming in pain where no one can hear you."

Rowdy's shoulders began to shake and tears formed. "Why?" he said, whining. "Why're you doing this?"

"Because somebody killed Cecil Holtzmeyer, a pretty good guy, and I've been pissed off about that. Somebody's going to take the weight for it and right now you're number one with a bullet."

CHAPTER FORTY-THREE

Rowdy gave up the name of the killer. Rowdy had been on the school campus to vandalize Saunders' office like he was twelve and it was Halloween. You can't figure dirtheads and how they think. Rowdy saw the killer get in a vehicle behind the superintendent's office before Pete Stanger entered the building. Jake was satisfied and within two minutes they heard the sirens.

"Where are the sirens headed?" Rowdy said.

"Coming here." Jake said.

"You called them before you got here, didn't you?"

"Yeah, don't you feel silly? You burned your ace in the hole on a busted hand."

"You're a piece of shit, Morgan."

"Think you're the first that told me that?"

Trooper Sam Ridley of the Missouri Highway Patrol was first on the scene followed by the Paradise County Fire Department and a county ambulance. The Firemen freed Rowdy from his truck and ambulance techs treated his wounds and set the leg break with a plastic blow-up splint.

Ridley looked at the truck in the quarry mire, then at

the bullet holes in the interceptor and said, "What the hell, Morgan? That looks like a brand-new vehicle and you..." Ridley paused to laugh and then said, "It's always the Wild West with you, isn't it? You are a lot of fun."

Jake shrugged. "Just another day of dodging bullets and fighting crime."

They looked up as the Ford Expedition, lights whirling, and siren wailing, arrived. It was Sheriff Buddy Johnson.

Jake lifted his chin, exhaled, and said, "Here comes an ass-chewing."

"Can I video it so I can watch later?" Ridley said. "I have so little in my life."

Buddy jumped out of his vehicle, quick-marched to Jake and Ridley. "Are you all right, Jake? There's..." Buddy stopped when he saw the damage to his brand-new Police Interceptor. His mouth fell open before he said, "I said, 'not a damn scratch'. Look at it."

"Actually, it's more than a scratch," Ridley said, smiling.

"What is it with cops?" Buddy said. "All you guys think everything is hilarious. It's the job, makes everybody crazy."

"I'm okay, bawse," Jake said. "Thanks for asking."

"You shut up." Buddy, worked up now, said, "We got a fire fight with two dead perps, one of those with a neck shot that nearly decapitated him, you and that damn .357 cannon, you didn't wait for back-up, and... How many times do I have to tell you not to call me 'boss', with that accent? You have not got one single friend on the city council already and...and, I'm going to take the repairs for that," He jammed a finger at the interceptor and said, "Right out of your narrow white ass."

"Are upset with me, Buddy?" Jake said. He turned to

Ridley and said, "He would be red-faced right now, if he was white."

Ridley, hands on hips, put his head down and laughed.

Buddy started to speak again but Jake interrupted and said, "I can cheer you up, boss—, I mean Buddy, I mean Sheriff. I know who killed Martin Saunders."

"And one more..." Buddy stopped and said, "You do?"

"Yeah," Jake said. "I've got him cold, too."

"He does," Ridley said.

Buddy started nodding his head, slowly at first, then bigger. "All right. That is good news. That's good work, Jake."

"So, I can call you boss again?"

It set him off again. "Hell no, you can't. Shit, you clowns are going to give me a stroke." He paused for a moment, started chuckling, and said, "Red-faced if I was white, huh?" Laughed some more. "Yeah, that's, a, that's funny, you worthless asshole. If you weren't my best friend, I'd strangle you with an appliance cord. So, who was it, the killer?"

Jake told him.

"Whoa." Buddy blew up his cheeks with air, exhaled, and then said, "God help us. Jake, you better be right. God almighty, we cannot be wrong about this one."

CHAPTER FORTY-FOUR

Jake briefed Chief Bannister and Buddy Johnson, regarding what he had learned and how he planned to corner the killer of Martin Saunders and Cecil Holtzmeyer at the City Council meeting. They were in Buddy's office with the door locked and the shades pulled low.

"At the city council meeting?" Buddy said. "The Cray-cray of that staggers me."

"Rowdy was on campus the night Saunders was killed. He had a partner with him. They were going to vandalize Martin Saunders' office to get back at him."

"That's juvenile," Cal said.

"Rowdy is a creepy guy but he's not stupid," Buddy said. "My sister-in-law, LaToya, says he is highly intelligent, but uses his intellect to do things most people would not."

"I have the murder weapon, the cause of death and now an eye-witness."

Cal said, "Got a report on a 'stolen' .308 Remington rifle a few minutes ago."

"Felicia must've passed on Bailey's visit," Jake said.

"What's next?" Cal said.

"We brief the city council about our homicide investigation as requested," Jake said. "Also, Cal, could you invite Winston Vestal."

"He may not like that."

Jake cocked his head and said, "Oh, I don't think he can't afford to miss it."

"What have you got in mind, Jake?" Buddy asked.

"Ever read any Agatha Christie?"

* * *

The shadow of the World War II Statue stretched out casting a facsimile on the façade of the 1912 courthouse, a stately building that reeked of tradition. Jake and Harper sat on a bench sipping coffee made by Sherry Hammersmith.

"You're sure this is the way to do this?" Harper said.

"In the immortal words of poet-philosopher, Randolph Scott, yup." Jake took a sip of the Guatemalan coffee Harper had brought him, and said, "Hey, this is pretty good."

"Makes Starbucks taste like mud," Harper said.

"That's a low bar." Jake settled back against the park bench and placed his arm around Harper. She settled in beside him and they watched the cars passing by. "So, I guess you're going into business with Sherry."

"In the immortal words of Randolph Scott," Harper said. "Probably."

"Cowboys don't say 'probably'. They are certain of their direction and purpose."

"Oh," Harper said, and looked up at his chin. "So, that's your problem. You know, some people hesitate before they jump into a snake pit full of people that don't like them. Are you really going to call out and arrest the killer at the meeting?"

"And anyone who had a part in it."

"A 'part in it'? What does that mean?"

Jake pretended to push back an imaginary cowboy hat and said, "Well, little missy, comes a time when a man's gotta ride herd on the owlhoots."

"Owlhoots, huh?"

"Yep."

"Jake," she said her voice softening. "This thing you have planned, you know, outing a killer in front of several people?" A leaf floated down and landed on Jake's shoulder. Harper reached up and removed it, held it in her hand and continued. "You make accusations in an open forum like that? Well, it could blow up in your face. Do the words 'lawsuit' and 'false arrest' mean anything to you? I love you, Jake, but I think you're addicted to jeopardy. About half of the city council wants to see you gone and looking for a reason. Are you sure about this? Aren't you worried? I am."

"Baby sister, all battles are fought by men who would rather be someplace else."

Harper rolled her eyes, then smiled. "That's about enough of the cowboy crapola for today." She twirled the reddish leaf in her hand, shook her head and said, "I don't know. Why did I pick such a macho shithead? I'm sure you know what you're doing, though?"

"I don't know what I could've done to make you think that."

She rolled her eyes and said, "Shut up and drink your coffee."

"Yes, ma'am."

CHAPTER FORTY-FIVE

Jake Morgan leaned against the wall standing between
Trooper Ridley and Leo the Lion. Prosecuting Attorney,
Darcy Foster, walked by, dipped her head slightly, and
said, "I cannot believe this is happening. If this doesn't
work, I'm just going to kill you, Jake. Oh my God. But,
good luck." Then she walked on.

Fred Ridley quietly said, "At least she wished you
good luck."

"An hour ago, she told me if I couldn't bring it off, I
was fired. Think I can get on with the Patrol?"

"I think we have a janitorial position open."

"Will they let me carry a weapon?"

Ridley said, "You know, the more I'm around you,
Morgan, the more I think there is something seriously
wrong with you. But, you got some serious balls."

On the other side, Leo the Lyon was saying, "I do
love this shit so much. Jake, you are a giant among shit-
stirring crazoids. It has been a pleasure knowing you

even as you slip into the cold waters of unemployment."

Foster Taylor called the meeting to order. The minutes of the previous meeting were read and accepted and Mayor Steinman rose to speak.

"I would like to thank everyone for their attendance at this special meeting," Steinman said. "I wish to thank our guests for being here to brief us on their investigation and to congratulate Investigator Morgan, Chief Bannister, and Sheriff Johnson on their arrest and confiscation of dangerous drugs and narcotics. We also wish to welcome Dr. Winston Vestal and Dr. Jackson Howard of the Paradise School district for joining us here tonight. Before we proceed Foster Taylor and Dr. Knox Sutherland have some words."

Taylor nodded at Dr. Sutherland and the Sutherland rose. Sutherland was resplendent in a dark blue wool suit, brilliant white shirt and rep tie. His salt-and-pepper hair was perfect.

"Ladies and gentlemen," Sutherland began, "There are many people involved in any successful undertaking. I would like to thank my good friend, Foster Taylor, who made the unique step of suggesting Madame Cynthia Wellstone who was integral in the arrest of Pete Stanger."

"Who is Madame Cynthia?" Ridley asked Jake.

"Spiritual Medium," Jake said.

"A what?"

"A seer. She sees the future."

"She tell you who killed the teacher?"

"That's the rumor," Jake said. "But she was wrong."

"And you're allowing this to happen?"

"Yes."

"Why?"

"Spite. And because it's fun."

Leo saying now, "This is superb. I may not want anything for Christmas."

Dr. Sutherland continued, saying, "...And now, I will turn over the podium to our law enforcement people who will brief us on all the details. A round of applause for Chief Bannister, please."

Council members and guests applauded, and Cal Bannister nodded at Jake. Jake pushed away from the wall, to address the council.

"I'm Jake Morgan, I am the investigator for both the Paradise Police Department and the Paradise County Sheriff's department. Like Henry the 8th said to his third wife, 'I won't keep you long'."

Scattered laughter.

Jake paused to take in faces. Foster Taylor sat imperious, assured of his position in the community. Felicia Jankowski, scowled, Beth Moreland smiled, and Winston Vestal wet his lips. Buddy Johnson looked every inch the Sheriff of Paradise County, while Buster Mangold checked his biceps and Deputy Gretchen Bailey watched the room.

Jake continued. "Homicide is a dirty business. People selfish or sick enough to take another person's life deserve whatever punishment we can provide. This particular murder managed to suck several people into its web of hate and jealousy. I'll tell you right now, despite what you heard Pete Stanger didn't kill anyone."

"What are you talking about?" Foster Taylor said. He turned to Darcy Hillman and said, "Darcy, you said you were going to instruct this officer to arrest Stanger."

"I gave him until seven tonight."

"You know," Jake said. "I was afraid Pete Stanger was going to take the fall for this homicide and the real killer fitted Stanger with a near-perfect frame. But only near-perfect. The mistake was killing Cecil Holtzmeyer and the person who made that mistake is right here in the room. And, that person is going to be arrested tonight."

Chairs scooted and voices buzzed.

"What are you trying to pull here, Morgan?" Foster Taylor said.

"It *was* Pete Stanger," Felicia Jankowski said, jumping up. "This is ridiculous."

"Felicia," Jake said. "Glad you're here. With your permission, would it be okay for me to have Leo Lyon to step forward and share an article we found in the Dr. Vestal's office?"

Felicia looked around the room like a cornered animal and sat down.

"I didn't think so," Jake said. "I'll have more for you here in a minute. How about you, Dr. Vestal? Here or afterwards? Your choice."

Vestal face blanched and he looked like was going to be sick. "After would be said," he said.

"Good. More on that later, also."

Felicia's jaw worked.

Jake saying now, "This investigation was complicated by the fact Martin Saunders has a lot of enemies. Almost like he courted them. I don't understand why that appealed to him. I've never come across anything like it. Several people in this room, had contact with Martin Saunders the night of his death. Two former students of Saunders', Ransom Eberhard and Ron Manners have been charged with assault and battery of Saunders', but they didn't kill him. Ransom has agreed to testify against Ron Manners, who most here know as Rowdy Manners. Manners has also been arrested for eluding and trafficking controlled substances. Two of his associates are dead and a third will testify against Manners. This has moved Mr. Manners to agree to testify in the murder trial."

Jake paused and looked around the room, taking every person into his view. "Nervous yet, killer? Eberhard and Manners had a grudge from years previous with Saunders. As high school students they acted in a play called "Failure Can be Deadly". A commemorative award with the title of the play was left at the crime scene. It was a golden apple on a base plaque. Rowdy and Eberhard wanted revenge on Saunders for various reasons by breaking into Saunders' office and stealing the commemorative. The two men, wearing stocking masks, were surprised when Saunders' showed up. Saunders was there to meet a person in this room. There was a scuffle and Saunders' was beaten and between the two men were able to carry the unconscious Saunders' into the Superintendent's office which they accessed utilizing Saunders' keys which they had taken from him. They brought the apple trophy with them to send a message."

"Wait," Dr. Sutherland said. "Saunders was beaten to death, right?"

"Only Dr. Zeke Montooth and myself, along with Chief Bannister and Sheriff Johnson knew the cause of death," Jake said. "The killer happened upon the scene and was happily surprised to find the unconscious Saunders in the central office reception area.

Here's where things get ironic. A third had issues with Saunders' and intended to kill the teacher and was prepared to do that. The person I'm talking about was and has been angry at Saunders for a number of reasons for some time." Jake stopped, motioned at Buster Mangold and said, "Officer Mangold, would you please go stand behind Dr. Sutherland?"

Sutherland exploded from his seat as if dynamited. "What the hell is this, Morgan? I will fucking ruin you for this insult, you arrogant ass."

The room buzzed with noise and surprised voices.

Mangold moved to a position behind the agitated Doctor. Fred Ridley joined him.

"You have no evidence of anything," Sutherland said. "Do you think this is a TV movie where you assemble everyone and then reveal the killer? Are you out of your ever-loving mind? Well you're not Sherlock Holmes, I'm no killer and you have no damn evidence. I cannot wait to take you apart in civil court."

"Terrible bedside manner," Jake said. "You're unconscionable and that's what tripped you up. Having no conscience limits your imagination. You haven't heard my evidence yet. Martin Saunders was killed by an overdose of a paralytic called Succinylcholine. Only a medical professional has access to this drug. You asked Saunders to meet you at school, planning to kill him, but when you got there you were surprised to find Saunders incapacitated. I'll bet you were excited to see it. Now you had the perfect crime. The cause of death would be by bludgeoning and you would be free of Saunders. You administered the hypo into Saunders' injured lip to disguise the needle puncture. Now, that part was genius. This was a brilliant move. Well done so far."

"This is the most fantastic thing I've ever heard," Sutherland said.

"Don't say anything, Knox," Felicia said. "Let your lawyer handle this."

"Why would I kill Saunders? He was my nephew for God's sake. And Succinylcholine is absorbed so quickly that is not possible for you to make the determination that it was the cause of death."

Jake swept a hand in the direction of Dr. Zeke Montooth and said, "Zeke, tell him."

"Jake is correct," Zeke said. "I suspected poisoning and preserved the urine from the autopsy for further examination. My work revealed a byproduct of Suxx in the urine." Zeke addressed the Mayor Steinman and Foster Taylor in way of explanation. "That's what we, in the medical profession call Succinylcholine. It is an exceedingly powerful paralytic."

The council members were stunned. Winston Vestal looked like he swallowed a wax candle.

"Even more ridiculous," Sutherland said. "A residual byproduct such as you mention, Dr. Montooth, you quack, is not evidence in a homicide."

"I'm going to have to disagree with your posit there, Knox," Zeke said. "It has already been admitted as evidence in two trials."

"Both of which ended in conviction," Jake said.

Sutherland started laughing. "I'll take my chances."

"Oh, I left out the best part, Dr. Sutherland," Jake said. "I have an eye witness. Two of them in fact. Both are going to be more than happy to testify against you for a reduction of their sentence. Rowdy Manners saw you. I won't even need Pete Stangers' testimony. Pete Stanger's appearance at school was a coincidence. You chased him, causing his wreck the night I had stopped Cecil Holtzmeyer. I saw your pick-up pass by at a high rate of speed. Neither I nor Holtzmeyer were able to identify your vehicle. You kept Stanger sedated with Narcotics until such time as you could have him overdose. You got worried about Stanger after I was able to talk with him so you got in a hurry. That was your next and biggest mistake."

Jake's eyes turned hot and he bore in on the Doctor. "You shot Cecil Holtzmeyer for no reason thinking he was an eyewitness. I have your .308 which you left at Stangers and then called it in as stolen."

"That was Pete's rifle," Sutherland blurted out. "I saw it at his home when I was treating him."

"You know I asked around and no one can ever

remember you making one single house call in your life. However, Deputy Bailey found your documentation whereby you listed every weapon you owned, including the date of purchase and serial number. I test fired and the bullet matches the one that killed Cecil Holtzmeyer."

"Then he stole it."

"Sorry, the timeline is off. You reported it stolen only after Deputy Bailey searched your home. That's when your girlfriend, Felicia Jankowsi—"

Vestal made a strange little cry and looked at Felicia.

"Yeah," Jake said, looking at Vestal. "You didn't know, did you? Martin Saunders wasn't popular, Dr. Sutherland, but Cecil Holtzmeyer was a nice guy and you killed him while he was watching a baseball game in his home. Officer Mangold, handcuff the doctor and read him his rights. Two counts, murder one."

CHAPTER FORTY-SIX

Jake and Harper sat in the leather loveseat in Harper's home. Bandit was curled up between them. They were watching the ten o'clock news on KCKS channel 12. Melissa Vanderbilt was showing footage of "Dr. Knox Sutherland being escorted from City Hall by Officer Buster Mangold of the Paradise Police Department. Sutherland has been arrested and will be indicted for the murder of Martin Saunders a teacher at Paradise High School…"

Harper said, "So, what happens to Felicia Jankowski?"

"She will be charged with adding and abetting for telling Sutherland about Bailey's visit. Of course, she knew about it. Why he told her I'll never understand. Telling a woman a secret is like—"

"Like what, Jake?" Harper asked.

"Like the absolute best thing a guy could ever do to demonstrate his love?"

Harper rolled her eyes and laughed. "Just not anyone like Felicia Jankowski."

"Exactly. But she'll beat the rap on aiding and abetting. It's weak and she'll turn on Sutherland. She's not the type to take a fall for any man."

"Except to fall back on a bed. What about Winston Vestal?"

"He'll resign and move to another school district. He's not going to allow the file Leo found become public knowledge."

"And you will hold it over his head?"

"Like the sword of Damocles," Jake said. "Leo's take on the file was that, quote, these pictures tell a story about Vestal, Felicia Jankowski and an unknown third person, the one in the mask. Leo said that this would not only would cost Vestal his job, it would end his career."

"You have to wonder who the cameraman was? Not to mention the person in the mask."

"I would imagine the person in the mask was Martin Saunders," Jake said.

"You're kidding?"

"No, we examined Saunders' home, and I was surprised all his cameras had been disabled. The scene in the photos was Saunders' bedroom."

"Ick. I see you allowed Buster Mangold to be filmed as the arresting officer. That was fairly gratuitous of you."

"He thanked me for that. Vanderbilt was shivering with lust watching him."

"Oh please," she said. "Why, after all Buster had done to screw up this investigation did you let him be seen as the arresting officer?"

"Yeah, he's kind of an idiot. But doesn't he look good in the uniform?"

IF YOU LIKE THIS, YOU ALSO ENJOY: COLE SPRINGER TRILOGY
A MEN'S ADVENTURE SERIES

"*Springer's Gambit is both fluent and riveting. Cole Springer is a comer and so is W.L. Ripley.*" —**Robert B. Parker, bestselling author of the Spenser and Jesse Stone mystery series**

COLE SPRINGER HAS A MUSICAL SOUL, A QUICK WIT, AND A CON-MAN'S MIND.

Ex-Secret Service Agent Cole Springer has exchanged his badge for a piano and the high-altitude life of Aspen, Colorado. But he hasn't lost his appetite for danger. Springer delights in playing button men and gangsters for personal gain and amusement. While an affable man, he's tough, hard to kill, and has an ironic sense of humor. Meanwhile, his girlfriend, determined CBI Agent, Tobi Ryder, doesn't know whether to love him, forget him, or arrest him for his escapades that skirt the edges of the law…

Don't miss the chance to dive headfirst into this thrilling men's adventure trilogy, where your heart will race as you immerse yourself in a world of action, vigilante justice, and adventure. Grab your copy today!

The Cole Springer Trilogy includes Springer's Gambit, Springer's Longshot, and Springer's Fortune.

"*Boston has Spenser. South Florida has Travis McGee. Now the New West has Cole Springer—a two-fisted piano player with a sharp wit and brooding soul. This is the best-written crime novel I've read since the debut of James Lee Burke's Dave Robicheaux.*"—**Ace Atkins, author of *Leavin' Trunk Blues***

AVAILABLE NOW

ACKNOWLEDGMENTS

Many thanks to my brother, Lt. Jim Ripley (Missouri State Highway Patrol, retired) and his wife, RN Mary Ripley for lending their professional expertise to provide details for this novel. Jim formerly served as a homicide and major crimes investigator for the Highway Patrol. Mary has worked in major Kansas City hospitals and has been an instructor teaching aspiring nurse candidates.

ABOUT THE AUTHOR

W.L. Ripley is the author of the critically acclaimed Wyatt Storme and Cole Springer mystery-thriller series' featuring modern knight errant Wyatt Storme, and Maverick ex-secret service agent, Cole Springer.

W.L. Ripley is a lifetime Missouri resident who has been a sportswriter, award-winning career educator and NCAA Div. II basketball coach. Ripley enjoys watching football, golf, and spending time with friends and family. He's a father, grandfather, and unapologetic Schnauzer lover.

In addition to the Storme & Springer series, Ripley has crafted two new series' heroes – Jake Morgan (Home Fires) and Conner McBride (McBride Doubles Down) for Wolfpack Publishing. Wolfpack is reissuing the Cole Springer series and Ripley is developing a new Cole Springer thriller for Wolfpack.

Ripley is represented by the Donald Maass Literary Agency.

Made in the USA
Columbia, SC
09 April 2024

34148732R00186